# French Twist

## Glynis Astie

ISBN: 0615874045
ISBN-13: 978-0615874043

*To my husband, Sebastien, for inspiring me to share our story.*

*And to my sister, Megan, for believing that I could do it.*

*Chapter One*

Repeat the mantra, Sydney. *Breathe.* "Good enough is not nearly as wonderful as perfect, but it is good enough." How often had my mother said those words to me? Countless times. She would always look at me with her warm brown eyes, smile reassuringly and squeeze my hand. During a particularly traumatic period in high school, she went as far as framing the words and asked me to read them—and take them to heart—at least once a day. Though I believed in the truth of these words on this day as I had on every other day, one thought kept occurring to me. Shouldn't your wedding day be the one day where perfection was expected?

I had tried to stay calm, but things kept going wrong and I *really* didn't like it when things went wrong. I was definitely not a "roll with it" type of person. From a very early age, any divergence from the plan I had formulated in my head was enough to send me into a tailspin. I thought if anything happened outside of what I had planned for, I would lose control. And losing control was not something I enjoyed. Therefore, I planned for every possible scenario and then worried obsessively that I had not planned enough. My father had always told me if worrying were a sport, I would be the champion of the world.

But, I digress. Let us return to the problem at hand. It all began with my wedding party. In my infinite wisdom, I had asked six women to be my bridesmaids. My older sister and best friend, Kate, my sister-in-law, Zoe, and four of my closest friends. Each woman had gladly accepted the role, but a week before the wedding all hell broke loose. First, Maya came down with mono. Who has *she* been kissing lately? I saw her every single day and the identity of the infector was a complete mystery to me. Then three days before the wedding, Amanda got the chicken pox. I'm sorry, but who didn't get it as a kid? The parents in the neighborhood where I grew up actually took their kids to "parties" to make sure they had the chicken pox when they were young.

Finally, the day before the wedding Holly broke her leg in four places and had to be immobilized for the foreseeable future. She had yet to tell me exactly what she was doing when she broke her leg, but I got the feeling it was highly embarrassing. *Seriously*?! *Three bridesmaids down*? Was this a bad omen for anyone involved in our wedding party? *Focus, Sydney*. Everything would be fine—Kate and I would reformat the ceremony along with the new bridesmaid/groomsmen ratio.

Sadly, the storm was not over yet. The breathtakingly beautiful gown I had planned to get married in was lost two days before the wedding. The fitted bodice was intricately beaded and the full tulle skirt hung perfectly. When I wore it, I felt like a princess, as every woman should on her wedding day. The hotel manager told me how sorry he was that my dress had been *misplaced* and would be happy to put in a good word for me at the costume rental shop down the street. He felt the Juliet gown would give "an exciting period feel" to our "incredibly lackluster" wedding. I informed him, as my fiancé held my arms back, that he would have a much better idea of what sorry was once I was through with him. He appeared completely calm, leading me to assume he had dealt with many a bride in his time.

I sat in the hotel lobby in a state of shock for an hour before I was able to move. I closed my eyes and tried to slow my breathing, but my mind wouldn't stop racing. Was this actually happening to me? What had I done to deserve this? And most importantly, what the hell was I going to wear?

Kate came to the rescue as usual. She pulled her exquisite wedding dress out of its protective cocoon and offered it to me. I felt relieved and guilty in equal measure as Kate was constantly coming to my rescue. Older and wiser was an understatement when it came to her; she was perfection personified. I both loved and hated her for it. How I could I ever live up to the standard she had set? It felt like an impossible task.

And as sweet as the offer of her dress was, if I wore it I would have the impossible task of wearing a long-sleeved satin gown in the sweltering July heat. Kate's decision to get married in December meant I had the choice of sweating in her perfect dress or sweating in Juliet's velvet monstrosity. I thanked my sister profusely and suggested padding the dress with lots of tissues. I took a deep breath and started to relax. Crisis averted.

Unfortunately, my relief was short lived. During the course of our rehearsal dinner, my mother and my aunt decided to have the biggest fight of their fifty-seven year relationship. My aunt began talking about her daughter's wedding and drawing pretty harsh comparisons to mine. My mother, of course, took great offense to my aunt's statements that her daughter's wedding was smaller, more tasteful and thankfully had far fewer "foreign" people. My aunt then exclaimed how glad she was that I had finally found someone who would marry me—even if he was a foreigner—since she thought I was going to be an old maid. (An old maid at the ripe old age of twenty-seven!) Her daughter, Cynthia, she reminded us, was married at the age of twenty-two—a far more appropriate age for women to capitalize on their childbearing years.

After a few glasses of wine, the conversation then degenerated into an argument over who chose the tiger lily china pattern first for their wedding registry, a bitter pill my aunt has never gotten over since my mother got married six months before she did. I knew this wasn't going to end well. That was when the shrieking and hair pulling started. My older brother, Charlie, and Kate's perfect husband, Nick, had to separate them. What a great impression my family had made on my fiancé's relatives!

My father, of course, was no help at all. He sat there, taking it all in, and laughed until he cried. My fiancé assured me passion of any kind was appreciated by his family, but I believed he was just trying to keep his bride from the edge of hysteria the night before her wedding. He stroked my hair gently and reminded me that in two days we would be on a plane to Paris. Focusing on taking a trip I had dreamt about for my entire life with the man I had dreamt about for my entire life allowed me to obtain a modicum of sanity. I should have known it wouldn't last long.

As I was preparing to leave my hotel room the next day (already sweating profusely in my borrowed wedding dress), I was handed a bouquet of bright green carnations. You heard me. *Bright* green. Not, let's say, a shade lighter than a jaunty Kelly green. We were talking *bright freakin' green*. My heart stopped. What had happened to my orchids and roses? I had chosen such beautiful shades of….something, but not green! Why couldn't I remember? I ran out to the balcony to check on the flowers at the wedding site below. They were all the same scary shade of green. The terrace resembled an exceptionally bad St. Patrick's Day hangover. My hands began to shake and I noticed green dye dripping down the front of my dress. Kate was going to kill me! I closed my eyes and tried to will the panic out of my body. Could this day get any worse? *Crap!* My father told me *never* to ask that question, because things could always get worse. I wish I had listened.

My nightmare wasn't over yet. As my mother and I approached the top of the staircase from which we would descend to the ceremony, the heel of my shoe broke. Fortunately, I didn't fall and make an absolutely unforgettable trip down the aisle. *Unfortunately*, all those in attendance of our wedding (as well as the wedding on the lower terrace) heard me swear at this occurrence. It seemed this final detail was the last straw for my strained wedding day psyche. The only thing that made me smile was the cackle my father let out following my outburst.

So there I was, standing at the top of the staircase with my mother, wondering if all these occurrences were a sign. How could my wedding day be this far from perfect? Was "good enough" really good enough on your wedding day? Was it actually possible for this many things to go wrong in one day? The questions just kept coming. Did my aunt and her daughter hatch a plan to ruin my wedding? Was Maya in on it? Why didn't I recognize most of my wedding guests? Where had I met my foreign fiancé? Was this really the man I was meant to marry? Why was I having trouble remembering his name or what he looked like?

As I tried to stop my disjointed thoughts from spiraling, I heard a faint beeping in the distance. What the hell was that? I started to seethe with rage as I realized the fire alarm was going off inside the hotel lobby. In a moment, all the hotel guests were going to be evacuated into the middle of my wedding. I starting shaking my head. *I couldn't do this!* I threw down my soggy bouquet and sobbed. My mother grabbed my arm and shook me, gently at first, but then more urgently. I kept trying to break her hold, but she appeared to be freakishly strong for a woman in her sixties. I knew something was wrong, but couldn't quite put my finger on it...

## Chapter Two

I woke with a start and sat bolt upright in my bed. I quickly assessed the situation and discerned I was coated in sweat and my roommate, Jess, was standing over me with an extremely annoyed look on her face. *Thank God!* It was just a bad dream. An actual nightmare! I sighed with relief and flopped back onto my pillows.

"Syd, your alarm was going off for, like, *ten* minutes!" she complained.

I frowned. Well, that explained the beeping.

Jess rolled her eyes. "I had to shake you for, like, another *five* minutes before you finally woke up."

And that explained the shaking. I knew my mother would never commit such unladylike behavior as shaking me—particularly on my wedding day.

"Get it together, woman!" She stormed out of my room and slammed the door.

I closed my eyes and searched for the will to get out of bed. My first order of business would be to find Jess and apologize. She had a very important presentation to give today and I had a sneaking suspicion my alarm had gone off before she had gotten her requisite nine hours of sleep. *Crap.* This was an excellent start to the day.

I opened my eyes and reluctantly swung my legs over the edge of the bed. I was still trying to defuse the anxiety lurking in my system from that crazy dream. It had felt so…real. I smiled and shook my head. I should have known I was dreaming considering: a) I didn't have a boyfriend, let alone a fiancé and b) I was *never* getting married.

I certainly didn't buy into my aunt's feeling that I was an old maid at the age of twenty-seven. (This part of the dream was disturbingly true.) But I did whole heartedly believe I was only capable of dating horrible men. This was a personality defect I had come to terms with. What was the point in getting married when I knew I was going to be miserable? My seemingly endless pursuit of the perfect man, which had later been downgraded to the pursuit of a decent man, had been fruitless.

Though I have gotten a little ahead of myself. I cannot expect you to understand my tenuous mental state on the subject of marriage without a little bit of background. As you have probably surmised by now, perfection was something I had pursued for my entire life. The perfect grades, the perfect schools, the perfect clothes, the perfect job…you see where this is going. And it all began with my perfect sister, Kate.

I had spent the majority of my life striving to fulfill the image of perfection I felt she embodied. From her beautiful blue eyes and golden hair, to her amazing intellect and kindness, Kate was the girl who made everything look easy. She was able to do anything she set her mind to and was able to talk to anyone—and I do mean *anyone*—with ease. (She once set a large, scary looking man in our subway car straight on his choice of cologne. And he thanked her! If I hadn't witnessed it, I wouldn't have believed it.) She was involved in a ton of activities in high school, graduated in the top of her class and was accepted to a top tier college.

It would stand to reason that attracting men had come very easily to Kate, since everything else did. She had had two boyfriends in high school: first a gorgeous Spanish exchange student and then the captain of the debate team. She let each down easily once she was ready to move on and had kept in touch with them to this day. She then met her husband at the age of eighteen as a freshman at Stanford. He approached her in the campus bookstore during her second day on campus and that was it. Nick was smart, handsome *and* funny. He was also a year older so he could guide her through her first year of college with ease. Of course, he swept her off her feet immediately, because he was perfect too. It was like they were made for each other. How could you not be happy for them?

I, on the other hand, was totally awkward around men. It was as though my brain disengaged from any rational thought processes and I started spouting absolute nonsense. I also had this nasty habit of blushing bright red when I was embarrassed, which was often when you sounded like a total moron. Thankfully, I had other assets, so I managed to attract a few men my way. I just tried to speak as little as possible.

Kate had always told me how gorgeous I was, but she was my sister; she was obligated to tell me that. The decision is yours to make. I stand five feet seven inches tall and have pale, but luminous skin. My mom always describes it as alabaster, but in my mind I look like a ghost. My long, dark hair falls in glossy waves down my back (after an hour with styling products and a blow dryer) and my dark brown eyes, I have been told, sparkle beautifully when I smile. I was also blessed with an amazingly fast metabolism, allowing me to eat whatever I want and still fit into a size two. Growing up, exercise was something I did for fun with my friends, most of whom hated me for only doing it recreationally and having such a trim figure.

Throughout high school and college, I was far too intimidated by any of the men I found attractive to attempt any kind of intelligent conversation. The only way I could talk to them was with a little "liquid courage" and it simply wasn't possible to be tipsy all the time. My sober self was not able to form coherent thoughts, so the result of my attempts at relationships amounted to a series of meaningless hookups (drunk self) and a few unbearable first dates (sober self).

I just couldn't understand it. I had tons of friends. People liked me! I was easy to talk to! Why did I become such an idiot once romantic interest raised its head? Kate had tried to give me pointers, but I was never able to carry out her instructions properly. After the latest debrief of yet another dating disaster, she would shake her head in amusement and tell me to relax. She would then tell me the right man for me was waiting just around the bend, out of sight. She said he would come along when I least expected it and I simply had to be patient.

I appreciated her optimism, but after the parade of challenging men I had dated, I believed her theory did not apply to me. Some of us were meant to be alone. While this declaration may seem overly dramatic, I have a number of interesting stories which illustrate my point. (Some will be left out as they are far too embarrassing.) Are you ready?

After I graduated from college, I moved out to California. I had always dreamed of living in a warm climate and the Bay Area was my idea of perfection. Twenty-two years of New York winters were more than enough for me. Kate and I shared the same "California" dream, which included living in the same town. She and Nick remained in Palo Alto following graduating from Stanford, much to the chagrin of the rest of our family who are all die hard New Yorkers. I, however, heartily approved of their choice since I couldn't wait to join them. With this fresh start, I felt some of Kate's trademark optimism and thought maybe things would be different.

My odds were greatly increased by the arrival of my good friend Maya, another escapee from the east coast. We had met during our freshman year at Northwestern and had commiserated over our shared hatred of winter. (She hailed from New Jersey, but I forgave her.) Maya was more than ready for all the opportunities California had to offer. She had her own dating scars and was determined to change her luck. Once we moved, she threw herself into singles clubs, chat rooms and alumni associations. The only problem was she didn't want to go alone, so she threw me in too— kicking and screaming, I might add. I wanted to be able to meet men a little more naturally, to let fate take its course. Maya believed even fate needed a little push.

After six months and ten awful first dates, I came to the conclusion that either all the bad men had followed me to California or good men were a seriously endangered species. Whatever the reason, I no longer felt the need to look for one of the good ones. Despite Kate's best efforts, my optimism was nowhere to be found.

A few months later, Maya set me up with a friend of her brother's—and, boy, did she do it with style. After my series of disastrous blind dates in the past year, I was not a willing participant in the dating process. My devious friend invited me to her apartment, introduced me to Mark (my date) and then raced out for an "emergency" bikini waxing. As she ran out the door, she informed me I wasn't the only one who would be getting lucky. "Mark," she whispered to me, was a "sure thing." She left me with a flushed face and butterflies in the pit of my stomach.

Mark was nice and easy going, but he had a bizarre sense of humor. I never got his jokes, which revolved around hunting 'gators, but I laughed anyway. I think I was ecstatic to have someone semi-normal take me out on a second date, so I overlooked a lot. He was twenty-seven years old and still lived with his mother, had spent his life savings on a pick-up truck and thought a romantic date was free hot dog night at the monster truck rally. I was so desperate to be "in love" like everyone else I knew, I moved in with him after six months of dating and hoped for the best.

Unfortunately, three months later I found him in bed with Tiffany and Tammy, the ticket takers at the monster truck rally. Evidently, the three of them had a lot in common and the girls moved in to my beautifully decorated apartment two days later. (I had high tailed it out of the apartment that night with nothing but my clothes, books and pictures. I had no desire for any of the furniture or linens as I had no idea what kind of, um, *residue* remained following their activities.) A year later I heard they started a matchmaking service for threesomes. Who knew there was a market for such a thing? Shortly after this bizarre news, I received a muffin basket with a thank-you note from the "wonder threesome" as I referred to them, stating they owed me a debt of gratitude for being so undesirable. *Ouch.* That one was going to leave a scar.

Fresh out of my "relationship" with Mark, I met James, a college student three years my junior. He was my roommate in a very hastily found rental following the discovery of the wonder threesome. I actually had five, no *six*, roommates. (I had almost forgotten how one of the girls smuggled her boyfriend in every evening, apparently to both satisfy her needs and to eat the contents of our fridge.) Alone and scared, I enjoyed the attention from this sweet young man. It was fun sneaking him into my room late at night for some very satisfying alone time.

A short while later, I realized our conversations consisted of the latest *Survivor* contestants and his deep and abiding love for Bob Marley. What the hell was I doing? When a group of sorority girls came over one night and gave me extensive advice on how to make myself over to be a suitable date for James' upcoming fraternity formal, I knew I was done. Honestly, what twenty-four-year-old woman wouldn't be? I told James it wasn't him, it was me, packed up my meager belongings and found an apartment for adults.

Two weeks later, I moved in with two professional women. Jess and Maggie had graduated from Stanford and were very active in the local alumni association. *Jackpot!* I would definitely meet a much higher caliber of men hanging out with these two. I was full of hope for the future.

For the first few months, things were looking good. My new roommates had wine and cheese parties and invited a bevy of captivating young men. Then I started to notice the men I was interested in always seemed to be escorted by their brilliant girlfriends. The single men were...well, let's just say they were single for a reason. I had never thought of myself as a shallow person, but wasn't it possible for men to be intellectually stimulating as well as attractive? I didn't need gorgeous, but there had to be some kind of spark.

Was I being too picky? Kate insisted that my standards were too high. This was pretty rich coming from someone who was married to the most perfect man on earth. She kept insisting he had flaws, but I had yet to see them. I was pretty sure she had embellished his deficiencies to make me feel better—and possibly to convince herself she was normal. *As if!*

I had nearly given up hope, when Maggie introduced me to her former coworker, Alex. He was attractive, funny and incredibly smart. He seemed almost *too* perfect. Seriously, what was wrong with me? I did my best to turn my brain off and enjoy dating Alex. We had a great time whenever we went out, but I couldn't bury the feeling something wasn't right. We had many a romantic evening in front of the fireplace of his condo (No roommates!) and he took me to the nicest restaurants in town. He gave me a beautiful necklace for Christmas and told me he loved spending time with me. I finally started to relax and allowed myself to believe I had found the real thing.

Shortly after Christmas, Alex told me he had planned the perfect New Year's Eve celebration for us. A few of his fraternity brothers had rented a suite at a fancy hotel in San Francisco and were hosting an elegant dinner to ring in the new year. Alex was in full party mode that night—which was actually kind of cute, right up until the moment he asked me to give him my favorite bra and panty set and call him Alicia.

I didn't sleep much that night and was desperately hoping we would laugh about it the morning. Instead, Alex told me he had been working up the courage to tell me about his lifestyle and hoped I would be a part of it. Had I ever thought about dressing up as a man? *Okaaay.* That was it. I was officially *done.*

Clearly, I was never going to meet the perfect man, but why did all the men who crossed my path have to have so many flaws? I mean, *come on*, a girl needed something to work with. Was it just me? My friends seemed to meet decent guys. In fact, more than half of them were already married. Why was I always behind? What did I have to do to find someone reasonable? Or was I destined to be the old maid my aunt had said I was? Maybe I was going to be the crazy lady who lived with her sixteen cats and told stories about them like they were her children. I really did *love* cats (they were such great listeners!), but they were hardly suitable companions for parties.

My only option was clear. I was going to have to learn to live without male companionship. Certain aspects of this, uh, situation would be very frustrating, but there were stores that could help take care of things...

*Chapter Three*

Following such a colorful—and very real—recounting of my history with men, you have a clear idea of why I wanted nothing to do with any of them. I firmly believed I was better off alone. Any man I met was painfully dissected and deemed unworthy. I was too scarred by the experiences of the last few years to see even remotely clearly. It was going to take a miracle to save me. Little did I know this miracle was just around the corner. *Damn it, Kate.* Why were you always right?

I will never forget the first time I saw Louis. It was a Saturday night in the middle of the summer and Maya was dragging me out yet again, full of positive words about meeting "someone special." She had even pushed me to wear something a little—okay *a lot*—out of my comfort zone. I had on snug-fitting low-rise jeans and a black lace tank top that exposed about two inches of my stomach and was not lined in the back. My chest was a modest enough size so no bra was necessary, but I felt totally on display. I kept pulling the tank top down, but it kept popping back up. Why did I let Maya talk me into this? I could be at home watching *Breakfast at Tiffany's*.

Maya scowled. "Will you stop fidgeting?"

"I should have worn the red scoop neck. In fact, I can run home and change..." I turned away from the door and tried to walk back toward the car.

Maya grabbed my arm. "Don't even think about it, Syd. It was enough of a struggle to get you here; there's no way I'm letting you go now. Just relax! You're *gorgeous*."

That was easy for Maya to say. She always looked flawless. She had short dark hair, perfect olive skin and a petite stature. She also gave the impression of having her own stylist and the most talented hair and makeup team in the world. It was not uncommon for men to stop their conversations and gape when she walked by, but somehow she was completely oblivious to the attention. As someone with massive insecurities, I found this *really* annoying.

The second my eye roll started, she grabbed my arm even harder. "Stop and listen, freak. You have to be willing to *try* to have a good time. And, as I said, you look incredible, so you're already off to a great start. Just give it a shot, okay?"

I was pretty sure she would say anything to make me feel better because she needed a wingman, so I reluctantly retraced my steps. As I tried to console myself with the idea of a hot bath later, I glanced up and saw Louis walking toward the club from the other side of the street. Our eyes met and I lost my train of thought—as well as my motor coordination. I tripped on the curb and almost fell flat on my face. Fortunately, Maya caught my arm before I could do any damage. I quickly righted myself, tried to restore what little dignity I had brought with me and turned my gaze back to Louis.

It wasn't just that he was handsome, the man had *style*. Style like none I had ever seen before. He was at least six feet tall and was wearing a pale blue suit with a matching pale blue sweater underneath. He had accented this ensemble with a chunky silver chain, massively spiked dark hair, a perfectly sculpted goatee and—wait for it—*pale blue sunglasses*. Clearly, this guy took coordination to a whole new level. It was immediately obvious he was either gay, not from this country or both. If he turned out to be gay, all the better. A new friend with great hair and makeup tips was always a good thing.

As I mulled this over, I noticed he had made his own assessment as evidenced by the slow, sexy smile he gave me. *Okay!* Most likely *not* gay, unless the smile was merely a show of appreciation for my fashion choices. I returned the smile and told him how much I liked his suit as Maya and I followed him into the club. Maybe Maya was right. Maybe tonight would be different. Maybe it was possible to meet someone special. It was a whole lotta maybes, but what did I have to lose at this point?

A few drinks and a few conversations with men trying to get into my pants later, I decided to approach the "flashy foreigner" as Maya and I had dubbed him. I started walking over to the edge of the bar where he was standing when I panicked. What was I going to say to him? Maybe I should borrow one of the lines I had been the recipient of earlier in the evening...

"My heart is aching from the sight of your awesomeness." Um, *no*.

"I don't need drugs to get high. I can look at your face. Want to see my van?" Definitely not.

"Come here often? I have since I divorced my cunt wife, but all the bitches have turned me down 'cause I told them about my crooked penis. Can I buy you a drink?" Wrong on *so* many levels.

*Oh, the hell with it!*
"What are you drinking?" I said and smiled, hoping I didn't look deranged after one too many shots.

He grinned. "It is called a coffin." Oooh, what kind of accent was that? I felt my knees buckle a bit from the sound of his velvety voice. Please don't be gay, please don't be gay, *please!*

"Sounds pretty deadly." *Oh, Sydney.* I felt heat instantly flood my face, confirming my suspicion that it had turned bright red. The verdict was in—I was officially going down in flames.

He took off his sunglasses and continued to grin at me. "Not as deadly as you. You are *very* beautiful."

Hmmm. Was he as full of it as the rest of these guys? Perhaps his incredibly sexy accent just made it sound better. I decided to reserve judgment for the time being. Maybe he was actually sincere. I mean, I had to give him credit for not laughing at my corny attempt at flirting.

"You're too kind." I dropped my gaze to the floor.

"No, not kind, just honest." He put his finger under my chin and tilted my face up until I was looking directly into the most achingly beautiful blue eyes I had ever seen. *Whoa.* I felt like my thighs were on fire. Was it the alcohol or because I hadn't had sex for such a long time? *Get a grip, Sydney!*

He released his hold from my face and offered me his hand. "My name is Louis, like your beloved Louis Armstrong."

I shook his hand and felt my heart skip a beat. Between his accent and his eyes, I was completely mesmerized.

"And you are?" he prompted.

"Dazzled." Oh. My. God. I was going to die right here in this bar. I did *not* just say that. A cross between a hysterical giggle and a cough escaped my throat. I took a deep breath and studied my shoes, hoping by breaking eye contact I could restore some semblance of sanity. "My name is Sydney. Sydney Bennett."

He waited until I found the courage to meet his eyes. "Well, it is a pleasure to meet you, Sydney Bennett."

He then took my hand and kissed it tenderly. Initially, I thought this was a cheesy move, but the sensation I felt when his lips touched my hand drove those thoughts out of my mind and into oblivion.

After a couple of minutes, I realized I was staring at him.
Would I *ever* stop embarrassing myself? Most likely not, but
in the meantime I should at least get a conversation going.
Think, Sydney, *think*

I said the first thing that popped into my head. "So,
Louis, where are you from?" I actually batted my eyelashes
at him. There was just no hope for me.

He chuckled. "You cannot place my accent, can you?
Many people have had trouble with this since I arrived."

It sounded like there was some serious competition out
there. No big deal! I could do this. (And if I couldn't, there
was always more alcohol.)

"Really? Let me guess...are you from Germany?"

"I am not, but I do speak German. This knowledge
helped me out of a few tight spots with the police."

So I had found myself a near convict. *Good going, Sydney!*
He must have seen the look on my face because he quickly
backpedaled.

"Please forgive me. I am sorry if what I said was
inappropriate. I am beginning to think I do not know how
to speak to American women. I have only been in the
country for two weeks and I have seen many of those
looks." He shook his head ruefully. "I am from France. I
grew up in the south, but I work in Paris for a small software
company. They sent me here to set up a few things in the
San Jose office."

So good news *and* bad. He wasn't a convict, but he
wouldn't be here for long. Well, there was nothing wrong
with a little fling, right? Except that I didn't know how to
do flings, managing to get my heart broken every time I
tried.

I cleared my throat. "How long are you here for?"

"Two more weeks. Then it is back to Paris for me." He
gave me his slow smile again.

Even through my drunken haze, I could feel the fear
coming. I knew very little about this guy and he was leaving

in two weeks with no plan to return. He was looking for a romp in the hay, nothing more. *I couldn't do this.* I had to run. It was the safe thing to do. *Come on, Sydney! Race you to the door!*

Something was keeping me there, standing in front of this man, gazing into his eyes. Why couldn't I just walk away? It was the easy way. It had worked for me very well over the past few years. No risk, no pain. But I couldn't get my body to agree with me.

"May I buy you a drink? I would like to know more about you." He pleaded with his beautiful blue eyes and I felt my willpower draining.

"Okay, *one* drink, but perhaps one less deadly than what you're currently drinking." *Seriously, Sydney, you need professional help. Just stop talking. He's going to change his mind!*

"Would you like a rum and coke?"

"Please." Keeping it simple—an excellent idea. This would greatly reduce your chances of saying something stupid.

Despite my usual moronic tendencies around attractive men, talking to Louis turned out to be pretty easy. (No doubt the alcohol helped.) He told me about growing up on a farm in the south of France, his collection of motorcycles and his hobby of building computers. He asked all about my family, my job and my childhood. Before I knew it, two hours had passed and Maya was tapping me on the shoulder.

She leaned forward and whispered in my ear, "I'm so sorry to do this to you, but I'm totally exhausted. I need to go home." She turned to Louis. "I'm sorry to take her away from you, but it's getting late."

"Please do not apologize," he responded, unleashing his signature smile. "I have had a wonderful time with Sydney. Please allow me to introduce myself. My name is Louis Durand "

Maya blushed. *Ha! Even she wasn't immune.* It was those eyes.

"My name is Maya," she said softly.

"It is a pleasure to meet you, Maya. I am happy you convinced Sydney to come out tonight. I owe you a debt of gratitude."

Maya blushed again. This just got better and *better*. "You're most welcome."

I sighed. "I'm sorry, Louis, but I have to leave." I think I was actually pouting. Wasn't that what French women did? It appeared his Frenchness was rubbing off on me.

Louis gently pulled me to a standing position and kept hold of my hand. "You have filled me with sadness, but I understand. Please give me your phone number so I may call you. I must see you again."

Was this guy for real? Did he feel obligated to ask? It was clear he wasn't getting lucky tonight. *It doesn't matter, Sydney. Just give him the number. Why not pretend?*

With no pen and paper available, I told him my number and he swore he would remember it. "I could never forget something so important."

Now I *knew* he was full of it. I wondered if this was how he got his kicks. Perhaps tonight would give him a good laugh for weeks to come. He and his French coworkers probably joked about the desperate, gullible American women they met each night. *Oh well!* I had a nice time nonetheless.

"Thank you for a lovely evening, Louis." I felt tears threatening—a sadness that none of this was real. I put my arms around his neck, planning on giving him a brief hug and running away, when he drew me to his chest and held me for a long moment. We just fit. It felt...right. Between the alcohol and his incredible scent, I had forgotten I was supposed to be in a hurry and jumped when Maya called my name.

"Be right there!" I smiled at Louis. "Take care of yourself. It was wonderful meeting you."

"Why do you say this? You sound like we will not meet again. I will call you tomorrow and we will, how do you say it, 'make a date?'"

As I walked away, I was sure I would never see him again.

*Chapter Four*

I woke up the next morning with an enormous smile on my face. I couldn't remember the last time I had felt this excited about a guy. Of course, it was all an illusion. I knew the probability he would call was right up there with my dad learning to knit. For the moment, I was choosing to ignore this and bask in the glow of my imagination. It was a lot more fun!

I had finished my delusion by planning what I would wear on our date when the phone rang. On Sunday mornings, Kate and I went to the farmer's market, so I figured she was calling to make sure I would be ready when she came to pick me up. She was always ready thirty minutes early and I always seemed to be ten minutes behind. Having a perfect sister was trying at times.

I nearly dropped the phone when I heard his voice. It was 10:30 in the *morning*, the *day after* I met him. I was with him *eight hours* ago. And he was actually on the phone with me. Now. And he sounded so good...

"Sydney?" he prompted. "Are you there?"

*Crap! Pay attention, woman!*

"Sorry! I'm here. I didn't get a lot of sleep last night." I giggled. *Pay attention* and *sound like less of a dork, please.*

"Was something keeping you up?" I could hear the sexy smile in his voice.

"Only thoughts of my favorite foreigner." I cringed at my particularly corny choice of words.

"What country was he from?" Louis asked innocently.

"He was German. Or Spanish...you know, I couldn't quite place his accent." My attempt at a throaty laugh sounded more like a deranged hyena. *Stop trying to flirt, Sydney. You don't know how!* I cleared my throat and tried a different tack. "How are you feeling this morning? Did you get any rest?"

He chuckled. "A little. My roommate brought a woman home with him last night and she was not very...quiet."

"How awkward for you," I replied hoarsely. Why in the world was I embarrassed?

"Nothing bothers me anymore. Not after working in a sex club."

*Sex club?!* Wait...he *had* mentioned that little tidbit. He had been a bartender—the first of three jobs he had in order to put himself through college. I shook my head in wonder. I had never met anyone like Louis before. His life had been so full, so interesting in his, um, however many years. *Did I forget to ask his age last night?*

"I can only imagine the things you saw." *Eww. Way too pervy, Sydney.*

"Be glad you did not have to see them. The darkness can only hide so much!" he exclaimed. "But this is not what I want to discuss with you on this beautiful morning."

Interesting. What did he want to discuss?

"I was wondering if you were free for dinner tonight?"

My heart stopped. Was he serious? Not only did he call less than twenty four hours after meeting me, but he asked me to dinner that very evening? Who *was* this guy?

"Sydney? Did I lose you again?"

"I'm sorry, Louis. You caught me by surprise. I would love to have dinner with you tonight."

"Why would you be surprised? I told you yesterday I

had to see you again. Are you not used to men doing what they tell you they will do? This makes me sad for you."

Seriously, was he for real? Or was this some elaborate scheme to seduce yet another American woman? Did I care at this point? I was drawn to him. I also had to face the fact that my bed hadn't seen any action in a very long time. It was time to dust off the cobwebs.

"Whatever you've heard about American women, Louis, is nothing in comparison to what I've experienced with American men. Forgive me for being a little gun shy. Let's start with dinner."

"How did the gun get involved?" Louis sounded completely confused this time.

"I'm sorry!" I spluttered. "It's an expression. It means it's hard for me to trust men easily."

"I see," he said dubiously. "It is a very odd expression. The French language makes a lot more sense."

"The English language is pretty crazy," I agreed. "Back to dinner, um, do you have a restaurant in mind?"

"*Magnifique!* I know a wonderful restaurant in Palo Alto. Do you like Italian food?"

"Love it! Let me know where and when I should meet you."

Louis gasped. "You American girls are so independent. There is no romance in courting. It is all business."

"You'll have to excuse me," I responded, smiling at the ease with which he teased me. "The years of dating American men have sucked the romance right out of me."

"Allow me to put it back in. Wait…I think you know what I meant." This was the first time I had heard Louis struggling for words. It was absolutely adorable.

I laughed. "Yes, Louis, I understood what you meant. We can discuss your theories of romance over dinner."

I was still smiling when I hung up with him five minutes later. Maybe he really was sincere. Maybe I would have a good time tonight. Maybe I should trust him. There were those whole lotta maybes again and I didn't like them. I needed to stick with definitive statements. They were safer. They didn't result in pain.

I raced over to my closet and yanked the door open. What was I going to wear? I didn't think the ensemble I chose in my imagination this morning would cut it. Dinner was totally different from clubbing. I wanted to look elegant, yet sexy, sophisticated, yet accessible, beautiful, yet relaxed. Only one woman could pull this off. I had to find my sister.

The doorbell broke me out of my reverie. *Kate!* I ran to the door. She would know the perfect thing to wear. She would know what I should say. She would be able to tell me what was going on. She knew...everything. It was *really* annoying.

I flung the door open to find Kate's smile fade quickly from her face. "You're not dressed yet."

I pulled her into the apartment. "Forget the farmer's market. We have much more pressing matters than which asparagus to roast. I have a date!"

"*What?*" The shock on Kate's face was a bit insulting.

I frowned. "Kate! You don't have to sound so incredulous!"

"I'm sorry, Syd. I'm not shocked that you have a date, because you're fabulous! I tell you that every day." She tapped her finger on my nose and broke into a huge grin. "I may have been a little *surprised* because I had no idea there was a man on the radar. When did this happen?" She was literally oozing excitement.

I felt relief wash over my body. If Kate (aka the eternal optimist) had lost faith in me, then there was serious cause for concern.

"Last night! Maya dragged me to Q Cafe and I met this *amazing* man. Well, he seems to be amazing. He could be completely full of it." I bit my lip. "I don't know...maybe I shouldn't go."

Kate rolled her eyes. "Will you relax? He obviously made quite an impression on you last night, so there must be something there. Did he ask you out last night?"

"No! He called me this morning. Can you believe it?" I was grinning like an idiot, but I didn't care.

Kate beamed and started jumping up and down. "That's awesome! Where is he taking you?"

"I'm meeting him at Il Fornaio."

Kate's face fell. "You won't let him pick you up?"

"Kate! I *just* met the guy. He could be a nut job—a beautiful nut job—but still!"

"Okay, I get it. It's not very romantic though," she sighed. "One step at a time. Agreeing to go on a date is a good sign. I was starting to worry about you."

It was my turn to sigh. "I needed a break, Kate. There are only so many awful dates you can put up with before you need to take a moment."

She giggled. "You're always taking your moments. I'm glad this moment is over." She grabbed my hand and pulled me over to my closet. "Now let's get down to business."

Kate's fingers flew through my hangars and two minutes later, she presented me with three choices. A black tank dress with beading around the collar, a gray pencil skirt paired with a sleeveless gray satin blouse and a red halter dress with a fitted bodice and a knee-length flared skirt.

"Here are the options." She cocked her head to the side. "It all depends what kind of look you're going for. The black dress is simple and elegant, the gray skirt-blouse combo is sophisticated and the red dress is hot!"

I pondered the choices. "What do you think?"

"You haven't been this interested in a guy in a long time. Plus, you don't know how long he'll be in the country. Go with the red dress, Syd! It looks *so* good on you."

"Really? It's not too much?" I asked nervously. "I feel so self-conscious in it."

"Sydney! Get *real.* You have an incredible body. You should show it off!"

I thought it over. "You're right. What do I have to lose? I may never see him again anyway."

Kate smoothed my hair back from my face. "Stop thinking about the future. You always take away the enjoyment you should be having *right now*. Live in the present for once!"

"Thanks, Kate," I murmured. "You know just how to snap me out of my craziness."

"That's my job," she said with a wink. "I'm your big sister! Now let's decide how to do your hair and makeup..."

⌒

Eight hours later, with my hair in loose waves down my back and my makeup expertly done courtesy of Maya, I was ready to meet Louis. At least, I was *physically* ready to meet him. Mentally, I was a mess. I couldn't remember the last time I had met a man with a genuine interest in me. It was too bad he didn't actually live in this country. I kept telling myself it would be a great experience, even if it was short-lived. With great effort, I swallowed my nerves and tried to focus on being more adventurous.

I gave myself a last look in the mirror. The red dress *was* an excellent choice. It hugged my body in all the right places and the elegant black heels I had chosen made my legs look even longer. *Breathe, Sydney.* Everything was going to be fine. Except...what if it wasn't? What if he turned out to be a jackass like all the others? I wasn't sure I could handle it. As my thoughts began to spiral, I considered my reflection with wide eyes. I felt my breathing become more and more shallow.

Kate grabbed me by the shoulders. "Syd! It's just a date. You aren't marrying the guy. Go and enjoy yourself. You can do that, right?"

I met her eyes. "Yes, I can."

Kate hugged me and murmured, "Don't overthink things. You're going to have a great time. I can *feel* it."

I hoped Kate was right this time. She meant well, but her "feelings" had been wrong before. Either way, it was time for me to leave.

"Call me when you get home, okay? I want to hear every detail." Kate handed me my black clutch and steered me to the door. "You know you're amazing, right? I've known it for a long time and I'm pretty sure Louis knows it too. *You deserve that*."

Her sincerity almost brought me to tears. "Stop it, Kate! If you make me cry, Maya is going to hurt you. Do you know how much this makeup costs?"

Kate giggled. "Maya *is* pretty scary. Although, sometimes I wonder if it's all talk." She hooked her arm through mine and walked me out the front door and over to my car. "Have fun, Syd! I love you."

"I love you too." I threw my arms around her. "Thank you for everything."

After one last squeeze from Kate, I got into my car. Along with the nervous butterflies, I had such delicious anticipation in my stomach. Louis was the first man to make me feel this happy in a long time. I was determined to enjoy our evening together. As I drove away, I did my best to stay positive, but in the back of my mind I kept wondering what was wrong with this seemingly perfect man...

*Chapter Five*

I parked my car outside the restaurant and took a deep breath. *One foot in front of the other, Sydney. You can do this.* I walked toward the restaurant and felt the familiar panic settling in my chest. Shocker! But seriously, I couldn't remember if I was supposed to meet him inside or outside the restaurant. I decided to wait outside since I was fifteen minutes early (thank you, Kate). The fresh air would help with my butterflies.

As I stood there trying to pass the time, my mind started to wander. What if he didn't show up? In my concern of what to wear, what to do and what to say, this thought hadn't crossed my mind. *Don't go there, Sydney.* He had given me no reason to think he would be a jerk, so I was going to give him the benefit of the doubt.

After a few minutes of waiting—and trying not to worry—I went inside to use the ladies' room. I chuckled silently as I thought of my dad's love of pointing out my "nervous" bladder. (He honestly believed he had missed his calling as a comic.) On my way through the restaurant, I could casually peruse the tables to see if Louis was waiting for me inside.

Ten minutes later, I was standing outside the restaurant

once again. Louis wasn't inside and I had done whatever primping I could—or "wishful makeupping" as Iona had said in *Pretty in Pink*. John Hughes was a wise man indeed.

I needed a sanity check. Before I could think better of it, I pulled out my cell phone and called Maya. She picked up on the first ring. "Why are you calling me? Aren't you on a date? Did something happen?" Her words rushed out at top speed.

I took a shaky breath. "He hasn't shown up yet. I'm nervous. I need you to talk me down. I feel like bolting."

"Syd, you got there early, right? Kate is a *such* a bad influence on you. You need to make men wait, you know, really make an entrance! Now, keep in mind Louis is European. They're known for not having the firmest sense of time. Do you have his cell phone number?"

*Rats.* "No, I don't. Come to think of it, he doesn't have mine either. I gave him our landline."

"Nobody uses landlines anymore, Syd," Maya scoffed. "Get with the times."

"Hey!" I spluttered. "I have trouble remembering my cell phone number after a few drinks!"

"Of course you do, hon," she murmured. "Okay, no need to worry. Everything is going to be fine. Just give him a little more time."

I nodded my head for a few seconds before I remembered she couldn't see me. "You're right. It's going to be great," I said, absently running my hand through my expertly gelled locks. *Shoot!* It had taken Kate an hour to get my hair to look perfect. Just as I was falling into a fit of despair, I glanced up to find Louis rushing down the street carrying a beautiful bouquet of flowers.

"He's here!" I exclaimed as quietly as I could. "And he brought the most gorgeous flowers!"

Maya sighed. "I knew you were overreacting. Later, crazy girl." She hung up before I had the chance to say anything.

Louis stopped in his tracks when he saw me. *Oh no.* Did

I smudge my makeup? Was my skirt tucked into my underwear? That happened to Maya once in a bar and it was hideously embarrassing. I was certainly nervous enough to have missed something along those lines during my trip to the bathroom.

As I quickly checked my appearance, he approached me with a wide grin. "You are stunning, Sydney. I did not think it was possible for you to look even better than you did last night, but you have proven me wrong."

I felt heat flood my face. Compliments always made me blush and coupled with his scorching gaze, I was pretty sure my face was a deeper shade of red than my dress. "Thank you, Louis. You look...handsome." Lamely put, but true.

Louis was wearing a black short-sleeved collared shirt with a metallic sheen and black pants. He seemed to go for the whole monochromatic thing—but his signature blue sunglasses were a nice touch. He too looked even better than he had last night.

"This is a high compliment, coming from such a beautiful lady." There was his sexy smile again. I felt a twinge of desire work its way through my body. Perhaps Kate and Maya were right—Louis *would* be good for me, even if it was only for two weeks.

Our staring exercise continued until a car alarm went off. Louis snapped to attention first and handed me the bouquet of flowers he was holding. I took them and beamed. They were blue irises, one of my favorite flowers.

"Thank you, Louis." I reached over and hugged him. He smelled unbelievably good and I didn't want to let go. As this was definitely not the time or the place for such activities, I reluctantly pulled back.

He contemplated me with his beautiful blue eyes. "Are you not used to a man who listens to what you say? You told me last night how much you love irises."

"Yes, I did," I replied. "The men I've been out with either wouldn't remember I had said that or wouldn't take the time to figure out what an iris was."

Louis raised his eyebrows. "What kind of men have you been dating?"

I couldn't help but smile at him. "I don't know, Louis, but I have no desire to think of them anymore. I want to hear more about *you*. Shall we go inside?"

At this Louis offered me his arm, walked me to the entrance and opened the door for me. He pulled out my once we got to the table and even asked the waiter to bring a vase for my flowers. He was a perfect gentleman. While Louis ordered a bottle of wine, I glanced at my watch. I was surprised to see the hands show six o'clock—exactly the time we agreed to meet. It was then I realized that Louis was rushing even though he was early. I had panicked for no reason. *Way to go, Syd!* I quickly turned my focus back to Louis, determined to enjoy our evening together.

I couldn't believe my good fortune. I had never laughed so much on a date before. As we ate our appetizers, Louis told me the most enthralling stories about his childhood. Growing up on a small farm in France may have seemed tame to the average person, but Louis managed to find whatever trouble there was to find. Since he was an only child, he felt it was up to him to keep his parents—Simone and Michel—on their toes. He jumped from rooftops, swung from ropes at great heights and raced motorcycles. He was even a national martial arts champion.

Louis was also valedictorian of his high school class, in the top of his graduating class in engineering college and regularly built computers for himself and his family. He was like a French MacGyver. I was sure he could have built some kind of communication device with the items left on the dinner table. It was mind blowing. I had never felt more ordinary.

"Is there anything you *can't* do?" I asked, a note of awe in my voice.

Without so much as flinching, he said, "No." Then his whole face lit up and he started to chuckle. "There are many things I cannot do, Sydney. For one thing, I cannot understand how it is possible that a woman like you is single."

I made no attempt to hide my massive eye roll.

He laughed. "I saw that! You are quite....what is the word, ah, sassy? Are you not?"

I broke into a grin. For the umpteenth time since I had met Louis (a whole twenty hours ago), I thought, "Is he for real?" He *had* to have flaws.

"Enough hiding, Sydney. I want to hear more about you."

"Well, after all the tales you've told me, my life is going to seem pretty boring," I admitted. "Besides, I gave you quite a bit of information last night."

"Not possible," he insisted. "And we barely scratched the surface last night. Please start from the beginning." He waited expectantly.

I gave him the basic rundown as we devoured our main courses. (Well, *I* devoured, he ate like a normal person. Another side effect of my extensive nervous energy was a voracious appetite.) I grew up in New York as the youngest of three children. My parents got divorced when I was six and my mom, Lyn, remarried two years later. I considered my stepfather, Ted, to be my real father as he loved and raised my siblings and me as his own after my biological father left us for his secretary. (Was it any wonder I had difficulty trusting men?) He even went so far as to adopt us, which was a huge deal considering he had already raised three daughters of his own. We, in turn, adopted his last name—Bennett. My brother, Charlie, and sister, Kate, were my favorite people in the world other than my parents. I had been the salutatorian of my high school class, had graduated *Magna Cum Laude* from Northwestern University and loved my job in Human Resources at a small biotech firm in Mountain View.

When we finished our desserts, Louis took my hand. "Sydney."

A shiver ran down my spine. "Louis?"

"Where shall we go next?"

I felt butterflies return to my stomach. I was having a great time, but I wasn't sure how much longer I could go without making a complete ass of myself.

"What about a walk down University Avenue? It's really pretty at night."

"A wonderful idea," he responded. "Let us go. I do not want to say goodnight to you yet."

As we walked out of the restaurant, he took my hand. I quickly suppressed a gasp (another of my annoying traits was how easily I was startled), before turning to him with a smile. He smiled back at me and suddenly stopped.

"Is something wrong?" I said, puzzled.

"No, not at all. I wondered...if it would be okay to kiss you?" he asked shyly.

My legs turned to jelly. "Um, that would be...nice." *Way to be definitive, Syd.*

He took a step closer to me and caressed the side of my face. His face was mere inches away, his beautiful blue eyes searching mine. He was so intense, so sexy and he smelled *so* good. Just when I thought I was going to hyperventilate from anticipation, he closed his eyes and pulled my face gently toward him. His lips brushed mine and it was absolute heaven. He kissed me softly a few more times and then gently released my face from his hands. Then he gazed at me and took my hand once more.

"You are extraordinary, Sydney. And you don't even know it."

I stared at him in a daze and nodded. I knew he had said something, but I couldn't process it. I was having enough trouble remembering how to walk.

After a few moments of strolling down the beautiful tree-lit street, I regained my composure and was able to engage in somewhat intelligent conversation. Before long, we walked into a bookstore and started browsing the latest titles. Somehow we ended up in the astrology section and I asked Louis when his birthday was so I could read about his personality quirks.

He frowned. "I do not have any personality quirks, but my birthday is July 22nd."

"That's a week from today!"

"Yes, I know," he replied. "Is something wrong?"

I touched his arm and smiled. "No, it's just, you'll be here instead of in France, right?"

"Yes, I will be here. Is that a bad thing?" He took a step closer to me.

I shook my head. "It's a shame because you won't be with your family."

He pulled me close to him and whispered in my ear, "Well, I guess it will be up to you to help me celebrate."

I giggled. "How old are you going to be?"

He pursed his lips. "I never remember how old I am. I know you will think me ridiculous. I will be...twenty-four years old."

The smile froze on my face. I was nearly *four* years older than Louis. *Holy crap!* Wait a minute...why did this matter? I had been totally fine—okay, sort of fine—before I knew his age. This was *so* not a big deal. I had dated guys who were years older than I was and they still sucked. *Stop finding reasons to disqualify him, Sydney!*

I regained my composure and grinned at Louis. "You're a baby!"

"French men mature faster. Why, how old are you?"

I laughed. "Don't you know it's rude to ask a woman her age?"

He winked. "I am French. We are known for being rude. Now, please answer my question."

I pouted at him. "I'm twenty-seven...soon to be twenty-eight."

He feigned shock. "Oh! You are *ancient*. I cannot believe you have fooled me for this long."

"You're so mean!" I swatted him on the shoulder. "I was going to ask you to dinner for your birthday, but now I'm not sure you deserve the invitation."

He drew me close to him. "I would love to go to dinner with you for my birthday, but only if you let me take you out again tomorrow night."

*Whoa!* Tomorrow night? I started to panic. How long could I keep up the charade of normalcy for Louis?

"Make it Tuesday and you have a deal. I promised my sister I would hang out with her tomorrow night." It was a total lie, but I needed a little breathing room.

"Okay. Tuesday it is." He released me from his hold and took my hand. "It is getting late, Sydney. I should walk you back to your car."

I nodded and we set off toward the parking garage. When we got to my car, he took my face in this hands once more. "I had a wonderful time tonight. I will call you tomorrow."

I was about to tell him I had a wonderful time too when he kissed me in such a way that would make my face turn a startling shade of crimson if I were to describe it to you. Suffice it to say, it was the most sensual, enthralling, stomach-flipping kiss I had ever experienced.

After what seemed like hours, Louis swept me into a tender hug and held me for a long moment. He reluctantly opened my car door and helped me gently inside. "Drive safely, Sydney."

I smiled, closed the door and started the car. With stars in my eyes, I waved to him as I drove away. I felt giddy at having experienced the most perfect first date *ever*, but couldn't shake the feeling that I had to be missing something. Could Louis really be this perfect?

## Chapter Six

My alarm clock woke me from a highly enjoyable dream of Louis. It was Monday morning and I had to get ready for work. I had snoozed through my morning workout since I had been up late last night telling Kate (and then Maya) all about my incredible evening. Between the reminiscing and retelling, my head was completely full of Louis. How was I going to concentrate on work?

Thankfully, the day went by quickly. Monday was the day I gave orientation for new employees and introduced them around the building. By the time this was done and their paperwork had been completed, it was the end of the day. I shut down my computer and called Kate.

She picked up on the first ring. "Hey, Syd!"

I really loved caller ID. "Hi! I'm on my way. Do you need me to pick up anything for dinner?" I had decided I had to make last night's statement to Louis true. I felt terrible for lying to him. Besides, it was always nice to see Kate and Nick.

"No, thanks. Plan B. We're going out."

"What happened to 'barbeque night?'" I asked.

She sighed. "Nick had a little trouble putting the grill together."

"*Shut up*! Mr. Perfect had trouble with something?" I couldn't control my laughter.

"Be nice, Syd. I keep telling you that Nick isn't perfect. *Do not* make fun of him when you get here. He feels bad enough as it is."

I suppressed another chuckle. "Of course I won't make fun of him. You know how much I love Nick. I would never do anything to diminish his masculinity."

"You'd better not. I'm your big sister, Sydney! I know how to get to you," she said darkly.

"Yikes! I'm petrified." Kate didn't have a threatening bone in her body. She tried, but she just couldn't pull it off. "I'll see you in half an hour."

"Wait, Syd! Have you talked to Mom lately?"

I thought for a moment. "Not since last week. The store is *always* busy. And even when it's not open, she's doing inventory or sales projections."

My mom and dad had opened a pottery painting studio a couple of years ago and though it had taken time to get off the ground, it had become very popular. Charlie, Kate and I were very happy for them, but because of the store's success, my mom was harder and harder to get on the phone.

"I know it isn't easy to catch her, but she really misses you. Why don't you try giving her a call tomorrow? Maybe you could tell her about Louis."

"I'm not ready to tell her, Kate!" I cried. "Let's see how tomorrow night goes, okay? I want to get know him a little better first."

"She just wants to you to be happy, Syd."

"I know. I don't want her to be disappointed if she doesn't have to be. She has enough to worry about with the store, she doesn't need to worry about me too."

Kate laughed. "She'll worry anyway, but I get what you're saying."

"Good. See you soon!"

I drove up to Kate and Nick's house exactly thirty

minutes later to find Nick outside with the grill and a toolbox.

"Hey, Nick!"

He glanced up and grinned. "Hi, Syd! I'm glad you're here. I need to hear more about this Louis guy. Kate says you're totally into him."

"Nice, Nick. You just set a new record. I love that your favorite game is to see how quickly you can embarrass me."

"You're my little sister now, you know. It's my job to make you uncomfortable."

"Gee. Thanks. I feel so loved." I gave him a big hug. "You're a total pain in the ass, but I love you anyway."

After messing up my hair, he put his arm around my shoulder and walked me inside.

Kate beamed when she saw us. "Hey, Syd! Are you up for some margaritas?"

"Definitely." I rubbed my hands together in anticipation. "Are you guys ready to go?"

"Let's go!" Nick and Kate said in unison. Sometimes perfection was really nauseating.

Dinner at Casa de Maria was delicious as usual. Carlos, the owner of the restaurant, loved Kate and was constantly sending over special dishes for us to try for free—just one of the many benefits of being her sister.

After dinner, Kate and Nick walked me to my car. "Thanks for dinner, you guys. It was *so* good."

Nick pulled me into a hug. "You're welcome, Syd. We're always happy to see you."

When he released me, Kate whispered in my ear, "Please give yourself a break and enjoy Louis. Stop second guessing everything. It must be exhausting!"

How right she was.

"Thanks, Kate," I murmured as I hugged her. "You always know what to say."

My stomach still felt like it was going to burst when I got home. I put on my pajamas and had just finished brushing my teeth when I bumped into Jess in the hallway.

"Hey, Syd! You have a message on the answering machine. Louis sounds *sexy!*"

I raced to the kitchen and pushed the play button on the answering machine. "Hello, Sydney. I am sorry to miss you, *mon coeur*. I hope you are having a good time with Kate this evening. Please know I am thinking of you and look forward to seeing you tomorrow. I will pick you up at six o'clock. Ciao."

I listened to the message again. My heartrate quickened at the sound of his voice. Jess had it right—Louis sounded incredibly sexy. I felt my stomach clench in anticipation of seeing him tomorrow night. Oh, the possibilities...

Much to Kate's delight, I had agreed to let Louis pick me up for dinner this time. Since he had chosen the restaurant for our last date, I chose tonight's restaurant. I opted for something more casual and fun—a pub down the street from my apartment. I was a regular there and hoped Louis would appreciate the food and crazy clientele as much as I did. Our conversations certainly led me to believe he enjoyed the unexpected.

I raced home from work and took a quick shower. Kate and I had already chosen my "casual" ensemble for this evening during our dinner last night. It had only taken us thirty minutes and four outfit choices. (Nick was thrilled!) We settled on a pair of dark jeans, a green satin camisole with cream lace trim and cream sling-back heels. I wrapped a soft cream sweater around my shoulders and added silver chandelier earrings for a little dazzle. Kate advised me to wear my hair up in order to show off my shoulders and the beautiful earrings she had let me borrow.

I twirled in front of the mirror. I had to admit I looked good and hoped Louis would agree. I smiled at the thought of him and then glanced at the clock. *Holy crap!* It was six-thirty. How did that happen? Wait, wasn't Louis supposed to be here at six o'clock? I went to the kitchen to check the answering machine. No messages. Did I get the time wrong? Wait! I hadn't deleted his message from yesterday. I pushed the play button. I listened to Louis' message and was almost immediately distracted by the sound of his velvety voice. *Focus, Sydney.* I listened intently. He did say six o'clock. Hmmm.

The familiar panic started to set in. *Stop!* He was probably just running late. I dialed his cell phone number and it went straight to voicemail. This was not good. I peeked outside my window, but didn't see his rental car in the parking lot. Where could he be? Was he stuck in a meeting at work? Did he have an accident? Or had I been completely taken in by his charming demeanor?

I jumped when the phone rang. I ran to it, almost upending a table in the process. "Hello?" I said breathlessly.

"Syd? Are you okay?" Maya asked.

"I'm fine, Maya. It's just...Louis is thirty minutes late to pick me up and I'm worried."

"Thirty minutes? Have you tried calling him?"

"Yes, I tried calling him," I snapped. "It went straight to voicemail."

"Get a grip, Syd. He probably got stuck at work. I know it's asking a lot, but why don't you give him a few more minutes before you lose your shit?"

I rolled my eyes. "Thanks, Maya. You're great at talking me down from the crazy." Knowing Maya, she completely missed the sarcasm, but at least being annoyed with her was distracting me. "What are you up to?"

"I'm on my way to the gym. I just wanted to see if you were free for a drink tomorrow night. You've been kinda busy lately."

"Indeed, I have," I sighed. "I'd love to. Seven at Charlie's?"

"You read my mind. Call me later to tell me how your date went. All the men I've met lately haven't been up to par. I need to live vicariously through you."

"If I'm not home too late!" I sang.

"You realize you owe me *big* time since I dragged your ass out that night."

"I know, I know. Drinks are on me tomorrow night."

"It's a start, my friend."

The sound of the doorbell gave me renewed hope.

"I have to run, Maya. Have a good night!"

"You too, Syd." Maya had the ability to make anything sound wicked.

I opened the door to find a very anxious Louis. "Sydney! I am sorry to be late. I got stuck in a last minute meeting and could not get out to call you. I was going to call you on the way, but my phone is out of battery. I hope you can forgive me." He handed me another gorgeous bouquet of flowers.

I threw my arms around him in relief. "I understand, Louis. Work comes first." I smiled shyly. "You didn't have to buy me more flowers, silly man."

"I wanted to buy them for you, silly *woman*," he replied, grinning. "I have missed you, Sydney." As he buried his nose in my hair, he sighed and said, "You smell wonderful."

I certainly knew the power his scent had over me. "You're making me blush, Louis. By the way, what does '*mon coeur*' mean?"

He laughed. "Ah yes, my pet name for you. It means 'my heart' in French."

My stomach flipped. "How beautiful. *Thank you.*"

"It is a fitting name for you," he said sincerely. "Are you ready to go? I am famished. I had to work through lunch today."

I grabbed my purse. "All set. We can walk. The pub is only a few blocks down the street."

He took my hand and kissed it softly as we walked out the door. "My day has just gotten *much* better, Sydney."

That was the beginning of another magical night with Louis. We talked and laughed for hours without a break. When he walked me home, I felt pure joy from finding this man. *Why* did he have to go back to France? I had avoided this subject like the plague, but the more time I spent with him, the more it pushed to the forefront of my mind. What was I going to do? The other nagging question was right beside it—what was wrong with Louis? He couldn't actually be this perfect...

*Chapter Seven*

The phone woke me with a start. I searched for the clock. Six-thirty in the morning? Who the hell was calling me this early?

I inspected the caller ID and hurled myself at the phone once I saw that it was Kate. *"Are you okay?"*

"I should be asking you the same question, my dear." Irritation colored her tone.

"Why? What's the matter?"

"You were supposed to call me last night, remember? I was worried when I didn't hear from you

"I'm sorry! I got home late and didn't want to wake you."

"You must've had an exceptionally good time." *Was that sarcasm, Kate?*

I giggled. "I did, but not the good time you're talking about."

"Good girl! You need to make him wait a little bit longer."

"I didn't say *nothing* happened, you know..." I smiled to myself. Louis and I had shared a very intimate and lengthy kiss in my apartment after he walked me home. It took every ounce of restraint I had not to pull him into my bedroom right then and there.

"Really? *Do tell.*"

"He is the most amazing kisser *ever.* Never in my life have I experienced anything like it." I became breathless just from the memory of last night.

"Oooh! When are you going to see him again?" She was pretty breathless herself.

"Tomorrow night. He's making me dinner at his apartment."

She chuckled. "Sounds like a *big* night."

I joined in her chuckle. "Hey, now. There's no need to be rude."

"Of course not. You're always perfectly virtuous, Syd."

"You're a bit smug for someone who's only slept with one man!"

We both started laughing. "I love you, Kate."

"I love you too, Syd. *Don't forget* to call me later!"

$\frown$

To my great dismay, I found myself buried in benefit audit paperwork for most of the day. In the late afternoon, my phone rang. Please, please, *please* let it not be another employee with an issue. I already had more than I could handle.

"Sydney Bennett, how may I help you?"

"There is no help for me, Duck. How's your day going?" My dad had been calling me "Duck" for as long as I could remember. He once told me that I looked like a duck when I was unhappy about something. Unfortunately for me, the name stuck.

"Hey, Dad. The day's going slowly. I'm totally bogged down with paperwork."

"Just shred it all. No one will notice," he advised. As his daughter, I knew he was completely serious.

I laughed. "That may have worked in your day, but now people would notice—and I'd get fired. I can't imagine you would be happy about supporting me again. I'm supposed to be financially independent, right?"

"You young people are so serious. It isn't a big deal."

"Easy for you to say, Dad. You were always your own boss. You never had to explain to anyone why you messed up. Although I can only imagine what you would have said if you did." The thought made me chuckle. My dad had a way with words, especially the profane ones.

"I have to explain it to your mother often enough. She seems to understand."

I had made the mistake of taking a sip of tea while he was speaking and started to cough following his revelation. Once I had regained the power of speech, I spluttered, "You *never* admit doing anything wrong."

"I didn't say *I* admitted doing anything wrong. I always have to explain to her what *other* people have done wrong."

I let out a full-blown cackle. "Dad, you're something else."

"I know. You're a very fortunate girl." My father could be quite smug, but it only make him more adorable.

A glance at the clock told me I had cut things too close. "I have to go, Dad. I'm meeting Maya for drinks in an hour and I have a stop to make on the way."

"Have fun, sweetheart. Say hi to Maya for us." My parents absolutely adored Maya. She was quite the charmer when she chose to be.

"I will. I love you, Dad."

"I love you too, Duck. Listen, don't forget to call your mother. She misses you."

"I won't forget. It's hard to catch her these days."

"She always has time for you, Syd."

"I know, Dad. I'll call her soon, I promise. 'Bye!" I grinned as I hung up. I was lucky to have parents who loved me as much as they did. Now I just had to find a man to help with the job. I wondered if Louis might finally be the one.

I ran down the sidewalk in a vain attempt to be a little less late for drinks with Maya. Picking out a new outfit for dinner with Louis tomorrow night took a little longer than I had expected. I should have had Maya come with me. Shopping was like second nature to her. Because of this, she had very little tolerance for those of us who were slightly challenged. She wasn't going to be happy about my lateness.

I pushed open the door to Charlie's and spotted her right away. She was at the end of the bar talking to a tall, dark and handsome man. There was no way I was going to get in the way of that. I nodded to Charlie at the bar and grabbed a table. Twenty minutes later, Maya came over to the table with a very satisfied smile on her face.

"Hey, Syd!" she said happily. "I've met the most wonderful man named Edmund." She sat down with a delighted expression on her face.

"Edmund? *Sweet!* You scored one of the kings of Narnia!" I frowned in response to her blank look. "Seriously, Maya? You've never read the *Chronicles of Narnia*?"

She shook her head. "I have no idea what you're talking about. Honestly, Syd, you're lucky you're so pretty."

Over drinks, Maya approved my outfit choice for dinner tomorrow evening. I had purchased a steel gray silk tank top and a pair of fitted black pants. Maya told me my chunky black Mary Janes would top off the outfit along with the silver hoop earrings and bangles she had brought me. She gave me a few hair and makeup tips and sent me on my way.

"Call me tomorrow night, Syd. There will be many details for you to share." She tossed a saucy wink over her shoulder.

"As long as I don't get home too late!" I called as I walked away.

The next day flew by in a blur and before I knew it I was

getting ready for my date with Louis. When I finished primping, I gave myself a last look in the mirror before leaving the apartment. I had followed Maya's instructions to a "T" in doing my hair (up in a bun with a few tendrils spilling out) and makeup (smoky eyes accompanied by plum colored lips) and was satisfied with the results. The jewelry she had lent me perfectly complemented my clothing choice and I felt rather sophisticated as I walked to my car. This night was going to be wonderful.

I arrived at Louis' corporate apartment five minutes before our agreed meeting time of six-thirty. I rang the doorbell, hoping he wouldn't mind that I was early. A moment later, Louis opened the door wearing a loud Hawaiian shirt and jeans.

I burst out laughing. "Nice shirt!"

He raised his eyebrows. "I think so! The saleswoman told me that it went perfectly with my complexion."

"That it does," I agreed with a grin.

After playfully tweaking my nose, he said, "It was Hawaiian shirt day at work. They are trying to create a more comfortable working environment." He shook his head. "The American workplace is just odd."

I laughed and threw my arms around him, inhaling his intoxicating scent. Except this time it was laced with...bacon? "What have you been cooking? It smells delicious."

"Veal wrapped in prosciutto." His relaxed expression suddenly changed to one of horror. "You do not have any issues with veal, do you? I did not realize Americans were offended by such a delicious meat."

Oh, how this man made me laugh! "No need to worry, Louis. I love veal—as offensive as it may be to some. Thank you so much for cooking tonight." I followed him into the apartment, relishing the mouth-watering scent of our dinner.

"You are well worth it, Sydney." He walked over to me and put his hands on my shoulders. I peeked up at him and completely lost my train of thought. His eyes should be registered as a lethal weapon. It really wasn't fair.

"You look enchanting, *mon coeur*." There was that suggestive smile again. I didn't stand a chance. He kissed me for the first time in two days and I was beyond ready. My hands found his face and I pulled him closer to deepen the kiss. He responded enthusiastically and I was pretty sure some very naughty things would have taken place on the kitchen floor had the smoke alarm not gone off at that very moment.

"Shit! I am sorry, Syd. Just give me a minute." He turned off the burner and raced out of the kitchen. A minute later, he returned with a broom and proceeded to hit the smoke alarm with gusto. Thankfully, it stopped ringing shortly after Louis' assault.

He smiled sheepishly. "You are far too distracting."

"I'm sorry, Louis. I couldn't help myself." I felt heat creeping into my face.

"You look so lovely when you blush. I am happy to cause this reaction in you."

"I bet you are." I smacked his arm and put my purse down on the kitchen counter. "Is there anything I can do to help?"

He came up behind me, put his arms around my waist and rested his chin on my shoulder. "No, thank you, *mon coeur*. Everything is ready, though some of it may be a bit well done."

He pulled out a chair for me at the dining room table and poured me a glass of wine. Then he disappeared into the kitchen and returned with the most colorful salad I had ever seen. It was filled to the brim with exotic fruits and vegetables, but the best part, hands down, was the dressing. It was the perfect combination of sweet and salty and turned out to be the result of his own development. Despite a lot of prodding, he wouldn't reveal the secret recipe.

He smirked. "I cannot spoil the mystery. I have to keep you guessing."

Next he brought out the slightly singed veal wrapped in prosciutto with rice and grilled vegetables. After we had eaten this incredible dinner, he served dessert wine and a chocolate soufflé.

"Louis!" I exclaimed. "I'm not going to fit into any of my clothes if you keep feeding me like this."

He winked suggestively. "That is the idea." I covered my face with my hands, causing him to laugh softly. "You are easily embarrassed. It is adorable."

"It isn't adorable," I grumbled through my fingers. "It's *embarrassing*."

Louis knelt in front of me and removed my hands from my face. "I am only teasing you! You do not have to be embarrassed." He stood up, bringing me with him. "Sydney, you are an exceptionally beautiful and captivating woman. It is perfectly natural for me to desire you."

When I felt heat flood my face, he sighed, "What will it take for you to relax?"

I gazed at him longingly. "Maybe we could go somewhere a little more private?" The last thing I wanted was for Louis' roommate to interrupt us.

He led me into his bedroom and closed the door. "Is this better?"

I wrapped my arms around him and nodded. "Much." Unable to resist any longer, I pushed him down onto the bed and kissed him.

Louis broke away and held my face in his hands. "Sydney, are you sure you want to do this?"

"Why don't we give it a try and see?"

All conversation ceased at that point. I was so distracted, I didn't even begin to wonder what was wrong with Louis.

## Chapter Eight

As it turned out, I was ready, but Louis wasn't. Well actually, we both weren't. Neither one of us had condoms. Way to spoil a party! I had never been so disappointed about anything in my life. The only positive thing I could think of was I would feel like less of a slut since our first time would have to wait until his birthday. At least I will have known him for a week by then.

I had spent the week being so distracted by Louis—talking to him, thinking about him, imagining kissing him, imagining doing *other* things with him—I had totally forgotten to buy him a birthday gift. It was now Friday night and I had to find a great gift by Sunday. He had to work all day Saturday, which meant I had time to work with, but it was still going to be tough. I wanted to give him something special, but we had known each other for less than a week so I didn't want to freak him out by buying him anything too meaningful. I knew I was overthinking this. It was time to bring in an expert.

Maya picked up on the first ring. How did she do that? She must have her phone permanently attached to her face.

"I need help."

She sighed. "Tell me something I don't know. What is

it this time?"

"Have I told you how obnoxious you are lately?"

"You'd better watch it, girl. You still owe me and clearly you need my help, so—"

"Fine!" I interrupted. "*I give up.* I need to buy a birthday gift for Louis, but I'm at a loss for what would be, um, appropriate."

She snorted. "Appropriate? Syd, you crack me up. Stop thinking so much! I'm sure you already have a great idea, but you've talked yourself out of it for some crazy reason."

"It frightens me how well you know me." I paused. "Or am I just that easy to read?"

"What do you think?" After we both had a good laugh, she said, "Now tell me your idea."

"Well, he loves the Bloodhound Gang and they're playing in the city next week. I went online and there are a few really crappy seats left for Tuesday night, but I thought it would be fun. Ugh! I don't know. Is it lame?"

"It's not lame! It's incredibly thoughtful, as usual. I totally give you props for going to such an awful concert for him. The Bloodhound Gang sucks!" She added sound effects for emphasis.

"Thanks! I *love* hearing your opinion on things. It's always so nicely put."

"Hey, honesty is important," she said matter-of-factly. "And you know you love me."

"Yes, I do...for some inexplicable reason. But seriously, the show is a nice gift, but I have to give him something on his actual birthday."

She burst into a fit of giggles. "I thought you had something very *special* to give him on his birthday." Her laughter became so boisterous, she dropped the phone with a loud clatter.

"Nice, Maya!" I cleared my throat. "I hope it'll happen, but it's not a gift. It's something I want too, you perv!"

Once she had regained her composure, she said, "Okay, I've got it. What about a picture frame? You could have a photo taken that night and put it in the frame for him to take back to France."

"No way! Too presumptuous. We'll probably never see each other again." I felt my eyes tear up at the thought and was thankful she couldn't see me. I didn't need any further mocking.

"Syd, I've seen the way he looks at you. He'll make something happen. I can tell."

"Maya, that's very sweet of you to say, but you're on crack. You saw him look at me the night he *met* me. There's no way he was in that place then—nor is he there now!" I didn't want to hear this. I couldn't allow hope to start burrowing in my heart.

"Have it your way, Syd, but I think I'm right. You wait and see."

Suddenly the idea I had been searching for smacked me right between the eyes. "A plant! I'll buy him a plant!" I allowed myself a good old-fashioned fist pump to celebrate my victory. "He was just saying the other day how bleak his apartment is and he *loves* plants. His mom has a huge garden back in France."

"Very sweet, Syd, but I think you'll be the one making his last week, uh, *memorable*."

"I'm glad you're enjoying yourself," I replied drily. "I have to run. Call you later!"

"Bye, hon! *Be good!*"

Why did she always make things sound dirty?

By Sunday afternoon, I was in good shape. I had bought Louis the concert tickets and a beautiful ficus plant. I had also borrowed my favorite dress of Kate's—a sparkly silver strapless sheath dress with a knee-length skirt. I straightened my hair, added light makeup (subtle hues on the eyes and lips) and a few pieces of simple jewelry, finishing off the look with silver strappy sandals. *Not bad, Sydney.*

Louis rang the doorbell at exactly six o'clock. I opened the door and stood back, taking a moment to admire him. He was wearing a French-blue long-sleeved collared shirt and charcoal gray pants. The blue of the shirt intensified the color of his eyes—if that was even possible—and the effect was breathtaking. I was stunned into silence.

"May I come in?" Louis asked, flashing his gorgeous grin.

I shook the steamy thoughts from my head. "Of course! I'm sorry, I was distracted by how handsome you look." I felt lust surge through my body following my admission.

"You are the one doing the distracting, *mon coeur*. You look...I wish I could find the right words." He thought for a moment. "I think *breathtaking* is the word I am searching for."

There was the tell-tale warmth in my face. *Blush much, Sydney?* I wondered if I would ever learn to take a compliment from him.

Louis approached me and ran his hands down my arms. "Sydney, you know what it does to me when you blush. We are not going to make it to the restaurant at this rate."

I gazed up at him and made a decision. I slid my arms around his waist and ran them down over his firm behind. Then I reached up and kissed him very slowly.

"Sydney," he whispered.

I pulled him toward me and led him to my bedroom without breaking the kiss. Once we were inside, I locked the door and turned to face him. He pinned me to the wall and kissed me hungrily.

"You have no idea how much I want you," he panted, feeling for the zipper of my dress.

"I think I have a very good idea, Louis." I kissed his neck and began to unbutton his shirt. His groan sent shivers down my spine.

He swept me into his arms and carried me to the bed. "I can't take any more waiting, *mon coeur*. I have wanted you since the first moment I saw you and the desire has only deepened the more time we have spent together."

My mind threatened to wander to a very sarcastic place, but I tuned it out. I wanted this man so badly and I didn't care if I would never see him again after next week. For once, I was living in the present. Kate would be proud.

The sex was extraordinary. Never in my life had I felt so cherished, so breathless and so *satisfied*. Louis really was good at *everything*. I had had orgasms before, but there were no words to describe this experience. I couldn't stop smiling, which amused Louis to no end.

He smirked. "You look pretty happy, *mon coeur*."

"Mmm...an accurate assessment, *Monsieur* Durand." I snuggled into his chest.

His eyes danced. "Well, with enough practice, you get good at things."

I smacked him in the chest. "Oh, so that's what you've spent all your time doing in France? I thought you were busy with school and work."

"Well, you can squeeze it in anywhere. You only have to be flexible!" He collapsed into laughter.

"What a heinous joke, birthday boy! We need to focus. Are you hungry? I'm sorry I made us miss our reservation." I did feel a little guilty. It was his birthday, after all.

"Do not be sorry, Syd. This was much better than any dinner could have been. In fact, I think I am ready for seconds..." He slowly ran his hand up my thigh.

"Louis!" I squealed. "I'm going to need sustenance before any further activity. I'm actually starting to feel dizzy." Having seconds was extremely tempting, but my blood sugar was at rock bottom.

He sighed. "You are right. Shall we order a pizza?"

"Are you sure pizza is what you want?" I frowned. " I mean, it's your birthday. Don't you want something special?"

"What I want is you and pizza is a quick meal. Let us

order it, eat and get back to celebrating."

"I like your style, Louis." I smiled as I got up and grabbed my robe. I stopped I my tracks when I realized that I was falling in love with this man and he was leaving in a week. I was suddenly struck with sadness.

As I tried to drag myself out of it, Louis stood up and caressed my face. "What is the matter?" His brow furrowed with concern.

I shook my head. "Nothing. It's silly. I was thinking about how soon you'll be returning to France."

His concerned look instantly morphed into one of joy. "Sydney! I was so distracted by you when I came in, I forgot to tell you. My company has been asking me to move to the San Jose office for some time now and I finally said yes." He gazed deeply into my eyes. "You gave me a reason to take them up on their offer. I will be moving here next month."

Completely speechless, all I could do was stare at him. He had agreed to be transferred to the US. He was *moving* here. My head was spinning. A normal person would have been ecstatic. A normal person would have immediately told Louis how happy she was and made mad passionate love to him despite the need for food. A normal person would have done something remotely sane. I, however, was descending into hysteria—using all my strength not to run away. It was probably a good thing I was naked or I might have tried to escape...

I snapped out of my thought spiral and threw my arms around Louis. "I'm so happy!" A true statement—but the happiness was mingled with a small amount of panic. What was wrong with me? Only moments ago I was filled with sadness over losing Louis. Now I wouldn't have to and I was terrified. Why was I such a freak?

For the rest of the evening, I pretended everything was fine. We had a pizza picnic on the living room floor and I gave Louis his birthday gifts. I was pleased to see the concert tickets met with so much excitement.

"Sydney, this is amazing! I have never seen them play live."

"I wish I could have gotten better seats." I shook my head sheepishly. "Those were the best of what was left."

"Are you kidding? This is great! You will finally see what I am talking about. These guys are musical geniuses." He was beside himself with excitement. I attempted a smile even though my anxiety was reaching an alarming level.

After I sang happy birthday to him, we fed each other the cupcakes I had baked and then retreated to my room for more magical lovemaking (cheesy, but true).

In the wee hours of the morning, Louis confessed that he had to go. "As much as I would love to stay with you, I have to get to work really early. I hope you have the chance to get some rest, Syd, you need it." He kissed my forehead, lingering for a final moment.

I linked my fingers through his. "What about you? How are you going to function with so little sleep?"

He gave me a knowing look. "Ah, you forget I was in the army for a year before I went to college. I have been trained to function with little sleep."

I had totally forgotten about his stint in the army. Louis had seen and done so much in his life. How was I ever going to catch up? Would I ever be enough for him? He was meant to be with a sophisticated, multilingual supermodel, not awkward, anxiety-ridden me.

Louis put his hand under my chin, gently bringing my eyes to his. "I have lost you again. Where have you gone?"

I quickly composed myself. "I'm sorry. I'm *exhausted*. I wonder why!"

"Allow me to tire you out again tomorrow night," he said softly.

I sighed with mock annoyance. "You're such a romantic, Louis."

"There is that sass again!"

"Yes, I'm full of it," I teased.

Louis laughed and kissed me again. "I must get up now

or I will never leave." He jumped out of bed, grabbed his clothes and threw them on.

I smiled sleepily at him. "I hope you had a good birthday. I know I enjoyed it."

"It was the best birthday I have ever had. Thank you, *mon coeur.*" He finished buttoning his shirt and came over to me.

I stood up and wrapped my arms around him. "You're welcome. Feel free to celebrate with me anytime."

He helped me into my robe and I walked him to the front door. "Drive safely, Louis. Call me when you get home, okay?"

He frowned. "Are you sure? You need to sleep."

"I won't be able to sleep until I know you're safe."

"I will call you the moment I get to my apartment." He kissed me tenderly, took his plant and walked to his car.

After I hung up with Louis, I closed my eyes and tried to sleep. I kept thinking about how happy I had been during this last week and how perfect everything seemed to be with Louis. *Seemed to be.* It couldn't possibly be perfect, since perfection didn't exist, right? Now that he was moving here, at least I would have time to explore being with him. This was a great thing—I knew that! Then why was I so scared? And what the hell was wrong with Louis? There *had* to be something. At least I would have the time to find out now.

## Chapter Nine

The good news, of course, was Louis was moving to California. The bad news was he would have to go back to France early for a few transitional meetings. Since he had to fly out Tuesday morning, this meant he would have to miss the concert.

"I am sorry, *mon coeur*. My boss just told me this morning I feel terrible that I will not be able to go. Especially since you went through so much trouble to get the tickets."

"Louis, *please* don't worry. You're staying in the country! We'll have plenty of time to go to other concerts."

"You are an extraordinary woman, Sydney. I am very lucky."

I felt a familiar swell of happiness, followed by the familiar sense of uncertainty. Louis continued to shower me with compliments and I had every reason to believe him, so why couldn't I shake the feeling that he was too good to be true? I wasn't sure what it would take to break me of this insecurity, but I had to try.

"I have to run, *mon coeur*, but I will call you later. Are you free for dinner tonight? Please tell me you are because I have to see you before I leave for France. Do not make me do something drastic."

I laughed. Louis' opinion of drastic was pretty extreme. "Of course I'll have dinner with you tonight," I gushed. "I need to see you *too*. I'm going to miss you! Do you really have to go back for two weeks?"

He sighed. "A project I have been working on for the past year is coming to a close and I need to be there to oversee a number of things. I would be able to finish it in a week and a half, but my mother's birthday is August first and if I did not stay for the celebration, she would never forgive me. French women cannot be trifled with, Sydney."

"I can only imagine. It's nice you'll be able to see her for her birthday." I faltered. "She must be pretty upset about your move to California." Louis had a very large, close-knit family and I felt terrible that he would be so far away from them.

"She is not surprised. She always told me I had a 'wandering spirit' as a child. When I told her I was moving here, she said she knew I would not stay in France for long. There is no reason to worry, *mon coeur*. My mother has always wanted to come to the US and is excited at the prospect of visiting California."

I secretly wondered what she would think if she knew he was moving to California because of me. In general, the rest of the world thought Americans were loud, fat and obnoxious. I had always thought of French women as sophisticated and elegant, so who knew what Louis' mother would make of her son's involvement with a lowly American. *Nice, Sydney. Way to be intimidated before even meeting her.* Sometimes even I was impressed with the depth of my neuroses.

"I have to go to another meeting, Sydney. I will call you later. I have an idea for dinner..."

The wicked tone of his voice made me chuckle. "Just what are you up to, Louis?"

"That would spoil the fun," he teased. "Have a good day, *mon coeur*."

"You too. Bye…b…uh...Louis." I hung up the phone quickly  *Crap*! I sounded like *such* a moron! I was trying to pull off calling him, "boo," but I chickened out at the last minute and ended up calling him what sounded like "Bluey."

I sighed and put my head on the desk. He was definitely going to ask me for an explanation later. Louis never missed a thing. What was I going to tell him? I picked my head up and smiled as a thought occurred to me. He had beautiful blue eyes and his name was pronounced "Louie." *Perfect*! "Bluey" would be my term of endearment for him.

I tried to turn my attention back to my work, but my mind was swirling with thoughts of last night. When I woke up this morning, I called Kate to tell her Louis was staying in the country. She was so excited she started squealing with delight. At that point, Nick took the phone and asked me to wait until his alarm went off next time before driving his wife into such a frenzy. I scanned the clock and saw it was only six in the morning. *Oops.* I quickly apologized to Nick, who merely grunted and gave the phone back to Kate.

Once I had her back on the phone, I began my freak-out.

"What's wrong with me, Kate? I should be thrilled, but I can't stop the crazy in my head. I feel sick to my stomach."

"Sweetie! This is *great* news. What are you worried about?"

"Before I wasn't worried because our relationship—or whatever you want to call it—was temporary. I knew it was going to end soon. Now he's here to stay. And he could break my heart."

"He could also be the love of your life," Kate pointed out. "Why do you always see the downside of any situation?"

"Look at what's happened in my life so far!" I exclaimed. "Every time I take a risk, it ends badly. How am I supposed to know it'll be different this time?"

Kate sighed. "You don't. You just have to try. You'll

never get anything worth having if you don't take a risk."

"That's easy for you to say. You met Nick when you were a teenager. I've had a much more colorful history. I mean, you remember the total parade of losers I have dated, right? I'm just so tired of it, Kate!"

"Syd, slow down. Take a breath." She paused. "Did you do it?"

"Yes." I rolled my eyes slowly and deliberately. It was satisfying even though she couldn't see me.

"Now take another one."

I exhaled slowly. "Okay. Now what?"

"Tell me how you feel about Louis."

"Um, he makes me happy."

"Good. What else?"

"He's funny, intelligent, sexy...he's, well, he's wonderful."

"So what are you afraid of?" she asked softly.

I took a shaky breath. "That it isn't real. That it won't last. That I'll get hurt. *Again.*"

"Has he ever given you a reason to not trust him?"

"I've only known him for a week," I responded irritably. "There hasn't really been time to establish much of a pattern."

"True, but I've never seen you fall for a man this hard, this fast. And he's picking up his entire life and moving it for *you.*"

"Come on, Kate. He isn't moving for *me.*"

"Really? Didn't you say he told you he'd been asked several times to move to California?"

"Yes, but—"

"Didn't he tell you he finally agreed because of you?"

"Yes, but—"

"No, buts! Have a little faith in the guy. He's obviously *really* into you. Stop thinking so much and enjoy being with him." She paused. "Or if you prefer, I know a number of women who would gladly trade places with you."

"There's no need for attitude," I retorted. "I know

you're right, I just don't know how to turn my brain off."

"One step at a time, little sister. Focus only on the day ahead of you. Stop thinking five years down the road!"

"Okay, okay. *I get it!*"

She laughed. "Good! It takes a lot to get through to you, Syd. I have to ask—am I going to need to do this on a daily basis? Because I don't think Nick can take it."

"So glad to amuse you this early in the morning," I responded, adding extra sarcasm to my tone. "I love you, goofball."

"I should be saying that to you, crazy pants!"

We both collapsed into giggles.

"Thanks for always making me feel better, Kate."

"I'd do anything for you, Syd. You know that."

I heard a beeping in my ear. "I have to run, Kate. I'm getting another call. I'll talk to you later."

"Say hi to Louis for me!"

I hung up on Kate and picked up the other call. "Hello?"

"Good morning, sunshine!" *Maya?* She was decidedly *not* a morning person. Something must be up.

"Hi! How are you?" I was unsuccessful at stifling a yawn.

"I'm fine. Out late last night?" I could hear the anticipation in her voice.

"Maybe. Who's asking?" I joked.

"Stop messing with me, Syd. Spill!"

I filled Maya in on my date with Louis, which involved answering a lot of highly inappropriate questions. She was a very nosy friend, but I loved her dearly. When she started going a bit too far, I abruptly cut her off.

"Stop being such a stick in the mud, Syd."

"Hey! You extracted way more out of me than Kate did. You've heard enough."

"How excited are you? He's moving to California!"

I held my breath for a moment. "Very excited."

"*Oh my God!* You're freaking out, aren't you?"

"Shut up! *I am not.*"

"*Sydney?*"

"*Fine*," I muttered. "I'm freaking out, but I'm doing my best to control the insanity. How bummed would Louis be to discover he's moving to California for a lunatic?"

"Looks like he's going to love himself a lunatic."

I grinned. "Okay, smartass. I have to get ready for work."

"Hey, Syd?"

"Mmm?"

"Stop thinking you aren't good enough."

It really shocked me when Maya hit the nail right on the head. She didn't go for sincerity often, but when she did, she left you speechless.

"I'll try," I murmured.

"I love you, Syd." And she was gone.

The morning flew by in a blur of paperwork. When I could no longer stand the feel of paper on my fingers, I ran into the kitchen to grab my lunch. When I returned to my office, the phone was ringing.

"Sydney Bennett. How may I help you?"

"You may have dinner with me this evening and then come back to my apartment for some, shall we call it, *entertainment*."

I felt the familiar heat flood my face. "Hi, Louis."

"What happened to Bluey? *I liked it.* You are a very clever girl." His smoldering voice sent my thoughts down a highly inappropriate road for the workplace.

I sighed with relief. *Thank God* he bought it. "Where would you like to go to dinner tonight, Bluey?"

"How about the Mexican place you often go to with Kate? It sounds good."

I smiled. "Carlos will be sad not to see Kate, but I'm sure we'll have a good time."

"You know, you can always bring Kate and Nick. It would be nice to meet them."

"No way! You're leaving tomorrow and I don't want to share you with anyone. You can meet them another time."

He laughed. "I see. Well, I am happy you want me all to yourself. What do you plan to do with me?"

"This is not a conversation I can have right now, but I'll be glad to go over my plan during dinner." I could feel the anticipation in my stomach as I thought about the possibilities.

"I cannot wait to hear this! Until tonight, *mon coeur.* What time should I pick you up?"

"How about seven? I need a little time to prepare."

"Now I am curious. I will be wondering all afternoon what you have in store for me."

"That's the idea."

He sighed. "I hate waiting!"

"Me too. But it will be worth it."

After we hung up, I was useless. All I could think of was what I wanted to do with Louis later.

I left work a little early to allow myself extra time to primp before his arrival. Thankfully, I was the only one in the apartment, so I was able to take a long soak in the tub without being disturbed. I added jasmine scented bath oil and lit the relaxation candles Kate had given me for Christmas. After an hour, I felt amazing and was ready to move on to phase two.

I decided since tonight was our last night together for a while, I would pull out all the stops. Following my extensive efforts, I was freshly shaved, tweezed and moisturized in all the right places. I put on my sexiest lingerie—a black satin bustier and matching panties—and a short black miniskirt. Next I put on a red scoop neck blouse, black chunky heels and silver hoop earrings. I wore my hair in a bun and applied a little makeup. With my choice of outfit, I didn't need much—only powder, mascara and lipstick.

Just as I was admiring my handiwork, the doorbell rang.

I glanced at the clock and noticed Louis was fifteen minutes early. I walked to the door (no running in these heels) and found Jess letting Louis in the front door.

"Hey, Syd!" she called. "Look at you, sexy girl!"

Surprise, surprise, I felt my face flush. "Thanks, Jess."

Louis laughed. "She cannot take a compliment, can she?"

"Nope. Get used to it. It's fun to make her blush though!" Jess grinned before ducking into her bedroom.

Louis put his arms around me and whispered, "You look wonderful."

I nuzzled into his neck. "I wanted you to have something to think about when you go back to France and see all those sexy French women."

"They have nothing on you, *mon coeur*."

"You're such a charmer."

"Only for you." He kissed me tenderly on the lips. "Are you ready for dinner?"

"Absolutely. It takes a long time to look this good."

Louis smiled slightly. "Are you sure you are hungry for food?" He kissed my neck and ran his hands slowly down my back.

"Louis," I whispered.

He pulled back and stared deeply into my eyes. My entire body was tingling as he took my hand and led me into my bedroom. Once I closed the door, our hands immediately went to work undressing each other. As he touched me, I began to shiver with anticipation. I had never been this attracted to any man—both mind and body—and it thrilled me almost as much as it scared me. I still suspected there was something wrong with him, but I just didn't care.

## Chapter Ten

I woke up the next morning feeling depressed. Two weeks without Louis was going to be hard. We had had the most amazing night together (with practically no sleep) and had a very hard time saying goodbye. Louis stayed until the last possible minute, but at seven o'clock he had to leave. As I walked him to the door, I vowed to keep busy so the time would go quickly. No sitting around and pining for me.

Louis pulled me into his arms. "I am going to miss you, *mon coeur*."

"I'm going to miss you more," I murmured. "What will I do without you?"

"I am sure you will find something to do." He smirked. "Please make sure Maya does not get you into too much trouble."

"You can never be too careful with those Jersey girls," I teased.

"So I have heard," he said, grinning. "I will call you every day, Sydney."

"Louis, you're going to be insanely busy! You won't have time to call me every day. Just call me when you can."

"I *will* call you every day," he insisted. "It will help me to get through all the bullshit if I can hear your voice."

I was incredulous, but I did my best to hide this from Louis. "What about your friends and all your plans? How will you possibly swing daily calls with a packed schedule *and* the time difference?"

He chuckled. "Do you not believe I can do anything? I thought we had discussed this."

I kissed him gently on the lips. "You're an incredible man, Louis Durand. Please travel safely. You're precious to me." It was nice to know Sydney the Dork was still present and accounted for.

He kissed me a little less gently on the lips and left me breathless. "I will call you later today. I have meetings all day and my flight leaves at seven. Just know I will be thinking of you."

I nodded. I felt tears coming and didn't want Louis to see them, so I threw my arms around his neck.

"We will be together again before you know it. You will soon become tired of me, *mon coeur*, and then you will cry for another reason!"

I swatted his butt playfully. "You're going to be late."

He kissed me one last time and then he was gone. I felt miserable, but had no time to dwell on it since I had to get ready for work.

I was putting my shoes on when the phone rang. *Louis!* "Hello?"

"Duck! Where have you been?" I could hear my father's booming voice full of concern.

"Dad! I'm sorry I haven't called mom. The last few days have been especially busy."

"No shit! I can't believe you're dating a Frenchman. What are you thinking?"

I inhaled sharply. I hadn't told either of my parents about Louis yet. *Thank you, Kate.*

Now I was going to be late for work so I could deal with my father's bias toward French people. My dad was a real piece of work. While he was one of the kindest and most generous men I knew, he was also the most opinionated. His strongest opinions revolved around politics, but he could pontificate on any subject under the sun.

I sighed. "Dad, there's nothing wrong with French people."

"Tell that to the many people they've negatively affected."

"Dad, can we *not* do this now? I'm late for work."

"Listen, Duck. You need to call your mother. She misses you."

"I'm sorry, Dad," I said, hoping I had captured the contrition I felt in my voice. "I've been a little distracted."

He chuckled. "I bet you have. Make sure you call your mother *today*. She wants to hear about this Linus..."

"*Louis*, Dad. His name is Louis."

"Whatever. She's hurt you haven't told her. We had to find out from your sister."

"Dad—"

"And before you try to blame Kate, she thought you'd told us. She feels terrible for spilling the beans."

"Again, Dad, I'm really sorry. I didn't want to get mom's hopes up. There've been too many disasters over the past few years and I didn't want her to worry."

"I'm happy for you, Duck. Now let your mom be happy for you too, okay?"

"I will," I said emphatically. "I promise. I love you, Dad."

"I love you too, Syd."

I felt like a terrible daughter. After all the horrible things my mom had held my hand through, I hadn't found the time to tell her about the amazing things that were happening now. On a mission, I grabbed my purse and ran out the door. I quickly dialed my mom on my cell phone as I got into my car. She must have been otherwise engaged because I got her voicemail.

"Mom, I'm sorry I haven't called. And I'm very sorry you didn't hear about Louis from me first. Call me when you can. You won't believe all the things I have to tell you. I think I've finally found myself a nice nerd." I laughed and hung up the phone.

My mom had insisted from the very beginning that what I really needed was a nice nerd. During my high school and college years, she had watched me engage in typical starry-eyed girl behavior—chase the hot guy and either get nowhere or get hurt. She firmly believed the smart men were there for the long haul. She had tried to remind me (unsuccessfully on many occasions) of the need for more than physical attraction to build a relationship. She had begged me to see the big picture and go for the man who was kind, funny, intelligent *and* attractive. She kept reminding me not to be short sighted and to realize the nice nerds were attractive too. (Perhaps not quite as attractive as the bad boys I used to pursue, but pretty damn attractive!) To my great embarrassment, it had taken me an extremely long time to figure this one out.

The first week Louis was gone went by pretty quickly. Kate and Maya had made it their mission to keep me occupied so I wouldn't let my mind go wild about what Louis could be doing back in France. I was in possession of a very vivid (read: irrational) imagination and they were committed to preventing any of my asinine ideas from catching hold. I was taken to dinner, movies, spa outings, shopping trips and even wine tasting.

Maya had a particularly enjoyable time embarrassing me during a shopping trip to the lingerie department in Bloomingdales. She picked out the most outrageous items she could find and dared me to try them on. Tired of her jokes at my expense, I took the challenge. Though I was sure my face was a scary shade of puce, I showed her each and every one of her selections and even decided to buy what I considered to be the most conservative of the bunch—a sheer black backless teddy. To celebrate my boldness, Maya took me out for cheesecake, our favorite shared vice.

"I'm impressed with you, Syd. You put on quite a show." She grinned as she took a huge bite of her chocolate cheesecake.

"You always push me out of my comfort zone," I complained. "I hate you for it at the time, but it generally pays off later." I paused. "Except for the lime green dress....that was *wrong*."

Maya laughed. "Sorry, Syd. Even the great ones make mistakes occasionally. Or maybe it was just for fun."

"Shut *up*!" I stared at her with wide eyes. "You *didn't*."

"I guess you'll never know, will you?"

As I was about to tell her to stick it where the sun don't shine, my cell phone rang. A quick glance at the screen made my heart leap with joy.

"I'm sorry, Maya. I need to take this."

She rolled her eyes. "Tell Louis not to keep you so long this time. We have more shopping to do." She grabbed her purse and left the table.

I took a deep breath before answering. "Hi, Bluey."

"*Mon coeur*! It is so good to hear your voice."

My stomach did a somersault. "You just talked to me ten hours ago."

"Well, it has been too long."

I laughed. True to his promise, Louis had called every day, at least once a day. I was absolutely gob smacked. (I *loved* that word! And it captured my feelings so well.) I was convinced he would forget about me once he returned to France, that somehow the spell would have been broken. Nothing could have been further from the truth. Louis had made it his mission to make sure *I* remembered *him*.

I found myself looking forward to our daily phone calls. Not only did I get to hear his beautiful voice, but I would also hear all about the latest adventures of his family. He had ten sets of aunts and uncles and more cousins than I could possibly remember. He was extremely close to two of his female cousins, who were sisters. They were very active in the late night social scene and had a variety of suitors who never lasted. Louis laughed and told me no one would ever be good enough for them, so he wasn't concerned.

He described his uncles as warmhearted and hilarious. (Hilarious had become one of his favorite words in the English language.) There was always some sort of farming or contracting disaster they would charm their way out of. His aunts, unfortunately, were very disappointed in his decision to move to the US, but his mother remained supportive of his decision. Though she was not surprised about the move, she knew there was something he wasn't telling her. Of course, she kept pushing until he revealed he had met an American woman. Then she asked him a ton of questions about me and was truly disappointed in my lack of fluency in French. She informed him in no uncertain terms that I would be expected to do something about this deficiency soon because she was too old to learn English.

Louis called me whenever he could, which sometimes meant I was awakened at three in the morning and had to try to form coherent thoughts. I received calls from friend's houses, stores, restaurants and even nightclubs, always involving loud music and/or yelling in the background. He said his friends had given him a very hard time about being so "whipped" and they were all astounded by his decision to date only one woman.

He then proudly informed me of his intention to bring me to France in the near future because there was a line of people who wanted to meet the woman who had finally tamed him. He laughed as he explained the men were upset because he was their hero and they felt let down in his decision to "give up the fight" and the women were upset that it took an American woman to do the job. Apparently, a few of the women thought he must have lost his mind to settle for an American, as the women were so fat, poorly groomed and crass.

While I found the stories amusing—and yes, somewhat

satisfying—after a week of hearing about the amazement of his friends, I started get nervous. Would I be able to keep him happy? Was this just something he was trying because it was different? Would he eventually grow tired of being with one woman? I had dealt with many different man problems over the years, but this was a whole other level of worry. I felt completely out of my element. I decided to call my mom for a sanity check. She had been very excited to hear about Louis when I called her last week and I knew she would be able to set me straight.

Thankfully, it was a slow day at the store so she picked up on the second ring.

"Paintables, this is Lyn. How may I help you?"

"Hi, Mom!"

"Sydney Bennett! How are you?"

Simply hearing her voice made me smile—and reminded me that I was freaking out for no reason. I thought about having her record herself saying calming things so I could play it when I had a bout of the crazies. Maybe I should have her record a few hours' worth...

"How's business?" I asked.

I was so proud of her. She had started this business completely on her own and managed all aspects of it herself. She was exceptionally intelligent and creative and was thrilled to finally be doing something she loved. Life as a financial analyst hadn't been too exciting, but it had paid the bills.

"Great! I just booked three more birthday parties. Kids love it here. It's such a fun experience to be part of."

I laughed. "You can't wait to be a grandmother, can you?"

"Well, I certainly don't want anyone to call me 'Grandma' since I'm much too young for that," she reasoned. "but I wouldn't mind taking care of a little one I'm related to."

"You don't say?" I teased.

"If only your brother and sister would cooperate."

"Give them some time, Mom. They're all still newlyweds! I'm sure you'll have your chance to be a, um, whatever you decide to call yourself, before you know it."

She sighed. "I hope you're right."

"I *am* right, but in the meantime, you must devote yourself to other things. Like your child's problems."

My mom gasped. "Did something happen with Louis?"

"No. Yes." I tried to organize my thoughts before speaking again. "Well, nothing happened exactly, it's just, the more I learn about him, the more worried I become that I won't be enough for him."

"Sydney." *Uh oh.* She was warming up her serious voice. "Has he ever given you a reason to think this is the case?"

"Well, no. But, he's led a very *exciting* life, full of different people and experiences, while I've lived a relatively boring life. I'm not sure I'll be able to keep his interest."

"It sounds to me like he's pretty interested in you, honey. He *is* moving to California for you."

"Mom! Not you too! It's only been a week. We can't say definitively that I'm the reason he's moving here."

"But Kate said he—"

"Mom! Kate believes what she wants to believe. I'm the realist, remember?" I paused, doing my best to choose my words carefully. "What if he's intrigued by the novelty of it all? He's never been with an American woman before. Plus, he used to be such a player. I'm not sure it will be so easy for him to change."

"Sydney Bennett! I'm surprised to hear you say such a thing! You've changed quite a bit since you were a child. After everything you went through, how could you *not* become at least a little different? I'd like to think you'd give Louis the benefit of the doubt."

I sighed. "I know, Mom. I just…I don't want to get hurt again."

"Listen, Syd, I know you want some kind of guarantee, but you aren't going to get one. Even if Louis told you right now that he wanted to be with you for the rest of his life, you wouldn't believe him. You have to give yourself time to trust him. Just be careful not to ruin your experience by second guessing everything, okay?"

I thought it over for a moment.

"Syd?"

"I'm here." I exhaled slowly. "I'll try."

My mom laughed. "Trying is all you can do—and it's good enough."

The second week Louis was gone passed excruciatingly slowly. Kate was really busy with work and Maya had met a new guy, so I didn't have my usual distractions. I went through my cell phone and tried to reconnect with old friends, but everyone seemed to be busy. Even Jess and Maggie were nowhere to be found. As a result of my newfound loneliness, I clung to Louis' phone calls like a life raft. Probably not the best idea when you're concerned about keeping someone interested. It would simply not do to appear needy.

Unfortunately for me, Louis' week was far busier than mine. He wasn't able to call as often, which fed my irrational notions that he was out philandering with buxom young women. After two days without speaking to him, I was starting to get the shakes. I finally gave in and called him, only to find a sultry female voice at the other end of the line.

I was so shocked, I hung up and immediately called Maya. She promptly gave me a lecture about jumping to conclusions and told me to "chillax." After two more days of not hearing from Louis, I considered our relationship to be over and began yet another post-dumbass rehabilitation process. Imagine how silly I felt when he called me later in the day with profuse apologies for not getting in touch with me due to a surprise hunting trip. He explained how he was carried out of his parents' house in the middle of the night four days earlier and his cell phone was left with his cousin

Monique...

By Friday, I was so eager for him to return that I became restless. Thankfully work was fairly slow, so I didn't have to worry about any major damage due to my major distraction. Instead of catching up on filing, I decided to surf the internet for potential activities once Louis returned. I wanted to show him all my favorite places in the Bay Area. We could go hiking in Muir Woods, go to the beach and boardwalk in Santa Cruz, have dinner in San Francisco and stay in a romantic hotel in Sausalito.

I suddenly realized I had no idea if Louis would enjoy hiking or the beach. From everything I had heard about his life so far, he enjoyed extreme activities the most. For someone like me, who was severely athletically challenged, this was a bit concerning. I was certainly willing to try new things, but there was a limit. Would he be willing to slow down for me? The familiar feeling of insecurity started to seep its way through my consciousness.

*Take a breath, Sydney.* Stop thinking so far in the future. One day at a time, just like the theme song says. I started humming the familiar tune (ba ba da da...) and felt a little better. When Louis returned we would get to know each other better. There was no need to panic. I decided then and there to stop wondering what was wrong with Louis and start working on making sure he didn't find out what was wrong with me. Otherwise, he would start running for those beautiful California hills...

## Chapter Eleven

The day of Louis' return had finally arrived and I was filled to the brim with anticipation. Two weeks without Louis was definitely my limit. I had last spoken to him yesterday since he had fifteen hours of flying to do to return to California. I woke at seven on Sunday morning absolutely bursting with excitement. His flight was arriving at three o'clock, so I only had to keep myself busy for the next six hours, allowing for travel time to the airport.

I tried going back to sleep, but my mind was whirling. The mild trace of Louis' cologne remaining on my pillow was extremely distracting. (I couldn't bear to wash the pillowcase and erase his signature scent.) I tried reading, but I couldn't concentrate. Finally, I put on a movie and managed to engross myself in something other than Louis for an hour.

By then I was restless. I decided to go food shopping so I could cook Louis a delicious welcome home dinner. But then I thought about how much better the food was in France and wondered if I could make him something that would live up to the standard he had become used to over the past two weeks. I also realized my cooking became disastrous when my mind was focused elsewhere. Perhaps dinner out was a better option.

After I had changed my clothes three times, it was clear I needed a break from obsessing about Louis. I decided to call my big brother, since I still hadn't told him about Louis. I wasn't sure why I was hesitating. Was I afraid he wouldn't approve? Even as I thought this, I knew it was unlikely. Charlie and Louis had many of the same interests and I had a sneaking suspicion they were going to be good friends. Whatever my subconscious had her panties in a twist about, Charlie had to hear about Louis from me. I took a deep breath and dialed his number.

"Hey, little sister!"

"Hi, Charlie! How are you?"

"Crazy busy, but otherwise fine. How's life with the Frenchie?"

I sighed. Could no one in my family keep a secret? "I'm sorry I haven't told you about him yet. Did you get the scoop from Kate or Mom and Dad?"

"First Kate, then Mom and Dad. Kate and Mom are happy for you, but Dad is seriously questioning your judgment."

I laughed. "When hasn't he? I think he'd be happy if he could make all our decisions for us."

"No kidding. He *always* has something to say. One of these days Zoe's going to tell him where he can go."

My brother's wife, Zoe, was as strong willed as my father, with just as many opinions. Unfortunately, most of their opinions were on the opposite end of the spectrum from each other. When the two of them got together, we all knew there would be some intense debating. It could be funny or it could be ugly. You never knew what to expect.

"I don't know how you handle the stress sometimes, Charlie. Those two might kill each other one day."

Charlie snorted. "My bet is on Zoe. Dad isn't as spry as he used to be. It must be all of those doughnuts."

"Or the chocolate bars or the ice cream..." I faltered. "Mom told me she's started hiding food from him. He really needs to lose weight."

Dad used to be pretty svelte when we were younger. Then his metabolism finally caught up with his outrageous eating habits and he morphed into a much larger version of himself. With his snow white hair and beard and his big round belly, he was the spitting image of Santa Claus. His poor mother wouldn't be happy with his appearance since she took her role as a good Jewish mother pretty seriously. It was a good thing she didn't live to see the transformation.

"So, tell me about this guy," Charlie said. "I want to hear about him from you, not everyone else in the family."

"Where do I begin?" I asked dreamily. "He's intelligent, funny, worldly, sexy...the list goes on."

"He does sound far more interesting than the last few guys you've been with. Dad said he was in the army?"

"Indeed he was. He had to serve for a year in the French army. He's a total adrenaline junky, so he opted to be a paratrooper and absolutely loved it. He keeps trying to get me to go bungee jumping."

"Like that would ever happen! He doesn't know you too well yet, Syd. How long has it been? A week?"

"Very funny!" I exclaimed. "You and Zoe were exclusive from the first night you met. Everything went pretty fast and *you* were still in college."

"You got me there," he admitted. "Please take it easy, okay? There's no need to rush into anything."

"Charlie, we're just dating. It's not like I've agreed to marry him. You need to relax!"

"That's pretty funny coming from you." He was right—the irony was ridiculous. "But seriously, you're my little sister. It's my job to protect you and it's hard to do from three thousand miles away."

"Don't worry! Kate considers herself to be your right hand 'woman.' She's close enough to help you get the job done." I smiled, pleased by his concern.

"I'm always going to worry about you, Sydie." I hated the nickname, but put up with it since Charlie gave it to me the day I was born.

I glanced at the clock and remembered I still had to finalize my outfit for the airport pickup. "I have to run, my brother. Give Zoe a hug for me."

"Will do. Tell Louis I'll break his legs if he hurts you."

"*Nice*, Charlie," I replied, stifling a giggle. "Um, while I'm sure Louis would absolutely show you the proper respect as my big brother, did anyone tell you Louis was a five-time national champion in Thai boxing?" Charlie was very smart and certainly strong, but no one in our family had any kind of athletic ability. It was a large deficiency of which we were all painfully aware.

"Seriously? He was a paratrooper *and* a national martial arts champion?"

"Oh...and a bodyguard."

Charlie made choking noises. "Where did this guy come from?"

"I have no idea," I confessed, shaking my head in bemusement. "Try to imagine me keeping up with all that."

"It does paint a funny picture," he replied. "But if anyone can do it, you can. And don't forget how lucky he is to have *you*."

I really loved my big brother. "Thanks, Charlie. I *miss* you."

"I miss you too," he said softly. We sat in silence for a moment, enjoying our warm fuzzy feelings. When he cleared his throat, I knew something serious was coming. "Now, I know you have to go prepare yourself for Louis' impending arrival, but there's one thing that we need to discuss."

*Uh oh.* I wasn't sure I liked the sound of this. "What is it?"

"When are you going to introduce him to Kate? I need someone on the inside to evaluate him."

"Charlie, I've only known the man for three weeks and he's been out of the country for two of them. I don't want to freak him out by introducing him to my family already."

"You know, I could just call Kate directly. I'm sure she would be able to orchestrate an *accidental* meeting.'"

I gasped. "You *wouldn't*!"

"Oh, but I would." I could hear the smile in his voice. "I'll give you one more week to set this up. If not, I'll have Kate work her magic."

"Charlie!" I whined. *Why did I become a five-year-old in his presence?* "I'm not ready to prep him for that level of interrogation. Do you know how hard I'm trying to make myself appear normal? This really wouldn't help matters."

He chuckled. "It's so easy to get a rise out of you. Though I miss seeing your face when I reduce you to whining."

"You're mean."

"I know. It's my prerogative as your big brother." Suddenly there was noise in the background. I heard a quick snatch of Zoe's voice and some scuffling.

"Syd?" Apparently Zoe had wrestled the phone out of Charlie's hand. "Don't listen to your brother. Relax and enjoy yourself. He's only giving you crap because he misses you so much."

"Thanks, Zoe. I miss you guys too."

"We wish you lived closer."

"I was just thinking same thing." I frowned. It's just so beautiful out here. You can't blame me for wanting to get away from those New York winters."

She laughed. "Not at all. I get it. He does too, but he totally blames Kate for luring you away to the sunshine."

"I'll be back for Thanksgiving. That's only three months away."

"We can't wait to see you. Now go get yourself ready to see this man." She lowered her voice. "And don't forget to call me at work and give me the good stuff. Your brother can't handle it."

I threw my head back and laughed. "You kill me, Zoe. I'll give you a call as soon as I can."

"Good! I love you. Here's your brother."

"I love you too. Bye, Zoe!"

Charlie's voice came back on the line. "What are you two conspiring about?"

"Nothing! Stop being paranoid. I love you to pieces, my brother. Even if you are extremely overprotective."

"Can't be any other way, little sister. I love you too. Talk to you soon. Remember what I said." He hung up before I could say anything else.

I shook my head and hung up the phone. I really missed my brother and my parents. I loved living in California and living so close to Kate, but it was hard to be so far from the rest of our family. With Louis' family in France, it would make sense to move back to New York in a few years. *Oh my God!* How did I end up on that train of thought? Wasn't I just telling my brother that it was too early to introduce Louis to my family?

After I shook the crazy out of my head, I perused my closet for the perfect outfit in which to greet Louis. None of the clothes I had tried on previously were quite right. I must have gone through ten more options before I registered the rumbling in my stomach. To pass the time, I made a big Sunday brunch for my roommates. They were so grateful, they cleaned the kitchen afterward so I could get ready to pick up Louis.

I took a long bubble bath and gave myself a mini facial. Then I dried my hair straight and used Jess' flat iron to create the fresh from the salon look. I felt so relaxed, I was *finally* able choose an ensemble. I put on my favorite jeans, a light blue beaded tank top and gray flats. I added silver drop earrings and pink hued makeup. When I finished putting myself together, I admired my handiwork in the mirror. I looked innocent and fresh. *Perfect!*

As I left for the airport, my thoughts of Louis were anything but innocent. Two weeks away from him had been hard. I mean, to have such amazing sex only to have it taken away so soon was downright cruel. I had plans for Louis the moment I managed to get him back to his apartment.

As my heartrate quickened, I noticed I was speeding. Not just "I didn't realize I was going five miles over the speed limit, Officer" speeding, but full-on bat shit crazy speeding. I *had* to calm down. It simply would not do to get into an accident on the way to the airport—that would only add to the waiting!

I turned on the radio and flipped around the stations until I found a song I liked. I settled on "Keeping the Faith." Anything by Billy Joel made me happy. I concentrated on the lyrics, feeling more relaxed with every word. *Keep the faith, Sydney.* Everything would work out for the best, whether I was meant to be with Louis or not.

I pulled into the airport parking lot and felt my excitement building. I took one last look at myself in the overhead mirror and adjusted my makeup. No "wishful makeupping" this time. I had no doubt I would see Louis. And I planned to see all of him as soon as possible. I paused, in awe at the change Louis had brought out in me. I was becoming much less inhibited. Was this a good thing?

*Focus, Sydney.* After one last deep breath, I got out of the car. I wrote down the floor and color of the parking section as I walked to elevator since I was very good at forgetting this vital information. It would be totally embarrassing to get lost in the airport parking lot—particularly when you had very important things you wanted to do *as soon as possible.*

I checked Louis' flight on the board and saw it was on time. He would be landing in ten minutes! Granted, he had to get his luggage and go through customs before I could actually see him, but I felt better knowing he would be safely on the ground and on his way to me within the hour. The anticipation only heightened my desire to see him.

Forty-five minutes later, the board flashed Louis' flight number, indicating the passengers had finally cleared customs. *This was it!* My eyes were glued to the large video screen showing the people who were about to come through the doors into the waiting area. Ten minutes later, there was still no sign of Louis, which made me pretty antsy.

Where was he? If he had missed his flight, he would have told me. I checked my phone again, but there were no messages.

My mind started to race. Did something happen to him? Wouldn't someone have called me? His family probably didn't have my number. *Shoot!* Should I call someone? Who would I call? I didn't have anyone's phone number.

Just then, I saw his face on the big screen. He was walking alone with his head down, smiling to himself. The sight of him made me lose my breath. He was wearing jeans and a light blue collared short-sleeved shirt. He looked *gorgeous.* I noticed he wasn't wearing his chain or his sunglasses. I briefly wondered if he was trying to adapt to his new environment—maybe have less of the "flashy foreigner" vibe. Quickly brushing the thought aside, I brought myself back to the moment. I felt a wave of emotion flow through me that this man was mine (at least for the time being) and couldn't wait to get my hands on him. I moved closer to the exit door and held my breath.

After what felt like an eternity, Louis passed through the doors. His eyes met mine immediately and he broke into the most spectacular smile I had ever seen. I ran over to him and flung my arms around his neck.

He buried his face in my hair and held me tightly. "I missed you, *mon coeur.*"

I breathed in his heavenly scent. "I missed you more."

He pulled out of the hug and held my face in his hands. "I highly doubt that, but we can debate this on the ride home if you like."

After a traffic-stopping kiss (seriously, we had an audience), I took his hand and we started walking toward the elevator. "How was your flight?"

He sighed. "Long. I was sitting next to this model who would not stop talking about the photo shoot that she was flying into San Francisco to do. All I wanted to do was sleep."

I felt a stab of jealousy. "Poor baby! You had to sit next

to a beautiful French woman for thirteen hours."

"You *should* feel sorry for me. You have completely ruined me for French women. They cannot hold a candle to you." He stopped and kissed me again. "You have no idea the power you have over me."

Even after everything that had happened over the last three weeks, I had trouble taking Louis seriously. I wanted to believe him, but a) how could I possibly have this effect on anyone? and b) he *had* to have some kind of hidden agenda. I decided if this turned out to be a total fantasy, it was still more interesting than anything else I had going on right now. Honestly, reality was often overrated.

"Cry me a river, Louis. You've forever ruined me for American men."

He laughed. "*Mon coeur*, how I have missed your sass."

As we got into the elevator, Louis put his hand on the small of my back. "So, what are we doing tonight?"

"What did you have in mind?" I asked huskily.

The elevator doors closed and Louis pulled me into a passionate kiss. All his luggage fell to the floor and we started reaching under each other's clothes. I hoped no one was watching on the security camera, since they would have been witness to some free soft-core porn.

"Louis," I gasped.

"I want you." He ran his hands all over my body, causing a most-enjoyable dizzy spell.

When the elevator stopped and the doors opened, Louis and I quickly rearranged ourselves, grabbed his luggage and exited past a group of people with very amused looks on their faces.

I laughed as we walked to the car. "That was quite a show in the elevator, Louis. Do you have a thing for having sex in public places?"

"No, I am not into any weird sex things," he replied. "Believe me, I have seen and tried enough for a lifetime. I simply could not contain myself."

A moment later, he pushed me up against my car and

kissed me until I thought I would melt into a puddle on the floor. With great effort, I pushed him away.

"That's it. You're cut off. We'll never make it out of here at this rate and I have no intention of having sex in the car." I ruffled his hair and opened the trunk. "Let's go."

Louis tried to look contrite. *"Oui, Madame."* He put his luggage in the trunk, climbed into the car and we were on our way. I concentrated on the fact that I would have him all to myself in less than an hour.

꩜

After far too much traffic for my taste, we finally reached the door of Louis' apartment. As he searched for his keys I felt a warm feeling spread through my entire body. *Finally!* I was seconds away from private time with Louis. When he put the key in the lock, I came up behind him and slid my hands around his waist.

"I'm so happy you're back." I kissed his neck slowly. Louis turned around and kissed me hard on the mouth.

As things started to heat up a little too much for the hallway of his corporate apartment building, Louis removed himself from the kiss. "We need to go inside, Syd. This would be quite a show for the neighbors."

I sighed. "You're right. Thank you for protecting my modesty."

Louis smiled and grabbed his bags. He opened the door and music spilled out into the hallway. *Crap.* Jean was home. My plans didn't involve having Louis' roommate in the immediate vicinity.

"Louis! How was your flight?" You had to hand it to Jean. He had impeccable manners. He insisted on speaking English to Louis when I was present.

"Long. I am glad to finally be back." He rubbed his eyes for emphasis.

Jean smirked. "I am sure you are."

Louis held up his bags. "I am going to put these down and rest. See you later, man."

"Enjoy your nap, Sydney," Jean said with a wink.

I felt my face burst into flames, but this wasn't going to stop me. "Thanks, Jean. See you later."

I followed Louis into his bedroom and closed the door. He grinned and I launched myself at him, knocking him onto the bed. My aggressive maneuver earned me quite the eyebrow raise. "You missed me a lot, did you not, *mon coeur*?"

"That's an understatement." I could contain myself no longer. I kissed him like my life depended on it. Louis responded and our hands started to wander. As I tried to reach the button of his jeans, deep laughter rumbled from his chest.

"I have missed you too, *mon coeur*. Just remember these walls are pretty thin." He sat up and regarded me with amusement.

"Are you worried Jean will hear something?" I asked innocently. "I seem to remember a few times when Jean was fairly loud with *total strangers* he'd brought home from a bar. Maybe it's time he got some payback."

"I was merely concerned for your virtue—as you call it." He couldn't get through his comment with a straight face.

"Hey! I'm perfectly virtuous." As I said this, I realized before Louis, the perception of my "virtue" would have been a real concern for me. After Louis, it didn't seem important. At this moment, I knew I wanted him and I didn't care who else knew.

I grabbed the back of his neck and pulled him back on top of me, into a slow kiss. My hands made their way back to his jeans and opened the button. Then I slowly worked the zipper down and began to tug his jeans off. I had pushed them down to just below the waistband of his underwear when I felt...skin. Louis took one look at my confused expression and burst out laughing.

I peered over his shoulder for a closer look. *Ah! Now it made sense.* "I had no idea your underwear collection was so varied, Louis. How long have you favored thongs?"

"I thought you might enjoy this." Tears of laughter sprang from his eyes. "You should see your face. You Americans are *so* uptight!"

I smirked. "You did that on purpose to shock me?"

"Of course not. I do not like my panty lines to show." He fell into another fit of giggles and I jumped on top of him.

"Ha, ha, *ha*. You've had your fun. Now come here." It wasn't too hard to get Louis to stop laughing.

⌒

A few magical hours later, Louis and I were lying in bed talking. Apparently, he had a lot of decisions to make in the next couple of weeks about his living arrangements.

"Now that I have been transferred to the US, I can no longer stay in corporate housing or drive a rental car. I need to find an apartment and a car of my own. So many decisions!" He tapped his temple as he thought. "Wait a minute...don't you help people with this kind of stuff for your job?"

"Why yes, *Monsieur Durand*, I do. Is there something I can do to help you?" I asked seductively. "Although, I will warn you—my fee is pretty steep."

"I think I can make it worth your while, Miss Bennett." With that, he drew me close to him and gave me a reason to want to do everything possible for him, whether there was something wrong with him or not. I was finally starting to let go. And it was about damn time.

## Chapter Twelve

Louis and I didn't get very much sleep his first night back, though we both agreed it was worth being exhausted the next day. I knew I should have gone home last night, but I couldn't bring myself to leave him. After being without him for far too long, my system was blissfully happy to be on overload.

When I opened my eyes in the morning, the sky was bright. In fact, it appeared to be a lot brighter than it normally was when I got up for work. I rolled over, searching for the clock. When my eyes settled on it, I noticed it was flashing twelve o'clock. *Uh oh.* I threw myself out of bed and frantically searched for my watch. *Crap!* It was eight o'clock in the morning! I was supposed to be work in thirty minutes. There was a very slim chance of that happening given my urgent need of a shower.

I raced over to Louis and gently shook him awake. "Wake up, Bluey! It's eight o'clock."

His eyes snapped open. "*No!* I am very late." He rubbed his eyes and got out of bed quickly. "Why did the alarm not go off?"

"Something must have happened to your clock." I pointed to the flashing numbers before starting the search for my missing clothing.

"*Merde*! Jean must have blown a fuse again," he said irritably. After giving me a quick kiss, he ran to the bathroom.

"Is this something he does often?" I called as I wrestled into my jeans. Getting dressed in a hurry had never been my strong suit.

Louis spat out a mouthful of toothpaste. "He has these late night cooking sessions and sometimes uses too many appliances at the same time. This is an old building, so it does not take too much to cause problems."

"Maybe he was lonely," I said. "For once you were responsible for providing the noisy entertainment."

He beamed as he tucked in his shirt. "I rather enjoy the sounds you make."

"On that note, I have to run. I'm going to be totally late." I wrapped my arms around Louis and kissed him soundly. "Have a good day, Bluey."

Louis held me for a moment. "You too. I will call you when I can. Today will be a busy day of debriefs."

He walked me to the door, pausing to kiss me one last time before we went our separate ways. "I am so happy to be with you again, *mon coeur*. I know I said this yesterday, but I must repeat myself—I missed you terribly."

"I missed you too." I gave his hand a squeeze. "Now, stop looking at me with those gorgeous eyes or I'll never get out of here."

"Yes, ma'am," he replied in a truly atrocious American accent.

When he covered his eyes with his hands, I made a run for it. Always one to multitask, I left a message for my boss during the speed walk to my car, letting her know my alarm didn't go off and I would be there as soon as I could. There was certainly no need to include my quick stop at home to shower and change into appropriate clothing for the workday. Everyone deserved a secret now and then.

I made it to work an hour late, but thankfully hadn't missed anything important. I didn't have any new hires for orientation, so it was only a matter of digging into what was sitting on my desk from Friday. No matter how much I worked, the pile didn't seem to go down. It usually bothered me—despite my boss' reminders that this was how it was supposed to be—but not today. I was on such a high, nothing could bring me down.

An hour into the mountain of paperwork, my mind wandered to a few particularly memorable moments from early this morning. Luckily for me, my phone rang shortly thereafter startling me back to reality.

"Sydney Bennett, how may I help you?" I lacked my usual perky tone, but I figured being able to form coherent sentences on only two hours of sleep was a good thing.

"You can spill all the gory details of your night of passion." Maya was not one to wait to be informed.

I giggled. "Good morning to you too, sunshine."

"So, you sound kind of tired, Syd. Were you up to anything special last night?" I knew she had an enormous smirk on her face. I also knew she was going to embarrass me within an inch of my life.

I sighed dramatically. "No, nothing special. It was actually kind of boring."

"Really? Then you're not having any trouble walking today?"

"*Maya!*" My face had to have turned the most ridiculous shade of crimson possible. I hadn't expected her to pull such a high level of vulgarity so fast. Thank goodness I had kept my office door closed this morning. Nobody needed to hear that level of shock in his/her HR representative's voice. It kind of blew the illusion of cool we tried so hard to project.

"Oh, don't be such a prude," she replied. "You know you had an *active* reunion last night."

"I'm thrilled to provide such lively entertainment for

you, perv."

Maya laughed. "You know you love me. Who else would coax you out of your shell?"

"Coax? *Really*? I would say you *yank* me out of my shell. Repeatedly. Against my will," I said pointedly. "But I do love you. You get a great discount at Bloomingdales."

Maya snorted. "Seriously, how was last night? I need details!"

"*Amazing.* Being with him is just...heavenly."

"You're totally high."

"I know! I'm *so* distracted. It's embarrassing!" I closed my eyes. "I need sleep. And Louis."

"Honey, it doesn't sound like those two things go too well together." She let out a huge cackle for emphasis.

*Totally walked into that one, Syd.*

Maya was still laughing. "I guess you're going to have to decide which one you need more."

"All right, missy. You've said quite enough! I have to try to make some sense out of the mess on my desk." Then I'll sort out the mess in my head.

"Sounds good, Syd. Then you can start on your head."

I shuddered. Sometimes Maya knew me a little *too* well. "Bye, Maya. I'll give you a call tomorrow."

"You'd better! Or I'll have to start stalking you. And if I don't get enough information, I can track down Louis..."

I hung up before she could say anything else. Maya was definitely crazy enough to do something like that. Just thinking about it made me feel queasy.

⌒

The rest of the day passed rather uneventfully, except for Louis' phone call right after lunch.

"Sydney Bennett, how may I help you?"

"I can think of a few things," his sensual voice replied. I felt a tingling sensation all the way to my toes.

I smiled. "I'm still recovering from last night."

"It was only a warm up, *mon coeur.*"

"As amazing as you are, I'm so tired I don't think I'm going to be of much use to you tonight."

"Do you think I am using you?" His voice had turned from sensual to edgy.

"Of course not! I'm sorry, Bluey, it's an expression. I only meant I'm so tired, I'll probably fall asleep very early."

"Oh." He paused. "The English language is very odd. I am afraid you will have to continue to explain these *expressions* to me for some time."

"I'm happy to provide the service." That didn't sound good. What did I have to do to get my brain working properly again? "So, when are you going to start teaching me French?"

"You would like to learn?" he asked eagerly. "Wonderful! You will *love* it. It makes a lot more sense as a language than English. The rules of grammar are consistent."

"Sounds good to me!" I said happily. "Consistency is helpful. Just don't expect me to master a French accent. I had very little success with my attempt at a Spanish accent and I have a sneaking suspicion this won't be any different."

"Do not worry, Syd. With me as your tutor, you will sound perfect." He cleared his throat. "I know you are tired, but I must see you this evening. May I come to your apartment after work? We can order some dinner and, if you do not mind, I will bring an overnight bag and stay with you."

I hugged myself. "I would love nothing more. But you'll have to keep your hands to yourself. I need some sleep tonight."

He laughed. "I cannot promise anything. And I do not think you can keep your hands off me."

"You Frenchmen are pretty full of yourselves, aren't you?" I observed drily.

"Full of honesty, *mon coeur*," he replied. "I have to run, but I will see you tonight."

"Bye, Bluey."

I hung up the phone and put my head on my desk. Even in my exhausted state I could feel myself starting to relax with Louis. I was actually starting to trust him. Maybe things were finally going to work out in my love life. Maybe I would be happy and spend my life with an incredible man. I was becoming pretty fond of those maybes...

When I dragged myself home from work at the end of the day, I found a message from Kate waiting for me.

"You are *so* on my list, Syd. Why haven't I heard from you all day? I'm sure there are many, *many* details I need to hear from last night, but you're leaving me hanging. Call me the *moment* you hear this message, even if Mr. Wonderful is there. I will *not* wait until tomorrow!"

If I valued my life, I would call her. I picked up the phone and dialed, hoping she would be home and I could give her enough details to hold her off until tomorrow. Louis was going to be here soon and I had absolutely no desire to discuss any of this in front of him.

"Where have you been?" *Uh oh.* Stern Kate was in the house.

"Hi, Kate," I responded brightly. "It's nice to talk to you too. How was your day?"

"Cut the crap. Tell me about last night. It must have been awesome!" Phew. Stern Kate had now been replaced by Excited Kate. She was way more fun.

I beamed. "It was...astounding. I'm really falling for him."

She squealed. "I'm so happy for you, Syd. You deserve to have a wonderful man in your life."

"I'm afraid to get too comfortable with the idea, Kate," I said softly. "What if he turns out to be horrible, like all the others?"

"Syd, we've been through this. You can't lock yourself away from the world because you don't want to get hurt. You have to stop thinking that every guy is going to be an asshole."

"Can you blame me for having issues?"

She hesitated. "Admittedly, you've had some, um, interesting experiences in your past."

"That's a nice way of putting it."

"The point is the past is the past. You're so smitten with this guy and it warms my heart to see you this way."

I laughed. "Did you just use the word *smitten*? Are you from a different era?"

"Oh, shut up. You know what I mean. Just let yourself be happy."

"Fine, but if he breaks my heart, I'm blaming you."

"Nice, Syd. I'm pleased to hear that you're behaving like a grown up." She paused. I knew that something else was coming. "So....when will Nick and I get to meet him?"

My heart stopped. "Have you been talking to Charlie?"

Kate sighed. "Syd, even if I hadn't spoken with him, I would still ask to meet Louis. Come on! Are you embarrassed by us?"

"Of course not. You guys are two of my favorite people in the whole world. That doesn't mean I trust you not to embarrass me. And it certainly doesn't mean Charlie and Nick haven't concocted some scheme to evaluate Louis." I knew them both too well to think otherwise.

"I promise not to embarrass you. Do you really think I would put you through that? I know how happy you are with Louis and I can't tell you how overjoyed I am to see the effect he has on you. The last thing I want to do is to make you uncomfortable. I just want to get to know the man who's brought the smile back to your eyes."

*Crap.* She was so sincere. How could I possibly say no?

"You don't play fair, my sister." I was about to agree when a thought occurred to me just in time. "Kate, before I answer, you have to tell me one thing. Have Nick and Charlie already come up with a plan for Louis?"

"They might have...discussed something the other day," she said in a small voice.

*I knew it!* "The answer is hell no."

"Sydney Julia Bennett, don't make me get Mom and Dad involved."

I scoffed. "What are they going to do from three thousand miles away?"

"Guilt is a pretty powerful weapon, sweetie. Dad has perfected it to an art form."

She had me there. Dad had heaped mountains of guilt on me over the course of my lifetime. I knew I wouldn't be able to hold out for long.

"*Fine*," I responded in exasperation. "I give up. But I need a little more time. How about we have dinner next weekend?"

"Great. I'll make your favorite."

"Please make your husband promise not to embarrass me," I grumbled. "I'm trying to convince Louis that I'm normal."

"Don't worry, I'll make Nick promise. If he doesn't listen, I'll have lots of wine for you to console yourself with."

"Not funny, Kate. You have to be on your best behavior too." Happy Kate often turned into Drunk Kate fairly quickly.

"What would I do to embarrass you?" she asked, clearly affronted.

"Are you kidding me? Once you have a couple of glasses of wine in you—which is a given when you host dinner parties—you start in with the stories from when we were kids. Somehow I'm the one who always ends up sounding like an idiot."

"I can guarantee this won't happen." She paused. "And even if it did, I'm sure Louis would find it charming."

"I'm hanging up now. Louis will be here soon and I need a moment to collect myself."

"Ha, ha. I love you. Have fun tonight and *call me* tomorrow. I refuse to let you off the hook for dinner."

"Bye, Kate. I love you too." I hung up the phone and

frowned. Kate and Nick were already asking to meet Louis. I loved them immensely, but the thought made me nervous. Maybe I was afraid I had been living in this amazing delusion and if I let anyone else in, everything would come crashing down. I couldn't sustain this forever though, so I guess I was going to have to deal with having them meet Louis. The only good thing was that for once my focus was on how to hide what was wrong with me and my family instead of my quest to find out what was wrong with Louis. It was a refreshing change.

*Chapter Thirteen*

The next week and a half flew by. Louis and I spent every possible moment together, causing me to take up residence on cloud nine. Never in my life had a man made me feel so special, so sexy and so cherished. Every woman should get to feel this good at some point in her life.

As I didn't have a personality transplant, the thought was still in the back of my mind that something was wrong with Louis. Lest you think I was actually living in a romance novel, our relationship was *not* perfect. I found Louis had flaws just like I did—he could be quite a slob, he often had a short attention span and he was extremely spontaneous. Though some women might find spontaneity to be romantic, I found it troublesome in anything other than small doses. I *liked* to plan. Planning was my *thing*. It made me feel secure.

Since we were still in the early stages of our relationship, I felt the obligation to roll with whatever Louis threw my way. Above all, I didn't want to appear to be high maintenance. So when he called me at work on Thursday afternoon with a spontaneous party invitation, I gladly accepted. Never mind my desire to go home and curl up with him in front of the fireplace with a glass of wine. I had to do everything in my power to appear to be the perfect girlfriend. (Not that we had discussed titles yet.)

The bonus to this little situation was Louis' request for Maya to join us. He remembered her from the night I met him and wanted to provide company for Jean, who would be tagging along. I told him I wasn't sure this was a good idea.

"What are you worried about, *mon coeur*?"

"You don't know Maya very well," I said, doing my best not to laugh. "I'm not sure Jean can handle her."

"Trust me. Jean can handle anyone."

I smirked. "You have *no* idea what you're in for, Bluey. Men have left her apartment in tears."

"They must not have been real men." He paused. "What do you think she is going to do to Jean?"

"I guess we'll have to wait and see."

"I am intrigued, Sydney Bennett."

"I'm sure you are," I teased. "I bet you're wondering now if you picked up the right girl that night."

"I have no doubt I did. There was no contest."

His complete certainty still caught me off guard. How could he have been so sure the night he met me?

"You're too kind, *Monsieur*. What time should we be ready?"

"How about I pick you up at seven? They will be serving food, so do not snack too much while you are getting ready."

He knew me too well. "I won't. I have to be able to fit into my dress."

"Only for the course of the party, *mon coeur*," he growled.

"It sounds like a great time will be had by all," I responded with a chuckle. "I'll call Maya about tonight. I hope for your sake she'll be free."

"For my sake?"

"Maya always provides an unforgettable evening."

Maya happily agreed to go to the party with us. She had one condition, which she reiterated to me when she arrived at my apartment after work.

"Don't expect me to sleep with Jean, Syd."

"Maya! When did I ever give you the impression this was expected? I don't think of you as a call girl!"

She laughed. "You're so easy to fluster. It's fun."

I swatted her in the behind as she walked by. "That was *mean*. You know I'm nervous about introducing you to Louis—I mean, having you spend more time with him tonight. Not to mention the wild card we know as Jean."

Maya went over to the mirrored closet doors in my bedroom to check her makeup, which was perfect, of course. She then straightened the hem of her teal mini dress. As if anything were ever flawed or out of place on her body. Sometimes it was hard to stand next to her as an average human being.

I joined Maya at the mirror and surveyed my appearance for the fifth time in the last hour. I had on a black tank dress with beading around the neckline, a light blue cardigan and high heeled black strappy sandals. I decided to keep my hair down and wear my favorite dangly earrings—silver with light blue stones. Maya had done my makeup, with the usual result of bringing me much closer to her level of perfection. This should have brought me some relief, but for some reason, I couldn't stop fidgeting.

Maya put her hands on my shoulders. "Will you please *stop* worrying? We'll all have a good time tonight. I'll keep Jean in check."

On that I had no doubt. Maya had a way with people. She told things like she saw them and didn't take crap from anyone. For some odd reason, people always listened to her. I wondered if it were the commanding tone in her voice, the expression of absolute certainty on her face or her incredibly attractive appearance. Perhaps it was a combination of all these things. Whatever it was, it worked.

I hugged her. "Thank you. Please promise me you

won't decide around your second drink that it would be funny to tell embarrassing Syd stories to Louis?"

She grinned. "I can't promise anything. I don't want to ruin *my* evening."

I sighed. "Maya, I'm taking Louis to dinner at Kate and Nick's tomorrow night. I can't have two nights in a row where I'm humiliated for sport. You know how hard I work to hide the crazy. You can't just hand it to him!" I stared imploringly into her eyes. "*Please.*"

"Fine, you win. I'll be good." With that, the doorbell rang and Maya and I were off for what I hoped would be a fun evening.

C⁓

The party was being given by Louis' coworker and newfound friend, Jake. Jake and Louis had quickly bonded over their love for mixed martial arts competitions and spicy food. The two of them were discussing the latest fight within five minutes of our arrival—as they chowed down on hot wings—which left Maya, Jean and I to fend for ourselves. Jean had taken to Maya from the moment he met her, but I could see she hadn't made her mind up about him yet. Jean left to find us some drinks and Maya and I found a comfortable couch in the corner of the living room.

Once Jean was out of hearing range, I leaned over to whisper in Maya's ear. "So? What do you think of him?"

She scrunched up her forehead. "I don't know yet. He's certainly good looking, but I don't know if we have anything in common." She shrugged. "He might make a good boy toy."

"Lovely. And you thought *I* was compromising your virtuous nature..."

Maya rolled her eyes. "I'm kidding. Besides, there are plenty of interesting young men at this party. I don't have to commit to anything yet." And by interesting, I was sure she meant hot.

As she surveyed the room, I followed her gaze and saw

how right she was. For Maya, it was like being a kid in a candy store. Poor Jean was going to have to vie for her attention.

"I think I'm going to take a little tour of the room." Maya gave me a quick smirk before sashaying over to a group of young men who seemed very happy to have their conversation interrupted.

Great. I had been at this party for ten minutes and had already lost everyone I had come with. Even Jean had been sidetracked on his way to the makeshift bar in the kitchen. Louis appeared to be in a deep discussion with Jake—probably about the merits of the top tier of the Ultimate Fighting Championship, given his rant earlier in the day—so I figured I would be on my own for a little while.

After I felt my stomach rumble for the third time, I set off in search of the food Louis had promised me. I managed to find some chips in the kitchen and was helping myself to some wine to go with my snack when I heard a voice behind me.

"Doritos and Burgundy? You can't be serious." I turned around to find a very good looking man with blond hair and green eyes smiling at me from the doorway.

I returned his smile. "There aren't many options. What would you suggest?"

He stepped further into the kitchen. "Well, for starters, Doritos should only be consumed with beer—or soda if absolutely necessary." He paused for effect. "You need at least cocktail weenies to warrant a glass of Burgundy."

I laughed. "I'm sorry, no one has ever taught me proper party food etiquette."

"Well, this must be your lucky day because I'm available for lessons."

*Party foul!* This man was flirting with me. What was I going to do? He seemed nice and was certainly attractive, but my interests were very well engaged elsewhere. Maybe I was imagining it. It wouldn't be the first time.

I would just keep things casual. "Do you have a syllabus?

I'd like to have an idea of what topics you'll be covering."

He took a few steps closer to me. "I have it right here in my room if you'd like to join me. It's a lot quieter in there, which would allow for better concentration."

*Okay.* Definitely not imagining it. I was trying to find a way out the situation, when I heard Louis' voice.

"Matt! I see you have met my girlfriend." Louis seemed cordial, but there was definitely an edge to his voice.

Matt took a few steps back. "Louis! I had no idea you had a girlfriend." Something in his tone didn't sound genuine. He turned to me with a grin. "But I can certainly see why you are interested in....I'm sorry, I never got your name."

I tried to speak, but nothing came out. I was a little freaked out by all the testosterone in the room. With some effort, I cleared my throat. "Sydney. Sydney Bennett."

Matt held out his hand, which I shook. "It's very nice to meet you, Sydney Bennett." He held my gaze and my hand for a little too long.

Louis came into the kitchen and slipped his arms around my waist. "I hope you will not mind if I steal my girlfriend back. We have much to catch up on." He kissed my neck slowly.

*Wow.* This was *really* uncomfortable—a feeling I was not used to when Louis kissed me.

Matt smiled stiffly at Louis. "Of course, I wouldn't want to come between the two of you." Matt picked up my hand and brought it to his lips. "I hope to see you again soon, Sydney." And with one last smirk at Louis, he left the kitchen.

I spun around to face Louis. "Who is *that* guy?"

Louis frowned. "He is an asshole." His irritation was absolutely adorable.

I laughed. "Clearly he is an asshole you know. Do you work with him?"

"Well, if you can call what he does work. He has no idea what he is doing. He takes credit for other people's work and tries to, what is it you say, *sweet-talk* all of our female coworkers into doing the rest of his assignments." He sighed. "Sadly, many of them have fallen for his bullshit."

I put my arms around him and kissed him on the nose. "He sounds like a *giant* asshole."

"I did not like him before, but when I saw him trying to flirt with you, I began to detest him." He clenched his hands into fists.

I grinned. "You're so cute when you're jealous."

"I cannot help it," he murmured. "You have quite a hold on my heart."

"I noticed you called me your girlfriend," I said softly.

He stared at me with surprise. "Isn't that what you are?"

"I would love to be your girlfriend, Bluey. We just hadn't discussed it yet. I didn't want to be presumptuous."

"You Americans are crazy!" Louis exclaimed. "You do not have to talk about *everything*. It is possible to just feel something."

"Well, I'm very happy to be your girlfriend."

"You say that now, but wait and see," he joked. "You have no idea what you have gotten yourself into."

I snorted in a most unladylike manner. "I could say the same to you."

Suddenly, there was a commotion from the living room. Louis and I immediately followed the whistling and catcalling. Seconds later, my jaw was on the floor. I had never expected to see Maya and Jean making out in the corner of the living room, completely oblivious to all the noise being made around them.

Louis and I burst out laughing. "We must have missed something big. Maya *never* shows physical affection in public. I wonder what happened?"

Oddly enough, no one seemed to know. All we could glean from a few onlookers was that one moment they were on opposite ends of the couch and the next moment they were all over each other behind a gigantic plant. Maya had some serious explaining to do.

I couldn't help but smile. After years of listening to her tease me about my idiotic behavior, I *finally* had something to tease her about. This night was getting better and better! True to my earlier statement to Louis, Maya always provided an unforgettable evening. And the best part? I was so distracted by the events of the evening, the thoughts of what could be wrong with Louis didn't even enter my mind. For once in my life, I was just happy.

## Chapter Fourteen

Getting Maya to spill the beans about Jean turned out to be much harder than I had expected. Louis and I drove back to his corporate apartment with Maya and Jean in the back seat (separated by a respectable distance). Though they held a perfectly pleasant conversation, there was no evidence of the passion exhibited earlier in the evening. It was *very* strange.

In the few seconds I had alone with her as I walked her to her car, I did my best to get the dirt. She politely refused to answer any of my questions, gave me a hug and got into her car without another word. I watched her drive away, shaking my head in confusion. It wasn't like Maya to be so tight-lipped. I mean, she *loved* to share the details of her escapades. In fact, she often overshared. What was going on?

As concerned as I was, I didn't have the chance to pursue matters further. I woke up the next morning with far more pressing matters on my mind. Tonight Louis was finally going to meet Kate and Nick. (*Finally* was Kate's word, not mine. I was perfectly happy to wait a few more weeks to introduce them.) After last night's outing with Maya, I was happy that dinner with the two of them would be low-key. Unfortunately, this also meant the spotlight was going to be on Louis alone. He was being very good natured about it, but I was slowly losing my mind.

Kate had promised me both she and Nick would be on their best behavior, but I knew how easily her love of wine could interfere with her promise. Not only would alcohol loosen her lips, it would prevent her from forcing Nick to stick to his promise. I was *doomed*. My only hope was Louis had been with me for long enough to care about me even after he had heard all the embarrassing stories which were bound to come out this evening.

I called Kate that morning to tell her about my status as Louis' "girlfriend" and to beg her not to interfere with this newly acquired status by misbehaving this evening.

"Hey, Syd!" she sang gleefully.

"Hi! What has you in such a good mood this morning?"

"Are you kidding? I *finally* get to meet Louis. *The* Louis. I'm excited!"

"You're freaking me out. Please, dear sister, take it down a notch."

I knew she was rolling her eyes at me. When it came to Kate, I could sense these things.

"Sydney, will you relax?"

Oh, yeah. Definitely rolling her eyes at me.

"Will you promise not to embarrass me, Kate?"

"I *promise*," she responded with exasperation.

"Good, because it wouldn't do for you to embarrass me in front of my *boyfriend*."

Silence. Hmmm. Kate always had something to say. Before I could ask her who she was and what she had done with my sister, a squeal pierced my eardrum.

"When did this happen, Syd? Last night? *It better have been last night.* You can't keep leaving these important details out. It's not fair!"

I laughed. "Yes, it happened last night. He introduced me as his girlfriend to one of his coworkers and then marveled when I told him we usually discuss the usage of such a term in this country."

"How adorable! I'm really excited to meet him."

"I'm really excited for you to meet him too," I admitted. "I'm sorry if I've been making you think otherwise. I'm happier with Louis than I've ever been. It's just hard to let my guard down."

"I know, Syd. It means a lot to Nick and me that we get to have him to ourselves. We promise to be good."

"I appreciate the repeat promise." I paused. "You're still serving wine though, aren't you?"

"Syd!" Kate cried. "Louis is *French*, we have to have wine."

"I hate to break it to you, but he doesn't like wine."

This seemed to stump her. "Really? Didn't you say his family owns a few vineyards?

"Yes, I did. His family *does* own a few vineyards, but he doesn't like wine. What can I say? It's bizarre."

"Should we have anything else on hand for him?"

"He's a big fan of rum and Coke."

"I'm on it."

"Thanks, Kate! I have to run. We're supposed to be there at six, right?"

"As I've told you *three* times already, you should come at seven. You seriously need to relax."

"Yeah, yeah." I chuckled. "Should I bring anything?"

"Only your smiling self. Oh...and your *boyfriend*."

They were totally going to embarrass me. Oh well! May as well get it over with. At least the entire family wouldn't be able to join in the fun.

Shoving my concerns aside, I said, "I love you, Kate. See you tonight!"

"I love you too, Syd. I can't wait!"

⌒

Several hours later, I was heading home from work to get ready for the big night. I had just enough time to freshen up before Louis arrived to take me to Kate and Nick's house. I quickly changed from my work clothes into a knee length gray cotton dress with a plum floral pattern. It had spaghetti straps and a nice sized slit up the side, so it was casual yet alluring. Louis had been very pleased with my decision to unearth some of the sexier items from my closet and I thoroughly enjoyed his inability to keep his hands off me as a result.

*Focus, Sydney!* Now was the time to do your imitation of a normal person. This meant I had to restrict my wine intake as well. Kate was not alone in the saying-humiliating-things-after-consuming-too-much-wine department. However, at least Kate was smart enough—even in her drunker state—to say embarrassing things about *other* people. I always ended up embarrassing myself. Badly.

Once I had finished lecturing myself in the mirror, the doorbell rang. I was glad to see Louis full of smiles on this very auspicious occasion.

He scooped me into his arms and squeezed me tightly. "Are you ready, *mon coeur?*"

When he released me, I considered him carefully. "You seem very excited."

"Is that a bad thing? I am looking forward to meeting the great Kate. You talk about her so much. She obviously means a lot to you."

I grinned. "Yes, she does. I hope the two of you will like each other."

He raised his eyebrows. "Who could possibly *not* like me?"

I laughed and felt some of my tension dissipate. "You always know what to say."

He kissed me gently on the lips. "Are you ready to go?"

"As I'll ever be." I grabbed my purse and we set off for his first encounter with Kate.

True to form, Louis had thought of *everything*. Not only had he bought a beautiful bouquet of flowers for Kate, but he had also brought a bottle of wine from his home district in France. Kate was completely charmed from the get-go. It didn't hurt that he had greeted her by kissing her on both cheeks.

"It's such a pleasure to meet you, Louis," she gushed. "Sydney has told us so much about you. And you certainly don't disappoint!"

Louis smiled. "Thank you for inviting me to your home. I am happy to meet you. Sydney talks about you both often."

Nick smirked. "Don't believe a word of it."

"She warned me about you, Nick," Louis joked. "I am ready for your questions."

Nick put his arm around Louis. "In that case, why don't you come out back and help me grill the steaks. We have a lot to talk about."

And just like that, they were gone. I turned to Kate with a panic-stricken look. She instantly rolled her eyes at me.

"Will you relax, please? It's going to be fine." She finished dressing the salad and brought it into the dining room, all the while shaking her head. "Why don't you let me pour you a glass of wine? It'll take the edge off."

Kate definitely had the right idea with the wine. Once I finished my first glass, everything I had been worrying about seemed inconsequential. I appreciated that this could be my altered state of perception, but I didn't care. Dinner was far more enjoyable this way.

Nick and Louis appeared to be getting along superbly and, to my great delight, Kate was completely taken with Louis. She waxed poetic about his impressive background and charming demeanor while we prepared dessert in the kitchen.

"You never told me he worked three jobs to pay for engineering college! Or that he was valedictorian of his high school class *and* at the top of his college class. Man! He was a paratrooper in the army, a national martial arts champion, a bodyguard *and* a volunteer firefighter. And he's so charming! He's amazing!"

Granted, Louis *was* amazing, but Kate's long declaration of this had more to do with the amount of wine she had consumed than the words she had exchanged with Louis this evening. She had already learned the majority of this information from me (and had passed it on to the rest of my family), but it was very cute to hear her profess her admiration nonetheless. I was thrilled they had all taken so well to each other. Not only would life be much easier since they got along well, but Kate would have lots of wonderful things to say when she reported back to our parents and Charlie. *Phew.*

"I'm delighted you approve."

She smirked and pulled me into a hug. "I know you don't need my approval. I'm just *overjoyed* that you've found such a great guy. I think he actually deserves you."

I felt a tightness in my chest. Kate had spent my entire life telling me how remarkable I was, but try as I might, I was never able to believe it the way she did. Her undying faith in me almost brought me to tears.

With a lump in my throat, I whispered, "Kate! Don't make me cry now."

She smoothed my hair away from my face. "I only wanted you to know how happy I am for you." She paused, biting her lip. "Plus, I'm pretty psyched that we don't have to hang out with a jackass. It's *such* a relief."

Leave it to Kate to bring me out of tears and into laughter. I tapped her on the nose and said, "You're too twisted for color TV."

Kate laughed. "Thank you, Ouiser." *Uh oh.* If the *Steel Magnolia* references had made their entrance, it was time to close things down.

Following that gem, we brought dessert into the dining room and enjoyed the rest of our evening. As far as I was concerned everything was far more than good enough, it was *perfect.*

## Chapter Fifteen

True to my expectations, Kate had raved about Louis to my parents and Charlie. It was sweet how she was able to put their minds at ease by confirming I had a worthy man in my life. If I had taken a moment to think about the fact that no one trusted *my* opinion about the man I was dating, I might have been insulted. Actually, even if I had, I would have been able to understand. My judgment hadn't been the best over the years.

Louis and I had been together for five weeks and had settled into a comfortable routine. We spent most evenings together and took turns staying overnight at each other's apartments. To an outsider, things probably seemed to be moving a bit quickly, but to me everything felt right. When you had spent as much time waiting for the right man as I had, you wanted to spend as much time with him as possible, just to soak it all up. In many ways I felt like I was playing catch up. My friends and family had all experienced love before in their lives. This was the first time in my life I had been in love. Real love. Louis made me feel like the most extraordinary woman in the world. He made me feel like...someone who deserved him.

We usually spent the weekend at Louis' place since Jean

was off gallivanting with one of his many lady friends. It was the Sunday morning following our dinner with Kate and Nick, and Louis and I had just finished a delicious brunch of pancakes and bacon. Completely stuffed to the gills, we were lounging lazily on the couch. Louis was reading with his head in my lap, when he abruptly put the paper down and gazed up at me.

"Do you have something on your mind, *Monsieur Duranc?*" I leaned down and kissed his nose.

"Yes, *mon coeur*, I do. I have a few apartments to look at today and I was wondering if you would come with me." Louis had seen quite a few over the past week, but hadn't found one to his liking yet. His company was getting antsy about his continued stay in the corporate apartment, so he had to make a decision quickly.

"Sure. I'd be happy to. Where are we heading?"

"There are a couple right down the street and a couple in the Belmont area."

I stroked his hair. "Okay. When do we need to leave?"

He glanced at the clock. "About an hour or so." He grinned and ran his hand up my thigh. "I can think of something we can do with an hour."

"Really?" I feigned innocence. In the blink of an eye, he had jumped up and flipped me onto my back.

"*Really,*" he whispered wickedly. He began kissing his way down my neck while his hands explored my body. I ran my hands under his shirt and up his back, pulling his shirt over his head. And just like that, we had the most amazing sex on the couch.

I couldn't believe the change Louis had affected in me in such a short time. If you had asked me two months ago, I couldn't have imagined having sex in the living room of my boyfriend's apartment—knowing his roommate might come home at any moment. Now, it didn't seem to bother me in the least. Louis had somehow managed to make me forget about my worries. (In all fairness, my more relaxed attitude could have resulted in part from the fact that nothing fazed Jean.  If he had come home while we were *in flagrante delicto*, he probably would have simply walked past and given us a thumbs-up.)

An hour and a half later, we were on our way to the first apartment.  It was about two minutes away, in a cute little apartment building I had often passed on the way to University Avenue.  The rental agent met us in the lobby and whisked us upstairs to the apartment.

It was a beautiful one bedroom, one bath apartment with a totally redone kitchen, a separate dining room and a little nook which would be perfect for Louis' office.  There were hardwood floors, tons of windows, three closets and a huge fireplace.  It was breathtaking.

"This is *beautiful!*" I stared in wonder.  The high ceilings made the main room seem even bigger.

Louis smiled.  "Do you really like it?"

"Are you kidding?  I *love* it!  It's incredible." I continued to gape.

Louis came over to me and held my hands.  "There is room here for you too, you know."

I regarded with curiosity.  "Well, I assumed I would stay here sometimes too."

"No, I mean, you could move in here with me."

*What?!*

"Have you thought this through?" My voice was shaky.

He held my face in his hands.  "Yes, I have thought this through.  I selected the apartments we are looking at today based on the two of us living in them." He kissed me lightly on the lips.  "I want to be with you, Sydney."

My heart started to race.  I took a few steps back.  "I just, um, need a minute...." To what?  To think?  To bolt?  What the hell was I going to do?  I was dangerously close to a meltdown and I had no one there to stop the crazy.  Louis was going to see exactly how messed up I was and then it would all be over.

"*Mon coeur?*  Are you all right?" Louis appeared genuinely worried.

I frantically searched the room for some semblance of a rational thought. *Okay, Sydney, slow down.* Focus on breathing. You can do this. Do *not* unleash the freak. He wasn't ready.

I gradually got my breathing under control and turned to Louis. "I'm sorry, Bluey. You caught me off guard." I paused "Have you honestly thought about what it would be like to live together?"

He walked over to me cautiously. "Yes, I have. And nothing would make me happier." He gazed into my eyes and stroked the side of my face. "I hope you feel the same way."

"Louis...I've never felt for any man what I feel for you. You're an incredible person and you make me *very* happy. I'm just scared because, well, we've only known each other for five weeks and you have no idea what you would be getting yourself into." I smiled weakly at him.

Louis pulled me into an embrace and kissed the top of my head. "You have no idea how you have changed my life, *mon coeur.* I have known many women and no one has ever touched my heart the way you have. I do not want to let that go." He sighed. "I know we have known each other for a short time, but why wait? I am sure I want to be with you for a long, long time."

Long, long time? This was getting weirder and weirder. I desperately wanted to believe this was it. I wanted to believe I had found the man I had been looking for...for what seemed like forever. But I couldn't stop thinking that it had only been five weeks since I'd met him.

I exhaled what felt like the entire contents of my lungs and held Louis tight. "This is a bit overwhelming for me. Could we take a little time to think about it?"

It broke my heart to see Louis look so disappointed, but I desperately needed time to figure things out. "Whatever you want, *mon coeur.*" He squeezed my hand and walked over to the rental agent.

Louis ended up taking the apartment, though I wondered if it was only because he didn't want to continue looking since our first experience became pretty uncomfortable. It would have been helpful had he not sprung this on me in such a spontaneous manner. I had made no secret of my love for planning. Maybe he was just trying to shake me out of my comfort zone. He had often told me how he thought my "reserved" personality was adorable, but maybe it was beginning to wear on him. I honestly didn't know what to think. I was completely confused.

After Louis dropped me off at my apartment (I claimed to have a headache), I called an emergency summit. Kate and Maya arrived at my apartment within the hour replete with bewilderment. I had given nothing away in my texts—only that they needed to hightail it to my place as soon as possible.

Kate was the first to speak. "What's going on, Syd?"

"Seriously, what's the deal?," seconded Maya. "I was in the middle of something important." Judging by her appearance, it was more like *someone* important.

"Not as important as this, my friend."

"Get to the point already," Kate said impatiently.

"I went with Louis to look at apartments today," I faltered, suddenly unsure of how to tell them.

"And?" Maya stopped to rolled her eyes. "They were too small? Too ugly? *What?*"

I exhaled loudly. "He wants me to move in with him."

They both stared at me. Kate's eyes were as big as saucers. Maya couldn't seem to pick her jaw up off the floor.

I gave them a satisfied smirk. "See? I *told* you it was a big deal!"

"No shit," Maya responded.

Kate regained her composure quickly. "You aren't ready to do this, are you? I mean it's only been, like, four weeks.

It's too soon, right?"

"It's been *five* weeks and yes, I think it's too soon. He's not ready to see behind the curtain yet. The relationship would be over before I even unpacked my boxes." I put my head in my hands.

Maya snorted. "Take it down a notch, drama queen. You may be a little neurotic, but you're predominantly awesome." She paused, searching for the right words. "The important thing is that you feel ready to do this. And if you don't, then just tell Louis."

Kate nodded. "Syd, he clearly cares for you very much. He won't push you if you're not ready. I mean, come on, he's a really good guy." She sounded pretty damn confident for someone who had met him once.

"What if I say no and he gets upset with me?" I wrung my hands nervously.

Kate glared at me. "Let me get this straight. You plan to move in with him so he doesn't get upset? That's not the right reason for doing this and you know it, hon. You need to decide what's right for *you*."

I sighed. "I know, *I know*. He caught me completely off guard."

Maya laughed. "He caught all of us off guard. No one was prepared for this! I guess he really digs you."

I frowned. "Thanks a lot, Maya."

She smacked me on the butt. "You know what I mean."

I glanced back and forth between the two of them. "So how do I tell him?"

Kate sighed. "Be *honest* with him. I'm sure he'll understand. You'll move in with him when you're ready."

I bit my lip. "If he still wants to..."

Maya smacked me on the butt again. "Why wouldn't he want to? He's *unbelievably* lucky. I can go over all your good points with him and show him how they greatly outweigh the bad points if you like. I have charts."

Maya ended up with a butt smack of her very own.

Kate and Maya left an hour later, once I had regained most of my composure. I called Louis and asked if he would have dinner with me that evening. He agreed and came to pick me up shortly thereafter. I was too spent from the afternoon's activities to care much about my appearance, so I threw on my favorite jeans, a black V-neck T-shirt and my favorite Converse. If Louis wanted to live with me someday, he was going to have to get used to Casual Sydney too.

We decided to walk down the street to the pub I took him to on our second date. The food was good and we both had fond memories of that night. When we sat down at the table, I got right to the point.

"Louis, I'm sorry if I upset you earlier today."

He smiled. "Don't be silly, *mon coeur*. I thought *I* upset *you*."

I shook my head. "No, not at all. I wasn't expecting your...pro—I mean, *idea*. I guess I just got scared."

"Scared?" he asked with worried eyes. "Am I *scary*?"

"No, you're not scary." I pursed my lips. "It's just, well, I've told you about the men I've dated in the past—all those, uh, colorful stories. All of *that* scared me." I waved my arms around to emphasize my point.

"But *I* won't treat you poorly, *mon coeur*. I care deeply for you."

I took his hand. "I know you do, Bluey. I care deeply for you too. I mean, I've never felt this way about a man before."

"But that is a good thing, is it not?"

"It is a *very* good thing, Louis," I replied, stalling for time. How was I going to explain this to him without sounding like an idiot?

"There is something you are not telling me, Sydney," he said with a hint of reproach in his eyes.

The time had come. I took a deep breath and blurted, "Everything is going *so* fast and I'm afraid if we move into together, you'll see how crazy I am and you won't want to be with me anymore."

Louis threw back his head and laughed. "*That* is what you are worried about?" He couldn't stop laughing. After a few minutes, I went from feeling relieved to feeling annoyed. It wasn't *that* funny.

"Louis? Should *I* be worried about *you*?"

He wiped tears of mirth from his eyes. "I thought you were not certain about your feelings for me. I thought perhaps you were changing your mind." He released a few stray chuckles. "But you are only concerned I will think you are too crazy to be with?"

I must have appeared *really* annoyed because he finally stopped laughing. "*Mon coeur*, I *know* you. You have to stop getting hung up on this sense of time, that it takes a certain amount of time to understand someone, to create a bond with this person. I have known some people for years and I have never felt close to them. But you! I fell in love with you the first night I met you."

I momentarily forgot how to breathe. He *loved* me?

"Sydney? Are you okay?" He examined me carefully.

"I...I'm at a loss for words."

"I will do the talking then. If you are not ready to move in with me now, then it is fine. I do not want to rush you. I was so caught up in how I feel about you, I wanted to move our relationship forward. The last thing I wanted to do was scare you." He took my hand and stroked it tenderly.

I gazed into those beautiful blue eyes I had come to know so well. "I'm in love with you too." *What?!* Where the hell did *that* come from? Though even as I had this minor freak-out, I knew these words were true.

Louis leaned over and kissed me softly on the lips. "This is certainly something to celebrate." He called our waiter over to the table and ordered a bottle of champagne.

I cocked an eyebrow. "I thought you didn't like champagne—well, anything from a vineyard."

He smiled mischievously. "You have to have celebration toasts with champagne." He frowned while perusing the menu. "Even if it is technically sparkling wine from California."

Now it was my turn to throw my head back and laugh. I mean really *laugh*. I was in full-on embarrassing cackle mode in public and I didn't care one bit. I had started out the evening completely freaked out about the status of my relationship with Louis and was finishing it completely sure of the fact that I was in love with him. He had gotten to know me better in five weeks than other men had in years. He accepted me for who I was and helped me to appreciate my best qualities. Sure, neither one of us was perfect, but we were more than good enough for each other. Without warning, it occurred to me—I didn't give a crap what was wrong with either one of us. We were in this together and we were going to make it work.

## Chapter Sixteen

The next week was a whirlwind of activities with Louis. He was able to move into his new apartment three days after he agreed to take it, but had very little to put in it. So we spent the week shopping for everything he would need to have a comfortable, yet functional, apartment. I was there to make sure it also looked nice—at least to me. Louis had his own sense of aesthetics and it was very...spartan. I planned to spend a lot of my time there and I didn't want to feel like I was in an institution.

My packed schedule annoyed Kate to no end. She called me at work on Thursday to give me a hard time about being so busy.

"Sydney Bennett, how may I help you?"

"You may tell me when I'm going to see my sister again."

"Kate! I've missed you." I really did. We usually saw each other every couple of days. It was a foreign feeling to have four Kate-free days.

"Well, whose fault is that?"

"I know! I'm sorry. It's been a weird few days." I barely had the chance to finish my sentence before I was overtaken by the mother of all yawns.

She laughed. "Not getting much sleep?"

"Not really. We've been spending our evenings in furniture stores, electronics stores, warehouse stores—you name it. Louis is really particular about his choice of television."

"Boys and their toys," she drawled. "Well, they think we spend too much time shopping for clothes, so I guess it all evens out." She paused to clear her throat, a clear sign that she was uncomfortable about something. "Mom and Dad have been asking about you. When's the last time you called them?"

"I actually can't remember," I replied, feeling more than a little guilt. "I'm a bit overwhelmed right now."

"I *bet* you are…being in love and all." She giggled. Of course I had found time to call her on Sunday night to tell her the big news. Kate and I had been waiting for a man as wonderful as Louis to come into my life for a very, very long time. She had to know we were in love as soon as I could possibly tell her.

I smiled. "I'm so *unbelievably* happy. It doesn't seem real. I feel like at any moment it'll all be taken away."

"You'll get used to it, Syd, just give yourself some time. And please, *please* do me a favor and call Mom and Dad. Otherwise they'll keep calling me and asking if you're all right."

"I'm sorry! I'll call Mom today."

"You'd better, *mon coeur*!" she joked.

"Ha, ha! I have to run, goofball. Give Nick a hug for me. I promise we'll get together soon."

"We hope so. Say hello to Louis for us."

After lunch, I decided I had better call my mom before she drove Kate insane. She picked up on the second ring, which meant she was actually sitting down for once.

"Sydney Bennett, where have you been?"

I chuckled. "I see you finally got caller ID."

"That's right! Your brother is helping us keep up with technology. I think I'd do okay on my own, but your father needs all the help he can get."

I giggled. "You'd better not let him hear you say that."

"I can handle him," she teased. "Enough about your dad. How are you, Syd? How is the wonderful Louis?"

"Ah! I see you've spoken with Kate."

"You bet. Kate and Nick gave us a nice rundown."

"You act like you haven't heard anything about him before! Don't you trust my account of him?"

"We all tend to wear rose-colored glasses when it comes to the people we're involved with. Your father and I only wanted to hear the opinion of someone who wasn't, um, intimately involved with Louis."

"Nice, Mom." I shuddered. "Do you feel better now?"

"Somewhat. I'll feel a lot better when I've had the chance to meet him myself."

Panic settled firmly in my heart. "I'm afraid you'll have to be patient. Unless you have a spontaneous trip to the west coast planned." I laughed weakly, silently cursing myself for planting the idea in her mind.

She sighed. "I'd love to come visit, but the store is simply too busy right now. You're still coming home for Thanksgiving, right?"

"I was thinking about it." I hadn't spoken with Louis about his plans yet, but I didn't want to leave him alone for a few days after he moved to a new country.

"Well, Syd, I was thinking..." I didn't like where this was going. "Maybe you could bring Louis with you." *Gah!*

I hesitated, thinking about the best way to phrase my answer.

"Syd?" my mom called. "Are you still there?"

"Sorry, Mom. I was just thinking. I...don't know if I'm ready for you to meet him yet. Louis is wonderful, but things have been moving so fast and meeting my parents is a *really* big deal."

"He met your sister, didn't he?" Her tone made it obvious that she felt insulted.

I exhaled slowly. "That's nowhere near as big a deal as *flying to New York and meeting my parents*. Plus, Dad's a total loose cannon! He could easily cause trouble. Or at least embarrass me to death."

"Sydney Bennett! I'm surprised at you. Don't you think you're being a *tad* overly dramatic?" Takes one to know one, Mom.

I felt a headache taking hold. "I'm sorry, Mom. I've been stressed lately. Louis, um, Louis sort of asked me to move in with him."

My mom gasped. "Already? Aren't things moving a little quickly?"

"Hence my stress. I've never felt this way about anyone before and I don't want to blow it."

"Well, what do you plan to do?" I could tell she had chosen her words carefully. She still fought the instinct to tell her children her opinion before we had formulated one of our own.

"I already told him I'm not ready and he's fine with it, but it's left me a little shaky." I sighed. "He seems so sure of everything."

"And you're not?"

"Yes and no. I'm in love with him. I'm sure of that. I'm just still having trouble trusting our relationship, you know? Believing it's all real."

"Has anything happened to worry you?"

"Of course not. It has nothing to do with Louis," I admitted. "It's all me and my buttload of crazy."

"Stop saying such things! You're not crazy, you've just had a few bad experiences. Give yourself some time to get used to him."

"I'm trying, but I think we can agree that meeting my parents right now is too much."

"Fine. I understand your concerns. I won't pressure you." Her disappointment was clear.

Relief flooded my system. "Thank you for being so understanding, Mom."

"You're welcome, sweetheart." Was it my imagination or was there a bit of guilt thrown in with those words?

A quick glance at the clock told me that my time was up. "I'm sorry to cut things short, but I have a meeting in ten minutes. I love you."

"You're not off the hook yet, Syd. Your father wants to speak with you too."

*Uh oh.* Cue the ominous music...

"Duck! Why has it been so hard to find you lately?"

"Hey, Dad. I've been helping Louis get his apartment set up."

"How is Linus?" Typical Dad. Using the wrong name on purpose just to push my buttons.

"*Louis* is fine, Dad. He's adjusting to life in California."

"And how are *you* adjusting to life with Linus?"

I laughed. "Enough, old man. I'm quite happy, thank you very much. Didn't you get enough info from Kate?"

"Your sister was helpful, but the only one who can properly evaluate this guy is me. So when are you bringing him home?" He waited expectantly.

"As I just told Mom, I'm *not* ready yet. Maybe we can come in the spring?"

"Not soon enough, Duck. I'm afraid I'll have to put your mother on a plane and come out there to meet this Frenchie."

Was he kidding? "Dad! Please tell me you're not serious."

"I am completely serious. You've never behaved like this with any of your other boyfriends. I need to go over a few things with him."

I put my head in my hands. "Dad, *please* don't mess with me right now. I'm ridiculously tired and may actually lose my mind."

"Chin up, Duck," he replied gleefully. "I'll give you another month to plan a visit. Then we'll discuss this further..."

I realized it would never matter how old I was, my dad would always worry about his little girl. "Okay, I'll think about it. I love you, Dad. I have to go back to work."

"I love you too, Duck. Make sure you call more often."
"I will. Bye, Dad!

Finally it was Friday—and not a moment too soon. I needed sleep in the worst way. Between shopping, unpacking, setting up furniture and spending, um, quality time with Louis, I hadn't slept much. I had to say his apartment was *gorgeous*, thanks in no small part to me. I was rather pleased Louis had finally compromised and allowed me to contribute a bit of my taste to his apartment. Otherwise it would have been completely devoid of color.

All the furniture was light wood and the couches were cream colored as were all the linens. (I did mention his penchant for the monochromatic, right?) After a little prodding, I was allowed to hang a few photos and paintings and to add a few splashes of color—a vase here, a throw pillow there. The apartment was a perfect blending of our styles and decorating it had been a good test of our ability to work together.

After we put the last piece of furniture together, we ordered pizza and ate it with gusto at Louis' new dining room table. After my third piece, I thought I was going to keel over.

Louis grinned. "You were hungry, *mon coeur.* I have never seen you eat like that!"

I stood up and patted my stomach. "It's one of the many things I've been hiding from you." I giggled. "Are you scared?"

He pulled me into his lap. "Completely terrified."

"I'll try to tone it down," I murmured before kissing him.

Running his hands down my back, he whispered, "I think you might feel a little better if you took your pants off."

I kissed him again, a little harder this time. "You think so?"

His hands wandered further down and ran over my behind. "You will feel much less restricted."

I bit my lip. "Maybe you can help me with this...restriction."

He stood up quickly and carried me into the bedroom. As he laid me down on the bed, my heart began to race. He slowly removed my pants, kissed his way down my legs and drove me wild with desire.

"I don't think you will be needing your shirt either." He held me in his smoldering gaze as he unbuttoned my shirt and slipped it off.

"Really?" I rasped. "And why do you need your clothes?"

"I would feel much better without them, but you have very rudely not offered to remove them for me."

I knelt on the bed. "Let me remedy that for you." I slowly unbuttoned his shirt, kissing my way from his neck to his navel.

"Sydney, *the things you do to me*." He pulled me on top of him and kissed me until I felt it in my toes.

Much later that evening, we were lying in bed talking. I was blissfully wrapped around Louis, inhaling his intoxicating scent.

"What do you feel like doing this weekend?" Louis asked me as he twirled a few strands of my hair around his finger.

I yawned. "I don't know. Something relaxing. This week was rough."

"I saw a great sale online for tickets to Vegas."

I propped my head up on my elbow so I could get a closer look at him. "Vegas? I didn't know you were into gambling."

He shook his head. "I am not. It seems like it would be fun."

"Don't even try to tell me you want to go see the shows." He grimaced and stuck out his tongue at me, making me laugh heartily. "So, I guess you want to lounge by the pool and be pampered after such a hard week?"

He studied me. "The pool sounds nice, but I was thinking we could get married."

I rolled my eyes. "You have a very interesting sense of humor."

"I am not joking."

My heart stopped. After the week we had, *this* is what happened next?

"Um...you're serious?"

"Absolutely."

My mind was reeling. What happened to not rushing me? What happened to waiting for me to be comfortable? It had only been six weeks since I had met him. What the hell was going on? Then a thought occurred to me.

"Are you going to ask me a question?"

He stared into my eyes. "I am not sure I want to ask you because you will probably say no."

I literally had no idea what to say.

Louis pulled me to his chest. "Relax, *mon coeur*. Forget I said anything. I got caught up in the moment. *Again.* You are exhausted. Let us go to sleep." He kissed me lightly on the lips and closed his eyes.

Like I was going to sleep after the most insane discussion *ever*! My mind wouldn't stop spinning. Was he kidding? Did he think this was a good joke? Was he really an asshole? Had I been completely taken in?

Suddenly, a hollow feeling crept into my stomach. I had *finally* figured out what was wrong with Louis. He needed a green card.

## Chapter Seventeen

I didn't sleep much that night. Whenever I could calm my mind enough to fall asleep, I would have these bizarre dreams about marrying Louis. One of them ended with our getting married and the minister saying, "I now pronounce you green card holder and wife." Each time I would wake with a start and Louis would toss a bit, turn over and go back to sleep. Ah, to be that peaceful.

Finally, at seven in the morning, I couldn't take it anymore. If I didn't get out of Louis' apartment, I was going to go crazy. I got out of bed, quickly brushed my teeth (Louis had proudly presented me with my own toothbrush the night before) and got dressed. I was going to leave Louis a note—because I was a total coward—but he woke up as I picked up my purse and was about to leave the room.

"Where are you going, *mon coeur?* Are you okay?" His eyes widened with concern.

I froze. "I...can't sleep. I thought I would go home and take a bath." Thankfully Louis didn't have a tub, so he couldn't suggest I take one here.

He eyed me suspiciously. "You want to go home to take a bath. At seven in the morning on a Saturday."

I nodded my head. "I need to meet Kate later this

morning for breakfast. She's really been after me lately for not being around. I thought it would be nice to take a bath before I met her." Did I sound as stupid as I thought I did?

"Is this about last night? Are you freaking out about our discussion of Las Vegas?"

I laughed nervously. "Of course not. Why would it freak me out?"

"Come over here and sit down." The expression on his face told me he meant business.

I moved slowly over to him and sat on the edge of the bed. He pulled me closer and took my hand. "If this relationship is going to work, you are going to have to learn to be honest with me. Stop worrying about how crazy you think you are going to look to me." He took my face into his hands and gazed deeply into my eyes. "I love you for who you are. You do not have to hide from me."

I let out a shaky breath. "You say that now, but if I ever actually let you in..." I shook my head.

"What do you think is going to happen?" He cocked his head to the side. "Do you think I cannot handle it?"

I raised my eyebrows in shock. "Do you think this is some kind of challenge? *This is who I am*, Louis." I knew he could tell from my tone that I was not amused.

He stroked my back. "I am not making fun of you. I am only trying to lighten the mood, which is what I think you need right now. You are taking things *far* too seriously. Whether or not you realize it, I have gotten to know you pretty well, *mon coeur*. In fact, I am sure I know you better than you think I do."

"Really? And what do you think you know?" I asked with a hint of sarcasm.

He sat up and faced me. "You are hungry *all the time*. You need to be fed every two hours or there will be serious consequences. You always want to choose the movie we watch and then you *always* fall asleep and snore through it. Romantic comedies are your favorite, but you are also addicted to murder mysteries, though you are often wrong about the identity of the murderer. You love Italian and Mexican food, but your absolute favorite is Greek. You love red wine and margaritas and hate white wine and all other hard liquor. All your desserts must contain some kind of chocolate or there is no point in having dessert. You buy yourself a new outfit every year on your birthday to make yourself feel better about getting older. You are completely self-conscious when you are wearing anything tight or short (or are naked), though you should not be because you are absolutely gorgeous. You put everyone else in your life first and often forget that you need things too. The first opinion you want on anything important is Kate, followed by a close second with Maya. I have absolutely no idea where my opinion factors in, but this is not important right now." He stopped to draw breath. "Shall I go on?"

*Whoa.* I totally wasn't expecting that. I guess he had been paying attention.

"Am I to assume from your stunned silence you realize I am right? That I do know you fairly well?" He shook me gently by the shoulders. "*I love* you, Sydney. I am very sorry if I scared you with my ridiculous idea to go to Vegas." He sighed heavily. "But I really want you to hear me when I say this. *Nothing you can say or do will scare me or will change how I feel about you.*"

I continued to stare at him. For the life of me, I couldn't think of what to say.

"*Mon coeur*, as I have said before, I have *never* felt this way for anyone. It amazes and overwhelms me. I sometimes get carried away. I know I want to spend the rest of my life with you and it came out. I am sorry."

"You're sorry that you want to spend the rest of your life with me?" I teased.

His shoulders slumped with relief. "There she is." He grinned and gave me a soft tap on the nose. "I knew you were in there somewhere."

"You sure know how to scare the crap out of a girl."

Louis threw his head back and laughed. "You have such

a way with words, Syd."

"I'm glad you're amused." I took his hand and contemplated how to explain my feelings. "I've never felt like this for anyone before either, Louis. It *terrifies* me. Everything has happened at the speed of light. I just need things to slow down."

He squeezed my hand. "As you wish, *mon coeur.* The last thing I want to do is upset you. Feel free to take a moment."

I threw my arms around him and felt tears welling in my eyes. "You *do* know me, don't you?"

"Yes, I do." After kissing me on the top of the head, he pulled out of the hug and handed me my purse. "Now go and visit with Kate. I am sure you have a lot to discuss."

"You're amazing." I kissed him slowly, savoring every touch of his luscious lips. "Are you free for dinner this evening?"

"I would love to have dinner with you. Shall I pick you up at seven?"

"Sounds great." I stood up and crossed the room. When I got to the doorway, I turned around to take one last look at Louis. "I love you."

He met my gaze. "I love you, too."

❀

By the time I left Louis' apartment, it was eight in the morning. I drove straight to Kate and Nick's house. I didn't care that it was Saturday morning and that Nick would probably kill me—there were important things to discuss. I parked my car in the driveway and walked up to the front door. As I stood there trying to decide whether to knock or ring the doorbell, Kate opened the door and scared me half to death. Not that I was jumpy or anything.

I clutched my chest. "Holy crap!"

"I should be saying that to you, Syd. What the hell are you doing here?" Hmm. This was most unKatelike. Somebody needed more sleep. Or to get laid. Or both.

"I'm sorry! I have a crisis! I had to talk to you right

away."

"Have you heard of the phone?" Seriously, you need *something*, Kate.

"I'm really, *really* sorry, but I need your help."

She sighed. "Fine, come in."

I followed her into the kitchen and put my purse on the counter.

Kate picked up her coffee mug and turned around to face me. "What's the big emergency?"

"Well, Louis, um, asked me to go to Vegas."

She examined me for a moment before saying, "Are you concerned he has a gambling problem?"

"No, but I *am* concerned that he wants to visit one of those chapels..."

Kate shook her head in confusion. "Why?"

"Because he mentioned going there so we could get married."

Kate put her mug back down on the counter. She paused for a moment, stared at the floor and then back up at me. "I'm sorry, would you please repeat what you just said?"

"Louis asked me to marry him. Well, technically he didn't. He suggested we go to Vegas to get married, but when I asked him if he was going to ask me the question, he said he didn't think he wanted to because he thought I would say no. Then we went to sleep, well, he did and I didn't..." I was on the edge of hysteria.

Kate came over and took my hands. "Syd, take a breath. It's going to be okay." It sounded like she was trying to convince herself of this too. "Let's go sit down. We need to...talk."

Kate made me a cup of tea, took me into the living room, settled me on the couch and asked me to go over the evening again. I relayed the conversations Louis and I had had, including the one from this morning. When I was finished, Kate sat for a few minutes with a furrowed brow.

She peered over at me. "This is crazy, isn't it?"

"It sure is." I paused. "You want to hear something even crazier?"

Kate nodded. "Love to."

"I think I would have said yes," I whispered.

Kate's eyes opened wide. "Really?"

I nodded. "It's strange, but I think I would have. I know I completely freaked out when he asked me to move in with him and I totally freaked out when he mentioned getting married, because I've only known him for six weeks." I let out a deep breath. "But this morning, when he told me how much he loves me and that nothing I could say to him would scare him or change the way he feels about me...after he described how he sees me...I knew. He's the man I want to spend my life with."

"Holy crap," she whispered.

"You got that right," I joked. "Now what?"

"What do you mean?"

"I mean, now what do I do? Do I tell him I want to marry him even though he never technically asked me? Do I propose a trip to Vegas?" I threw my hands in the air. "Or do *I* propose to *him*?"

Kate took a deep breath. "This is just crazy."

"What's crazy?" Nick called from the kitchen.

I glared at Kate in a panic. She glared back at me. "You're going to have to fill him in, Syd. It's not like we can hide it."

Nick came into the living room. "Hide what? What's going on?"

I regarded him cautiously. "Don't worry, Nick. Everything is fine."

"Really?" he scoffed. "That's why you're here before nine in the morning—wearing your clothes from yesterday, I presume?"

I sighed. "Fine. Ten points for your astuteness, Nick. Louis asked me to go to Vegas to get married."

"Holy shit!" Nick almost dropped his coffee. "He asked you to marry him?"

"Technically he never asked her," Kate supplied helpfully.

Nick sat down on the couch between me and Kate. "Please explain."

I massaged my temples. "Exactly what we told you. He asked me to go to Vegas to get married, but technically never asked me to marry him since I freaked out."

"Huh. Didn't see that coming." He patted me on the back. "So what are you going to do?"

"We were just wondering the same thing," Kate said as she curled up in his lap.

"What do you think, Syd? I mean, I'm not sure he's good enough for you. I don't think we've had time to figure that out yet." Nick had shifted into full big brother mode.

"Well, I'm in love with him. And I just told Kate that I would have said yes if he had asked me to marry him." I bit my lip. "I want to be with him for the rest of my life."

"That's amazing!" Nick exclaimed. "I'm so happy for you, Syd. I have one question though—make that two questions."

"Okay," I said warily.

"First, does it have to be so fast?"

I leaned my head back against the couch. "No, it doesn't. It seemed way too fast before, but somehow, now it doesn't. It may sound silly, but I feel like, when you know, you know." I smiled at his furrowed brow. "What's your second question?"

He took a deep breath. "Please don't get upset, but is it possible...do you think he needs a green card?"

There was that hollow feeling in the pit of my stomach again. I had thought about this a lot over the last ten hours and had let my heart win the argument. I had decided that Louis really loved me and just wanted to start our life together as soon as possible.

I met Nick's gaze. "I've thought about it, but I don't think it's true. He could get one through his company. His transfer made him a regular employee of their San Jose office, which is a US owned company. He's on a visa right now, but he could easily start the green card process in the next few months."

Kate perked up. "So you guys talked about this?"

I frowned. "If you're asking me whether or not I asked Louis if his suggestion of getting married had anything to do with the need for a green card, no I did not."

She eyed me with concern. "Syd, I'm worried about you. I want to make sure you aren't rushing into anything. It's only been six weeks—"

"I know, Kate." I reached over and hugged her. "I'm sorry. My mind is all over the place right now."

Nick put his hand on my shoulder. "We're both worried about you, but the bottom line is, this is your decision. We'll back you whatever you decide, but please think seriously about it first."

I moved over and put one arm around each of them. "I love you both so much. I promise to think everything over carefully." I got up from the couch and brought my mug into the kitchen. I then grabbed my purse off the kitchen counter and came back into the living room.

"I need to go home and figure some things out." I gathered my hair in a ponytail and secured it with the elastic band I always wore around my wrist. "I'll call you later."

Kate came over and hugged me. "I love you, Syd. Call if you need anything."

"I will. Though, I definitely think *you* need something, grumpy girl." I winked at her.

She swatted the back of my head and laughed. "Maybe."

As I drove home, I knew I had already made my decision. Actually, my heart had made the decision and my head was pretty pissed about it. There was a good chance I was going to get my heart broken and I was walking into it willingly. (Perhaps sprinting was a more accurate description.) This behavior was completely contrary to how I had lived my life for nearly twenty-eight years. What was I doing?

One thing was clear—there was something seriously wrong with *me*, like bat-shit crazy wrong with me. Whether I was crazy or not, nothing was going to stop me now. I was going to propose to Louis.

## Chapter Eighteen

As soon as I got home, I called Maya and asked her to meet me at the Nordstrom in the Stanford Shopping Center. She grumbled about the early hour, but I told her it was urgent and I would buy her lunch at the Peninsula Creamery. She couldn't resist their milkshakes, so she eventually agreed to my request. I parked outside Nordstrom at ten to eleven and wondered for the hundredth time if I were completely insane.

I had asked Maya to meet me in the jewelry section so I could start browsing. Her flexible sense of time meant her arrival window was fairly large and I wanted to keep my mind busy with something while I waited. I had been browsing for five minutes when I heard her voice behind me.

"Okay, Syd. What was *so important* that—"

I turned around to find her staring at me. "What?" I checked my appearance to make sure I hadn't forgotten something important, like pants. Laugh if you will, but I had a lot on my mind this morning.

Maya bit her lip as she perused her surroundings. "Why are you looking at costume engagement rings?" She glanced at me once more before picking up a ring and sliding it onto her finger. "Is there something you want to tell me?" she joked.

I smiled nervously. How was I going to explain this? *Just spit it out, Sydney.* "Louis asked me to go to Vegas for the weekend to get married."

"*Are you fucking kidding me?*" Maya's voice carried all the way down to the lingerie department.

I suppressed a giggle. "Maya! You're shocking the customers."

"He asked you to marry him?" she whisper-yelled. "When did this happen?" As petrified as I was, I still took a moment to enjoy this rare reaction from my confident friend.

"Well, technically he didn't ask me to marry him, only to go to Vegas to get married. Ugh. Whatever. It happened last night."

"What did you say?"

"Nothing! I was in shock. We talked about it this morning after he caught me trying to sneak out of his apartment." I sighed. "Not my finest moment."

Maya stared at me expectantly. "And?!"

"And he said some incredible things about how much he loves me and how nothing I can say or do will scare him off. He told me he didn't want to rush me, he was just…following his heart."

"And you believed him?" Maya slapped her hand over her mouth. "Sorry, Syd. Old habit."

I rolled my eyes. "Nice." Although I was pretty sure I would have said the same thing in her shoes. We East Coasters are pretty cynical.

Maya surveyed her surroundings once more before asking, "So, what are we doing here?"

"Um….you're going to think I'm nuts."

"I already know you're nuts," she snickered. "Please enlighten me as to why I will continue to think so."

I cleared my throat. "We're buying a costume engagement ring."

Maya's eyes widened. *"Really?"*

"Really." I grinned. "I'm going to propose to Louis."

In the blink of an eye, she grabbed me and started jumping up and down. *"Oh my God!* That's awesome!"

Her excitement was so contagious that I started jumping and squealing right along with her. Soon everyone within a fifty-foot radius was watching us like we were complete lunatics—which we were, of course.

I couldn't stop smiling. "I know this is crazy, but I don't care. I want to do this. I *really* want to do this!"

"I'm so excited for you," Maya gushed. "Now let's pick out a ring!"

"These are the ones I've found so far." I gestured to the line of rings on the counter.

While poking through my selection, she said, "Question—why is it that you're buying a costume ring?"

I had come up with a carefully worded explanation to answer this question on my drive to the mall. You always had to come prepared with Maya. "Well, Louis is very traditional and he wouldn't want his manhood undermined by his fiancée purchasing her own engagement ring. This will be a prototype. He can buy the real one later."

Maya snorted. "I see, so you don't want to 'undermine his manhood' by buying your own ring, but you have no issue with *proposing* to him." She emphasized her point with air quotes and loads of sarcasm. Maya had real talent when it came to vexation—she managed to irritate me with words and gestures simultaneously.

"He basically asked me already," I replied, giving her a healthy smack on the butt for her impertinence. "He just didn't formally state the question since he was afraid I would turn him down."

"I love your reasoning." She shook her head and held up a ring, twirling it in slow circles around her index finger. "This one is my favorite."

I held out my hand eagerly. She placed her find in my palm and I peered down at it in fascination. It was a silver ring with a large round cubic zirconia surrounded by a ring of small cubic zirconia. The band was plain silver. I knew it was fake, but the effect was still overwhelming, in both the sparkle and the significance of the ring. For one brief moment, I lost my breath.

"It's my favorite too," I whispered, slipping the ring on my finger. It fit perfectly. It *had* to be a sign. "This is the one." I looked over at Maya. "Am I crazy?"

"Absolutely! But this is one of the smartest decisions you've ever made." She sighed. "Honestly, Syd, I know it's only been six weeks, but I've never seen you this happy. If this is what your heart is telling you to do, then I think you should do it."

I studied at my shoes. "What if I get hurt? What if he *is* after a green card?"

Maya touched my shoulder. "Syd, look at me."

I reluctantly withdrew my gaze from my shoes and met her eyes.

"If you don't want to go through with this, then you don't have to. Take all the time you need. But if you're simply afraid of getting hurt, well, you can't safeguard against that. I know you want to be able to, but you can't. And if you don't risk anything, you won't gain anything."

"Is that so?" I asked softly.

She nodded. "It sucks, but it's true."

I knew she was right. In my heart, I knew I wanted to marry Louis, but that didn't stop the concerns from popping up all over the place. I kept obsessing about what everyone in my life would think. My parents were *definitely* going to flip out, but really, who could blame them? My dad might even get on a plane so he could check out "this Linus character" as soon as possible. Charlie and Zoe would think I had finally lost my marbles and even though Kate and Nick had tried to be supportive this morning, they didn't really think I would do it—because Sydney Bennett would *never* do anything so crazy! And everyone would probably think this was about a green card.

I mulled it over for another moment and came to a conclusion. I couldn't live my life worrying about what other people thought I should do, I had to decide for myself.

I locked eyes with Maya. "Let's do this." I walked over to the cashier, handed him the ring and took out my credit card.

"That's my girl!" Maya cried.

As promised, I took Maya to the Peninsula Creamery for lunch. She was in heaven with her strawberry milkshake and burger. As she devoured everything on her plate, I sipped my chocolate milkshake and went over my plan. When I was finished, she had a huge smile on her face.

"You've outdone yourself, Syd. He's going to love it."

I let out a huge breath. "I hope so. I'm *nervous*." I paused, a horrific thought occurring to me. "What if he's changed his mind?"

"Will you stop? He hasn't changed his mind. Relax! And if you're too overwhelmed right now, you don't have to do it. You can always abort the plan if you change your mind."

I smirked. "Way to be definitive, Maya."

"Hey, now! You know once I make a decision, I stick with it." She finished her milkshake with a huge slurp. "This *is* a big deal and I think it's great that you're doing it. But if you're unsure at any point, it's fine to wait."

I had to laugh. I wasn't sure if it was the lack of clarity or the slurp. Either way, I felt a little better.

"Thanks! Your certainty astounds me."

She rolled her eyes. "Shut up! You know what I mean."

"I know," I murmured. "Thanks for doing this with me. And for not thinking I'm crazy."

A look of surprise crossed her face. "Of course, Syd. I always have your back. You know that, don't you?"

"I do." I beamed. "Now, finish up. We have things to do!"

Maya and I worked our way through the Stanford Shopping center selecting the perfect outfit for my date with Louis this evening. First, we found a beautiful black strapless dress with a knee length skirt and a generous slit up the back. Next we found a pair of black patent leather peep toe heels and matching clutch. To top it all off, Maya snagged the last crimson cashmere wrap—out of another woman's hands, no less—from the accessories counter at Bloomingdales. The woman looked like she was about to bitch slap Maya until she shared with her that I was getting engaged tonight and desperately needed this wrap to complete my ensemble. I felt guilty until I remembered this was actually true and not one of the crazy stories she usually made up to relieve others of items she wanted.

We raced back to my apartment and began the long process of beautifying. While I was in the shower, Maya came in holding the phone, indicating Kate was eager to speak with me. *Sweet!* I was hoping she would call me back before Louis picked me up. It wouldn't seem right to ask him this very important question without Kate knowing about it first. After rinsing the last of the conditioner out of my hair, I quickly dried myself off and took the phone from Maya.

"Kate!"

"Hi, Syd! What's up?"

I took a breath. "I've made my decision."

"Already?" she asked, a hint of apprehension in her voice.

"Yes, already," I confirmed. "I'm going to ask Louis to marry me."

No response. This didn't bode well. Kate *always* had something to say.

"Are you there, Kate?"

She coughed. "Sorry. Yes, I'm here. I was just, um, *surprised*."

"I'm sorry. I know it's crazy. But when you know, you

know."

"So, when are you going to propose?" Her voice was barely audible.

I didn't hesitate. "Tonight. I'm taking him to dinner at Il Fornaio." I heard a thud and then a clatter. "Kate? Are you okay?"

It took a moment, but she responded. "Fine! Totally fine. Sorry about that, I, uh, missed the couch. I was going to sit down and, well, I guess didn't pay attention." She chuckled. "I fell on the floor."

I giggled. I had never shocked my big sister like this before! Not even when I almost set fire to the kitchen. (I was only seven years old! And it wasn't my fault that the toaster had faulty wiring.)

"I'm sorry, Kate. I didn't mean to alarm you. Are you sure you're all right?"

"Absolutely. Don't worry. When is your reservation?"

"Seven-thirty." I checked the clock. It was already five, which meant I had to go so I could finish getting ready.

"Is Maya helping you get ready?"

"Yes, she is, but I would love it if you were here too." I felt tears come to my eyes. Kate had been there for every single important event in my life. I wanted to share this with her too, even if she wasn't so excited about it.

"I wouldn't miss it for the world," she said breathlessly. "Be right there."

I swallowed the lump in my throat. "I love you, Kate."

"I love you too, Syd."

⌒

Kate arrived twenty minutes later with a bag full of accessories and makeup. My sister didn't mess around. She and Maya consulted for a few moments on hair and makeup while I read a magazine. They never involved me in these decisions since they felt they knew better than I did. I wanted to be insulted, because I felt like a child, but sadly, it was true. They always made me look amazing, even when

I thought their ideas were ridiculous.

An hour later, I was almost ready. Kate had put my hair up in a French twist and had artfully arranged tendrils around my face. Maya then applied light blush, perfectly executed black eyeliner, silver eye shadow and lash-extending mascara. My eyes were sparkly and amazing. She finished with a deep crimson lipstick which matched my wrap exactly. Maya didn't mess around either. She and Kate were the perfect team.

When Maya finished applying my makeup, I put on my dress and shoes so we could make the final jewelry selection. We opted for diamond drop earrings, courtesy of Maya, and a white gold and diamond bracelet, courtesy of Kate. We decided not to add a necklace, allowing for the focus to be on the beautiful neckline of the dress.

I checked the clock and felt my heart start to race. Louis was going to be here any minute. I had asked him to pick me up a little early so we could walk down University Avenue for a few minutes before our reservation. I was sure this request seemed a little strange to him and in my nervous paranoia I was completely convinced he knew what I was planning. When he didn't make a comment, I decided to believe he hadn't noticed anything. You can certainly attest to the fact that he had seen some odd behavior on my part on more than one occasion. This was one of the benefits of being *slightly* crazy—people didn't necessarily notice when you were up to something.

I examined myself in the mirror. Everything seemed to be in place. I turned to Kate and Maya and asked their opinion with my eyes. They both gazed at me with love and happiness.

"You are absolutely beautiful, Syd," Kate said, her voice thick with emotion.

Maya grinned. "You do look really hot."

"Good," I responded with a laugh. "Hot is what I was going for."

"*Duh*," Maya replied. "You can't go wrong with hot."

Suddenly, I felt a giant wave of nausea. "I'm *nervous*!"

"Of course you are! This is a *big deal*," Kate breathed. "But you're ready, Syd."

"Damn straight you are!" Maya hooted.

Kate blinked back tears before whispering, "Louis is a very lucky man."

"We can remind him of that when he gets here if you like," Maya declared just as the doorbell rang.

"Please do *not* embarrass me tonight. I might have to kill you!" I told her, perhaps a bit too sharply.

"Look at me, Syd." Maya put her hand on my shoulder, waiting patiently until I turned toward her. "You're going be fine. *You've got this*."

I put my arms around her and squeezed tightly. I then found Kate and hugged her within an inch of her life.

Kate held my face in her hands. "*Enjoy* this night, Syd. You've planned something truly special for him and he's going to love it.

"You're right," I responded, trying to sound confident. "It's going to be great." I did my best to let her optimism take hold of my mind instead of the usual insanity that resided there.

As the doorbell rang again, I ran to answer it and almost wiped out in the hallway. Thankfully, I was able to catch the umbrella stand and right myself before any damage was done. Maya and Kate burst into peals of laughter at my utter lack of grace.

"We promised not to embarrass you, but you did that completely on your own," Maya said between cackles.

When I opened the front door, Louis came in and surveyed the scene in front of him. Kate had regained her composure, but Maya was still hopelessly lost in a fit of giggles.

"What is going on?" He threw a confused glance at me, then Kate and then Maya.

Kate laughed. "We have no idea, Louis. She does this sometimes." She approached him with a smile. "It's so nice to see you again."

Louis kissed her on each cheek. "It is nice to see you too, Kate." He turned to Maya, who was still stifling a few rogue giggles. "And you too, Maya. By the way, Jean asked me to say hello for him."

This stopped Maya's giggles and turned her face a deep shade of red. What was that about?! I had *never* seen such a reaction from her before! Not *ever*. What happened between them? I desperately wanted to know, but had more important matters to attend to at present. She wasn't off the hook yet though...

Louis returned his attention to me. "*Mon coeur*, you look absolutely gorgeous." He kissed me tenderly on the lips. "Many men will be jealous of me tonight."

I regarded my soon-to-be fiancé (or so I hoped) with wonder. He called me gorgeous, but he looked *incredible*. He was wearing a dark-red long-sleeved collared shirt and fitted black pants. (Had Maya called to coordinate my outfit with his?) He was freshly shaved and smelled delightful, as usual.

"Women are *always* jealous of me, Bluey. And tonight will be no different. You are...magnificent." Hmm. Perhaps not the most expressive choice, but I was a bit distracted by the daunting task ahead of me.

"Thank you, *mon coeur*. You flatter me immensely." Louis took my hand. "Are you ready to go?"

I nodded. "I only need to get my purse and wrap." On cue, Kate came over and handed them to me.

"Thanks, Kate." I stared at her with fearful eyes. Perceptive as ever, she squeezed my hand and winked.

"Have fun you two." Maya grinned mischievously at us. I immediately felt annoyed with her for possibly giving something away to Louis, when I remembered he was used to all manner of mischief from Maya.

We said goodbye to our send-off committee and started walking out to the parking lot. I felt my phone buzz twice as Louis opened the car door for me. Who was calling me now? I picked up the phone prepared to hit the decline button, when I noticed I had received two text messages. One each from Kate and Maya with the same idea: "Call as soon as you can afterward!" I waved my assent as I carefully got into the car. I had planned what I imagined to be the perfect evening and hoped I would have good news for them later. Unless there was something seriously wrong with my judgment of this entire situation...

## Chapter Nineteen

I did my best not to fidget on the car ride to the restaurant, but it was extremely difficult. I knew if I didn't control myself, Louis would know I was up to something. He didn't miss a thing when it came to my body language. My heart started to race as I thought of his body language, *Focus, Sydney*!

"You are very quiet, *mon coeur*," he observed quietly.

"I was just thinking."

"Thinking can be dangerous." He laughed. "What were you thinking about?"

"Oh, just the last time we ate at this restaurant." It was funny to think how nervous I was that night. It seemed like nothing in comparison to what I was feeling now.

"That was one of the best nights of my life."

"Really?" I smiled mischievously. "Why?" I expected him to say it was the first time he kissed me.

"Well," he said softly, "I was sure I had met the woman I wanted to spend the rest of my life with."

Hearing him say those words sent shivers down my spine. I was still anxious, but at least I felt more confident about the outcome of the evening. I slipped my hand inside my clutch for what felt like the thousandth time to make sure the ring hadn't fallen out.

We pulled up to the restaurant and Louis got out of the car and handed the keys to the valet. I glanced over at him, surprised. There was a public parking lot right across the street and Louis wasn't a valet kind of guy. He didn't want anyone else driving his car, even if it was a rental.

"Wow! What's the occasion?"

"Only the best for my girlfriend." He winked and my heart froze. Did he know something?

I extended my hand to him. "Are you ready for a little stroll before dinner?"

He took my hand and his gaze dropped to my shoes. "Are *you* ready for a stroll?"

Sadly, I hadn't thought about the comfort level of these shoes when I bought them today. They looked great with the dress, but I would probably end up with blisters. Ah, the things women did to look good. I scanned the area quickly and remembered that the hotel next to the restaurant had a little courtyard. I smiled and led him to the path.

As we walked toward the fountain in the center of the courtyard, Louis pulled gently on my hand. "What are you up to, Syd?"

I gave him my best innocent eyes. "What makes you think I'm up to something?"

"I have told you," he responded, laughter coloring his tone. "I *know* you. Something is going on."

I stopped walking and turned to him. "You sure know how to suck the romance out of a situation, don't you?"

"Well, I think you know by now I am not your stereotypical Frenchman. So are you going to tell me what is going on or not?"

I had planned this whole beautiful speech about how much I loved him, how special he made me feel, how sure I felt about his feelings for me—with or without the crazy— and that he had come along at a time when I thought I would be alone for the rest of my life. As these thoughts swirled around in my mind, I looked at him and realized two things. One, I would *never* get through all that without either crying or saying something stupid. And two, he *already* knew. Louis was a man who didn't need to hear these things again. There was just one thing he needed to hear.

I took his hands in mine, gazed into those achingly beautiful blue eyes I loved so much and whispered, "Will you marry me?"

His expression of pure shock spooked me for a minute, but his face quickly morphed into the biggest smile I had ever seen. He picked me up and twirled me around until I was dizzy. When he finally put me down, he held my face in his hands and kissed me gently on the lips. He then leaned his forehead against mine and ran his hands down my back.

"You have made me the happiest man in the entire world." He was breathless and couldn't stop smiling. It was utterly adorable.

I grinned at his excitement. "Well, are you going to answer my question?"

"Yes! Yes! Yes! I will marry you." He snatched me up and twirled me around again.

Once my feet touched the ground, I reached into my bag and pulled out the ring. "Okay, then. You'll need to put this on my finger to make it official."

He took the ring from me and studied it. He then cocked his head to the side and stared at me. I laughed nervously. "It's only a prototype, Bluey. I wanted to have something on hand for this evening." Maybe this had been a stupid idea.

His brow was deeply furrowed. "A prototype?"

"You know, a model of a ring I might like..." I trailed off, wondering if I had totally ruined this.

He gawked at me again. "It is fairly large. Is this what you want me to buy for you?"

My hands flew to my face. "I'm so sorry! There isn't a lot of choice when it comes to costume engagement rings. All the ones I found were about this size. I chose the shape and general style I liked."

He laughed and pulled my hands down from my face. "Syd, I was kidding. Though I think we will have to go a bit smaller than this. French companies do not pay as much as American companies."

I squeezed his hands happily. "I don't care how big it is. I'm just happy you said yes." So that was *mostly* true. We could always upgrade later.

There was his million dollar smile again. "How could I not say yes? I am *amazed* you asked me." He brought my hand up to his lips and kissed it softly.

"Yes, at least I had the courage to ask the question." I poked him in the ribs.

"Only because I had basically asked you already." He poked me back.

"It's a whole lot scarier to ask the actual question!" I teased.

He stroked the side of my face. "I will have to take your word for it." He reached over and took the ring from my hand and I started to tremble. The moment I had dreamt about since I was a little girl was finally here. The moment the engagement ring would be put lovingly on my finger by the man I was going to marry. I didn't care that it was a costume ring or that I had purchased it or even that technically *I* had proposed to *him*. It all came down to this.

Louis took my left hand, gazed into my eyes and said, "Sydney Bennett, will you do me the honor of becoming my wife?"

Even though the matter had already been settled, I felt a massive surge of happiness as I murmured, "Yes."

After slipping the ring on my finger, he kissed me sweetly on the lips and whispered, "Thank you, *mon coeur.* Thank you for agreeing to become my wife."

We stood there for a long while just smiling at each other and kissing. It must have been quite disgusting to anyone passing by. Suddenly, I remembered we had a dinner reservation. "Louis, do you know what time it is?"

He looked at his watch. "It is seven forty-five. I am afraid we have missed our reservation."

I took his hand and led him toward the restaurant. "We'll see about that!" We quickly walked inside and I approached the hostess. "Excuse me, we have a seven thirty reservation under Durand." I flashed her a grin.

She frowned. "You're fifteen minutes late, ma'am. I'm sorry, but we had to give your table away."

I wasn't going to let it go so easily. "I'm terribly sorry that we're late, but we just got engaged!" I held up my left hand to show her my ring. "I'm afraid we were a little distracted. Is there any way you can find a table for us?" I smiled at her again. This event had to be celebrated in style.

She glanced from me to Louis. "Let me see what I can do."

"Thank you!" we said in unison. Wow. It was even nauseating to be part of the couple speaking in unison. Who knew?

Louis pulled me aside and nuzzled my neck. "Very nice, *mon coeur*."

I smirked. "It's true, isn't it?

"Indeed it is, but the last thing I feel like doing right now is eating." I stared into his hungry eyes and felt my thighs go up in flames.

"Louis Durand! We're going to have a nice dinner to celebrate our engagement." I dropped my voice to a whisper. "Then I'm going to take you home and rock your world."

He slowly ran his hands over my hips and along my behind. "I look forward to it very eagerly."

Just then the hostess called us over. "I can seat you now."

"Thank you so much," Louis responded, unleashing his beautiful blue eyes on her. "We greatly appreciate your help."

The hostess looked like she might melt on the spot. I certainly couldn't blame her. (My *fiancé* was smokin' hot, after all.) She brought us to a lovely table next to a window overlooking the fountain where I had proposed to Louis. It was absolutely perfect.

I beamed at Louis as he pulled out my chair. Once he had settled himself at the table, he reached across and took both of my hands in his. "You are an exceptional woman, Sydney Bennett. I feel so lucky that you have chosen to spend your life with me."

It was all I could do to stop the tears from falling. I knew the effort Maya had taken with my makeup and had no desire to ruin it and leave the restaurant with raccoon eyes. Instead, I focused on how happy he made me and what a crazy miracle the past six weeks had been. I felt like the luckiest woman in the world.

Louis ordered a bottle of champagne and we toasted our engagement with joy. The hostess had told the restaurant manager about our news, which prompted him to send over complimentary appetizers and desserts, I believe, in a bid to have us book our wedding reception with them. The food was phenomenal, but we had a long way to go before choosing a venue.

As we were finishing our delicious desserts, Louis hit me with his best smoldering gaze. "You look absolutely beautiful this evening, *mon coeur*."

I felt desire run through my body. "Thank you, Bluey."

"Your hair is particularly elegant. What style is that?"

I adjusted the tendrils surrounding my face. "It's Kate's specialty—a French twist."

He grinned. "How appropriate, as I am your French twist."

"You're so corny! But I love it."

Louis gave me a puzzled look. "Corny?"

I paused for a moment to think about how to explain corny to him. Louis and I had encountered a number of moments like these already. Many American sayings didn't translate well to French and vice versa.

I tapped my finger on my temple and said, "Let's

see....corny means overly sweet, um, romantic to the point of illness?" I shrugged. "It sounds bizarre, but I think my description gets the point across."

"Corny, I am not," he declared, feigning vexation. "I was merely saying I am the twist—the plot point you were not expecting. And I am French."

"I take it back. You aren't corny at all. You're a genius!" I dissolved into giggles.

"Well, now you are mocking me."

I fought to regain my composure. "I promise I'm not mocking you. You're *absolutely* my French twist." I thought for a moment. "I think I'll call you my plot point instead of my fiancé."

He laughed. "I am over the moon to be your plot point."

I considered the wondrous man before me. "You know, everyone is going to think we're crazy."

"*Crazy in love*. Now that was corny!" he said proudly.

"I bow down to the master," I responded, executing the best bow I could from a seated position.

Louis stood up from the table. "Please excuse me for a moment *mon coeur*. I am sure you would like to send texts to Kate and Maya. But when I come back, I will take you back to *our* apartment and show you what a master is." He smiled darkly.

My heartbeat quickened in anticipation. I hurriedly took out my phone and sent messages to Kate and Maya. As expected, both texted back almost immediately. Their messages were filled with smiley emojis and exclamation points. I was so elated that I almost forgot I would have to tell my parents tomorrow. My dad was going to unleash an unprecedented number of expletives. I knew he was going to think something was seriously wrong with me.

# Chapter Twenty

Louis and I spent a magical night in our new apartment. I was sharing an apartment with my *fiancé!* I couldn't believe how much my life had changed in the last six weeks. Suddenly, I had a million things to do—give my roommates notice, pack up my things, move in with Louis and oh, tell my family and friends I had gotten engaged. I wasn't quite sure where to start, but I was excited. And nervous. Who was I kidding? I was *screwed*.

Kate, ever the saint, had promised to help me develop a plan to tell our parents. She and Nick had invited us over that morning for the major purpose of celebrating our engagement and the minor purpose of figuring out a way to tell Mom and Dad without them wigging out. On the drive over to their house, Louis tried to assure me I was panicking about telling my parents for no reason.

"You are a grown woman, *mon coeur*. What exactly do you think they are going to do?"

I sighed. "Ah, Louis, sweet, naive Louis. You've never met my parents. There are plenty of things they can do."

He regarded me skeptically. "From three thousand miles away?"

I nodded. "Guilt knows no boundaries, my love."

"I am confused. I thought they wanted you to be happy?"

"Of course they do," I hesitated. "It's more complicated than that."

Just then we stopped at a red light and Louis turned to me with a serious look on his face. "What are you not telling me?"

"What do you mean?" I asked, refusing to meet his eyes.

"Sydney Bennett! I know when you are hiding something from me. What are you afraid of?"

I bit my lip, trying to find a way out of his current line of questioning.

"I *knew* it," Louis crowed. "Biting your lip is a dead giveaway. There *is* something. Out with it!"

I exhaled a long breath and met his eyes. "It's only my theory." Okay, so that wasn't entirely true, but there was no way I was going to throw Nick under the bus. "I'm concerned my parents are going to freak out...because everything has happened so fast."

His look said it all—*and?*

"And...I'm worried they might think you're in need of a green card."

An expression of indignation appeared on his face in an instant. *Shit.* I shouldn't have said anything.

"This is what they think of me," he said quietly.

"No!" I yelped, trying not to panic. "I'm only concerned this will cross their minds. They aren't the most romantic people—my father in particular—and they've always known me to be an extremely cautious person. This will seem very out of character for me and they'll worry." I threw my hands up frustration. Why couldn't I find the words to explain this in a way which made sense?

Louis remained silent, so I decided to try again. "Bluey, *please.* I'm *deliriously* happy. It will take a little time to for my family to get used to this. It's hard for them to be so far away while all of this is happening. And they haven't had the chance to meet you," I finished lamely.

Once he parked the car in Kate and Nick's driveway, I took his hand in both of mine and kissed it. "Please don't be upset."

Louis sighed. "I am not upset with you. I only hope your family will be able to see your happiness and celebrate with you, instead of making you feel I am using you for a green card."

"I don't want to give you the wrong impression of my parents or of Charlie and Zoe. They're all wonderful people." I paused, considering my words carefully. "They're protective of me. They've seen me get hurt so many times." I squeezed his hand. "As soon as they meet you, they will have no doubts. Trust me."

As we approached the house, I concluded that given this latest development, we were going to have to go to New York for Thanksgiving. I decided not to bring this up to Louis for a few days. We had to get through telling our families about our engagement first.

We rang the doorbell and stood looking at each other for a few seconds while we waited for Kate or Nick to answer the door. I could see some of the happiness from last night come back into Louis' face and felt relieved. I never should have said anything to him about my suspicions of how my parents would respond. Maybe I was overreacting. Maybe they would be supportive. Maybe my estimation of how they would react was way off base. And maybe I was on crack.

Kate opened the door with an enormous smile on her face. "Congratulations, you two!" She threw one arm around each of us, squeezing us tightly, and squealed for good measure. When we were eventually released, Louis smiled genuinely. Thank God for Kate. She always made everyone feel good.

Louis kissed Kate on both cheeks. "Thank you, *ma belle-soeur*. Well, soon to be."

She giggled. "I'm looking forward to being your sister-in-law, Louis." Kate had much better knowledge of French than I did. I was going to have do something about that before it became embarrassing.

"Where is our new family member?" Nick called from the kitchen. We followed the sound of his voice to find him flipping pancakes on the griddle.

I inhaled the heavenly scent of butter-laden pancakes. "Nick! Those pancakes smell *good*." I rubbed my stomach in anticipation. "When do we eat?"

He chuckled. "I bet you've worked up quite an appetite, little sister."

Louis laughed and clapped Nick on the back. "I think we are going to have some fun, man."

I felt heat flood my face. "You both suck."

Kate handed me a cup of tea. "Like two peas in a pod, Syd. At least now Nick has someone to keep him company while we gossip."

While I knew Louis and Nick would spend many an evening laughing at my expense, it warmed my heart to see how easily Kate and Nick had accepted Louis into their lives. They loved him because I loved him. If only it could be this easy with my parents.

I hooked my arm through Kate's and brought her into the living room. She studied me briefly and sighed. "You're worried about telling them, aren't you?"

I stared at her incredulously. "Wouldn't you be?"

"Of course," she replied. "I'm not trying to downplay your concerns. I know how important their opinion is to you. Just try to remember that you're an adult and you've done nothing wrong."

"I know, Kate. I...I don't want them to worry."

She laughed. "Syd, they're Mom and Dad! They're going to worry. There's nothing you can do about that. And you have to admit this has all happened rather quickly. The best thing you can do is to tell them how happy you are. Help them see why you proposed to Louis."

I put my mug on the coffee table and sat on the couch. "I am pretty damn happy," I said, grinning for all I was worth. "Do you think they're going to be reasonable or go completely nuts?"

Kate thought for a moment. "Well, Mom will appear composed on the outside and will most likely have a thousand theories running through her mind. Dad will say everything he's thinking, which will most likely include a high degree of profanity."

"At least I'll learn a few new swear words," I joked.

She sat down and put her arm around me. "Then they'll both calm down and realize you're happy for the first time in a long time and they need to get with the program. It's going to be fine. Besides, you keep forgetting about the big picture."

"No surprise there," I said with a hint of sarcasm. "Please enlighten me."

She took my hands in hers. "You're engaged to the man of your dreams! *That* is something to celebrate."

After a quick tap on my nose for emphasis, she took me into the kitchen to begin our celebratory brunch.

Kate and Nick had made an amazing meal for us, which they started with a champagne toast. They both said incredibly sweet things and congratulated us on deciding to spend our lives together. Louis and I thoroughly enjoyed ourselves and I started to feel like telling my parents wouldn't be as scary as I had originally thought. After three wonderful hours, I could put off this unnerving task no longer. On our way out the door, Kate made me promise to call her the minute I hung up with them so I could tell her every single detail. It was a good thing I loved her as much as I did, because she sure was nosey.

As we walked through the front door of our apartment, I felt my heart skip a beat. I put down my purse, picked up the phone and stared helplessly at Louis.

"It's now or never," I murmured.

He smiled. "Are you ready?"

"Not really, but that's not going to change any time soon." I took a deep breath and dialed the number for my mom's store.

"Duck!" *Oh shit.* I wasn't prepared for my dad to answer the phone.

I cleared my throat. "Hi, Dad. How are you?"

"Oy vey, all the usual crap. You just made my day better though. How are you? How are things with Linus?" Nice, Dad. You'd better get his name straight soon.

"Great, Dad. Louis is doing really well." I had to get this over with, but there was no way I was going to tell him first. "How's business? Is Mom crazy busy?"

"The store is a bit slow today. She'll be thrilled to talk to you. Hang on, let me see if I can find her." I heard him walk to the front of the store in search of my mom. (He kept a phone in the back so he could help my mom with the phones while he ran the kiln. In addition, his *interesting* customer service skills led my mom to believe it was best to keep him hidden from the general populace.)

"Lyn! Duck is on the phone!" *Gah!* I had forgotten how loud he could be. The phone actually vibrated in my ear.

I heard the sound of classical music as my mom picked up the phone. "Thanks, Ted. You can hang up now."

"Actually," I stammered, "...would you stay on the phone, Dad? I have something I'd like to tell you both." I knew they were within sight distance of each other, exchanging quizzical looks.

"What is it, Duck?" Dad was *always* impatient.

"Um...well...Louis and I have exciting news." I paused, gathering strength for my next statement. "We're getting married."

Silence.

After dislodging the frog in my throat, I asked, "Any opinions on this?"

My mom was the first to recover. "We're sorry, Syd. We weren't expecting that."

I laughed nervously. "I bet you're glad I didn't say I was pregnant!"

"You're not?" My dad sighed with relief.

"No, Dad, I'm not. We aren't having a shotgun wedding."

My mom exhaled. "Wow! Congratulations! How did this happen? Fill us in!" *Uh oh.* Her voice had climbed about three octaves—which meant she was totally freaking out.

I told them about Louis' suggestion of Las Vegas (so they would know he had alluded to the idea first) and finished with a brief version of my proposal.

"Oh, Syd. How beautiful!" my mom cried. "I'm thrilled for you!" *Phew.* She sounded genuine. Although I certainly wasn't dumb enough to think this was over. I knew she would interrogate me at a later point in time.

"Well! You certainly are a modern woman," my dad said with a note of gruffness in his voice. He didn't get emotional often, but it wasn't every day that his youngest daughter got engaged.

"You taught me to be strong and independent, didn't you, Dad?"

"That I did. And I'm proud of you." He cleared his throat loudly. "Now, I think I need to have a talk with Linus."

"Dad, stop pretending you don't know his real name. This man is going to be my husband and a very important part of our family. Be nice to him!"

"I'm always nice!"

I laughed. "Mom, please make him promise."

"Don't you worry, Syd. I'll make sure of it. Now, please, put Louis on the phone so we may congratulate him too."

"Okay, but don't scare him," I warned. I nervously handed the phone to Louis. "They want to congratulate you."

He grinned. "Hello, Mr. and Mrs. Bennett. It is so nice to meet you...over the phone."

He listened to my parents for a few minutes, interjecting

small comments here and there, all the while smiling. Five minutes later, he thanked them, said goodbye and handed the phone back to me, keeping the receiver covered.

"You see? I told you it was not going to be so bad! They were very kind."

I was still skeptical, but I took the phone from him with a smile. "So? What do you think?"

"He sounds as lovely as you've described," my mom gushed. "I can't wait to meet him!" I breathed a sigh of relief. Louis definitely had a way with the ladies.

"Yes, Duck, we are really looking forward to meeting our future son-in-law. When will this be happening?" Before I had the chance to answer, he added, "Let me suggest it be soon."

"Well, Mom asked me a little while ago if I would bring Louis home for Thanksgiving. Is that soon enough?"

"I suppose so," he replied slowly. "But plan on staying for a few days. I have some grilling to do and I need to see his facial expressions and body language while I do it." *Was he serious?* My dad was an accomplished interrogator—a skill he had honed in the army—but I didn't want Louis to be subjected to this process during his first visit with my family.

"Dad, promise me you won't go crazy. I do actually want to marry this man." I tried to laugh, but was unsuccessful. The fear had taken over once more.

His silence was answer enough. He still didn't trust Louis.

"Sydney Bennett, of course your father will treat your fiancé with respect," my mom soothed. "Don't you worry, we'll show Louis a good time. We know how special he is to you."

I choked back a sob. "You're both very special to me too. I hope you'll love him as much as I do."

"I'm sure we will, Duck," my dad said grudgingly. Witnessing his children's raw emotions always softened my father's resolve.

"Thanks, Dad," I murmured. "Well, now it's time to call

Louis' parents."

My dad chuckled. "Good luck, Duck. At least you'll have no idea what they're saying!"

"Dad!" I scolded. "From what Louis has said, they'll be completely blasé." This may have been a bit of an exaggeration, but it made me feel better.

I heard a muffled yelp from my father and knew my mom had swatted him in the back of the head.

"Syd, what your father meant to say was they'll be lucky to have you as part of their family. I'm sure they already know that from everything Louis has told them about you."

I suddenly realized I had no idea what Louis had told his family about me. I had often heard him on the phone with his family, but I knew very little French, so he could have been plotting a bank robbery and I would have been none the wiser. *That was it!* Tomorrow, I was going to sign up for French lessons. I had to be able to communicate with my new family.

I felt tension building in my stomach. "I hope you're right, Mom."

"Of course I'm right. Now, promise me you'll call me later today to give me the extended version of your proposal. And I want to hear about your ring!"

I winced, wondering what my mother would think of my *nontraditional* choice. "Sure, Mom. I'll call you later." I was about to say goodbye when an important thought occurred to me. "Please don't tell Charlie or Zoe. I'll call them as soon as I can after we speak to Louis' parents."

"You've got it, Duck. We won't say anything to them, but make sure to call them *today.* I can't hold on to gossip this hot for too long," he teased. "We love you."

"Thanks, Dad. I love you both too."

After I hung up the phone, Louis smiled and said, "It wasn't so bad, *mon coeur.*"

I felt a sense of relief that the conversation was over. I knew my parents were very far from being used to the idea of my having a fiancé, but at least they knew about it now.

I returned his smile. "Are you ready to call your parents?"

He shook his head. "It will have to wait until tomorrow. I am sure they are in bed by now."

"I'm sorry, Louis!" I gasped. "We should have called them first." I had totally forgotten about the nine hour time difference.

"It's fine, Syd," he said. "It was already too late to call them when we got back to the apartment. I will call them tomorrow morning."

I wrapped my arms around his waist and buried my head in his chest. "I'm so, so sorry. I was so worried about telling my parents, I didn't think about yours."

"*Mon coeur,* there is no need to worry!" He ran his hands down my back. "You know, I can think of a way for you to make it up to me."

I raised my eyebrows. "Really? And what might that be?"

He grinned wickedly. "Let me take you to the bedroom and show you." He took my hand and led me toward one of the most perfect afternoons my life.

*Chapter Twenty-One*

Charlie and Zoe were categorically shocked when I called that afternoon to tell them I was engaged. They had a barrage of questions which I answered in painstaking detail. I felt terrible about leaving them in the dark about the proposal and thought they deserved to know everything there was to know about Louis and our remarkable experience so far. Once they had extracted every last piece of information, they made me promise to let them have time alone with us when we visited in November. Charlie took his big brother responsibilities very seriously and I loved him all the more for it.

After I hung up with them, I thought about how crazy this whole situation would seem to an outsider. I could only imagine what my friends were going to think. Some of them would be thrilled by the romance of it all and be delighted for me. And some of them would involve themselves in a good old-fashioned group gossip session, ending with the decision to have an intervention for the sake of my mental health. They would be convinced I had finally lost it. Either that or they would go with the theory that Louis needed a green card and poor, lonely Sydney agreed to help because she was so desperate to get married. Sadly, there was nothing I could do. People were going to think what they were going to think.

My night was filled with fitful sleep. Now that my family knew about our engagement, I was free to worry about what Louis' family would think. From everything he had said, they would be happy for him. I wondered how much of what he had told me had been the truth and how much had been at least partial fiction to make me feel better. For better or worse, he would call them in the morning and we would deal with the results then. I hoped they wouldn't freak out that he was marrying an American. We didn't have the best reputation in France—well, really most of Europe. And perhaps a few other places. Dating an American was one thing, but *marrying* an American was a whole other ballgame. (Totally unintentional but fabulous pun.)

Louis called his parents before we left for work the next morning. Again, my knowledge of French wasn't great, but he was smiling a lot, so I figured things were going well. He put me on the phone with his parents at the end of the call and they sounded very excited. Of course, they could have been cheerfully telling me to go screw myself and I would have had no idea. I had no choice but to go with Louis' reaction. He was happy, so I was happy.

I left for work feeling a lot better. My family had been told and appeared to be on board. Louis' parents had been told, appeared to be on board and had started the massive phone tree to notify the entire family. Since his family was huge and loved to gossip, all of France should be aware by this evening. I still felt a little unsure of his family's opinion, but I had to accept the fact that I wouldn't be able to verify anything for myself. If there were any negative comments, Louis would filter them for me to protect my feelings. He knew me too well. I took a moment to mull it over and decided to hope for the best.

When I arrived at my office, I wondered how I was going to concentrate on work after my eventful weekend. As I sat down at my desk and turned on my computer, I realized I was going to have to tell my boss and my coworkers about the engagement *today*. They were probably going to notice the rock on my left hand. I didn't have to tell them it was a costume ring right away...

I quickly skimmed through my emails, answered the urgent ones and checked my voicemail. The third one was from Maya. It was a demand, not a request, to have lunch with her today. She was eager for the details of my proposal and was quite put out that I hadn't found time yesterday to call her and fill her in—especially because in her world, she was at the top of *everyone's* priority list.

After answering all my voicemails, I decided to call Maya at work. As I reached for the receiver, the phone rang.

"Sydney Bennett, how may I help you?"

"It's about time, Syd. Where are we going for lunch?"

I laughed. This woman literally had no patience. "Good morning to you too, Maya."

I knew she was rolling her eyes at me. "There's no time for pleasantries, my dear. I have a meeting in two minutes."

"Got it. How about the brewery?"

"That works. Meet you there at noon?"

"Sounds good. See you then."

I spent the rest of the morning trying to get work done as the news of my engagement spread across the company. My boss was the first one I told. We were having our usual Monday morning rundown of projects for the week, when she saw my ring, grabbed my hand and started squealing. She must have asked me dozens of questions in the span of three minutes. Naturally, everyone in the vicinity came by to see what the commotion was and the news traveled like wildfire. I loved the people I worked with and was flattered by their interest in my life, but I felt completely on the spot. As expected, the level of shock was fairly high—many employees had no idea I was even dating someone. I closed my mind off to the inevitable gossip, since nothing makes a better story than a possible scandal (read: shotgun wedding) in the Human Resources Department.

I pulled up to the brewery at exactly noon. I felt chills run down my spine, knowing Maya was preparing for one of her famous interrogations. My dad had *nothing* on her. And he was trained by the army! Where in the world had Maya developed her skills?

I walked into the restaurant and noticed she was already waiting at a table near the bar. I could tell by the look on her face she was primed and ready. I took a deep breath, straightened my shoulders and walked over to her.

"Hey, Syd," she drawled. "Are you ready?"

"Give me a minute to sit down, stalker," I quipped, lamenting that it was a work day. A glass of wine would have been really helpful for this exercise.

She rolled her eyes. "I'm excited! You're lucky I'm as interested in your life as I am. And don't forget that if it weren't for me, you wouldn't *have* a fiancé."

I smirked. "Are you going to hold this detail over me for the rest of my life?"

She tapped her temple, pretending to mull this over. "Yes, that's my current plan. Now stop stalling! Tell me *everything*."

I launched into a very detailed description of the night I proposed to Louis. This took a good forty-five minutes to explain which, fortunately for me, left only ten minutes for her questions, since we both had to get back to work.

"Did I give you enough information, Maya?" I feigned exhaustion.

"You did pretty well," she admitted. "But I do have a few questions." Her eyes danced with anticipation.

I groaned inwardly. I didn't like where this was going. Maya's questions were…embarrassing.

"How was the sex that night? It must have been pretty awesome, right?"

I felt my face heat up. "Yes, Maya, it was *awesome*. But as I have told you before, it always is with Louis.

He's...incredible." I had to redirect my thoughts to something else quickly or I wasn't going to get any work done for the rest of the day.

She smirked. "Lucky girl. I hope you appreciate your good fortune."

"I certainly do." I paused, gathering the courage to ask for some information of my own. "Now that I've spilled many, *many* details about a very private night, I think you owe me some information. What exactly happened between you and Jean?"

The smile on her face vanished immediately. "I have no information to share with you about Jean."

I regarded her with my poker face (or at least my attempt at one). "Really? Nothing at all."

Her face remained impassive. "Nothing at all."

I pursed my lips. "You're hiding something from me, Maya. Something *big*. I'm going to find out what it is, whether you want me to or not."

"Is that a challenge?" she scoffed. "Because you're a horrendous detective. You can't even figure out who the murderer is on *CSI*, when it's *so* totally obvious."

"Not true!" I exclaimed. Or was it? I had figured it out lots of times—with a little help. No matter. I would crack Maya's mystery. "*Fine.* You don't have to tell me."

"I wasn't planning on it."

"So I guess you have nothing to worry about."

She kept her mask of serenity firmly in place. "I guess not."

I was intrigued. What in the world went on between the two of them? Maya was never secretive about anything. In fact, I was always asking her to share *less* information. I would have to enlist Louis' help. Since Maya wasn't being forthcoming, I was going to have to try to extract the information from Jean.

"What are you plotting, Sydney Bennett?"

I smiled devilishly. "I guess you'll have to wait to find out."

She finished signing the check and got up from the table. "I'm quaking in my boots."

As we walked to the exit, I was even more determined to find out what she was hiding. Maya was going to learn what it was like to have her friends sticking their noses into her business—well intentioned or not.

~

Over the next few days, I worked my way through telling my friends about the engagement. As expected, there was quite a bit of shock—especially given this was the first that many of them had heard of Louis. (It was hard to keep in touch with people across different time zones, work schedules and phases of life. Even more so when you were spending all your time with an amazing Frenchman.) I patiently told an abbreviated story of our whirlwind romance and, yes, of my proposal. Everyone gave me their best wishes and said they couldn't wait to meet Louis.

I had no doubt there were a flurry of phone calls between my different friend cliques speculating as to the circumstances for such a quick engagement. Was it actually a whirlwind romance? Was I pregnant? Was he in need of a green card? Did we have some kind of business arrangement or was I simply naive? As much as I hated to admit it, I could certainly understand their concern. I knew I would have been skeptical if I had received the same phone call from one of them.

My roommates were completely shocked by my revelation, but very happy for me. Jess shrieked and threw her arms around me, all the while congratulating me on landing such a great guy. She had developed quite a relationship with Louis' voicemail messages, as she found the sound of his voice to be "exceedingly alluring." Maggie was speechless, but quickly recovered and offered her services as a wedding planner. (A rather lucrative side business she had started this past year.) I thanked her profusely as I had no idea where to start. After all the giddiness had died down, I let them know I would be moving in with Louis and offered to pay rent until they found a new roommate. Luckily for me, Jess already had someone in mind.  Louis and I had to start saving immediately if we had any hope of paying for this wedding. I knew my parents would want to contribute something, but I had no idea of the amount and had absolutely no idea how much the wedding would cost.

It suddenly dawned on me that Louis and I hadn't discussed any wedding details yet. I, of course, had been thinking about this day since I was five years old. I hadn't planned every aspect (which was surprising given my personality), but I had a good idea of what I wanted—a beautiful outdoor wedding, overlooking the ocean, maybe one hundred people or so, with a DJ and a chocolate wedding cake. *Slow down, Sydney*! First things first: pack your stuff and move in with Louis. We had to make sure we were indeed perfect for each other before we attempted to plan the perfect wedding.  No pressure or anything...

## Chapter Twenty-Two

Miraculously, it had taken me only two evenings to pack up all my things and then two additional evenings to move them into our apartment. (Given that the wonder threesome had acquired the majority of my furniture long ago, I shouldn't have been surprised by the ease of this move.) By Friday evening, I was happily installed in my new home. While I was excited about the direction my life had taken, I was still nervous about living with Louis. I gratefully remembered the many times he had told me he could handle my neuroses, but saying this and actually living it were two completely different things. I resolved to do my best to keep the crazy in check—and maybe living with Louis would cause some of his confidence to rub off on me. There was always hope.

Our first weekend of officially living together was heaven. We went out to dinner, spent lazy mornings in bed and took long walks through town, stopping occasionally to browse in bookstores and have coffee. Not to mention the many amazing hours we spent in our bedroom. I felt totally at peace. I started to think living with Louis was going to be easier than I thought. Maybe I was I finally learning to relax and accept that nothing was going to go horribly wrong. *You go, Sydney!*

Unfortunately, the bubble of our domestic bliss burst with a resounding crack on Monday morning. Louis and I had spent a particularly satisfying thirty minutes in the shower before work and I was still floating on cloud nine when he called me at work just after ten.

"Sydney Bennett, how may I help you?" I heard a huge sigh on the other end of the phone, but no dialogue to go with it. Did I have another obscene caller on my hands? I had one last year who was extremely persistent. He kept calling me to talk about the insurance coverage for his penis enlargement operation. And, no, he *didn't* work for my company. I finally had to have my extension changed. As I wondered what new horror awaited me, I heard a familiar voice.

"*Mon coeur*, I am afraid I have some bad news."

Fear struck me as I imagined every possible disaster he could throw my way. He was only kidding when he accepted my proposal! He received a phone call from the love of his life and was moving back to France! He was having a sex change operation and was pursuing his lifelong dream of becoming Louisa! (Not entirely farfetched given my relationship history, right?) When I mentioned the crazy I was trying to protect Louis from, this was what I meant.

"Syd? Are you there?"

I shook my head in a vain attempt to clear all the nonsense. "Yes, I'm here. I'm sorry! It's been a busy morning. Is everything all right?"

"Yes and no. I just got out of a meeting with my manager. I have to go back to France."

*Oh shit!* I actually *wasn't* crazy. He was moving back to France! My eyes started darting around the room as though I would find some type of helpful information hiding somewhere. Perhaps under my desk? If nothing else I could hide there for a while.

"Syd, rein yourself in. I am not moving back to France for good. I have to go back for two weeks to assist with a project I used to manage. I wrote the code for the program and the new project manager just got the specs from the client for an update." He sighed again. "They only want me in the same time zone."

"You know me too well," I said softly, feeling an immense sense of relief wash over me.

He chuckled. "Yes, I do. And I am hoping one day soon, you will learn to trust me.

"Louis! I do trust you." Right? At least I thought I did. "I need to learn to stop being insane."

"You are *not* insane. You have just been burned before. It is understandable that you are a little...cautious."

I thanked my lucky stars I had found this man. "Thank you for being so patient with me."

"You are well worth it, *mon coeur*," he replied. "Now, back to the discussion of my trip. I am afraid I will have to leave for Paris rather soon."

"When do you have to leave?"

"My flight is tomorrow evening, but I have meetings all day, so I will have to leave for the airport directly from the office."

I felt my stomach drop. We had just gotten engaged and he had to leave for two weeks! This *really* sucked. "Well, I can't say I'm happy about it, but you have to go. We'll have a wonderful time together tonight to help us last through our weeks apart."

"I am sorry, Syd. I hate to leave you." The dejection in his voice nearly broke my heart.

It was my turn to be the positive one in the relationship. "We survived the last two week trip, right?" I made my tone as cheery as possible, hopefully not erring on the side of artificial.

"Barely," he murmured.

"Well, at least you'll get to see your family. You'll have time to go down south on the weekends, won't you?" Something good *had* to come out of this for someone. His mom, for one, would be thrilled.

"I hope so. My mother would be pretty upset if I didn't. Plus my cousins have been after me to visit so they can take me clubbing."

"Sounds like fun." Hmmm....I didn't like the sound of that. Too many hot, drunk French women hanging all over *my* fiancé.

"Not really. I am over the clubbing scene. I think I have seen enough over the past seven years."

I laughed. "Especially working in that sex club." After the stories he had told me I had a much greater awareness of the extent of, um, *sexual experimentation* in the world.

"It was crazy back then," he said, clearly amused. "But you know I would much rather be alone with you than be anywhere else in the world. At least it will make my cousins happy. I really miss spending time with them."

"I can't wait to meet them." From all the stories Louis had told me, his cousins seemed pretty adventurous. Monique worked for the tourist service office in her hometown and her favorite activity was bungee jumping. In fact, she wouldn't date a man if he wasn't willing to jump off a bridge with her. According to Louis, Monique felt that a man must have a truly courageous spirit in order to be able to handle a relationship. Sophie was an accountant by day and a club dancer by night. She was exceedingly well networked and had a lively personality, so the club paid her both to dance and to provide unofficial publicity. I was pretty sure these two had had a heavy hand in Louis' thrill-seeking childhood.

"They feel the same way, *mon coeur*. I have been getting a lot of pressure to bring you back to France."

I felt my heart stop. I was *so* not ready to go to France. I had serious doubts as to what his very large, very intimidating family would think of me. I was the stereotypical American who couldn't speak their language and had no knowledge of their culture. I had to do something about this *tout de suite*. I opened up my internet browser and started searching for French classes in the area.

"Syd? Have I lost you?"

"I'm sorry, Louis. The work is piling up. I got distracted for a second." No reason to worry, Louis. This was only your fiancé still trying to cover up the complete and total insanity whirling around inside her brain.

"I understand," he replied. "I will let you go. Think about what you want to do for dinner tonight. I want to take you somewhere special."

I couldn't help but smile. "I love you, Bluey."

"I love you too, *mon coeur*. More than you can possibly imagine."

I hung up the phone with mixed emotions. I was thrilled to have this wonderful man who loved me exactly as I was, but I couldn't contain the sadness I felt at the prospect of being without him for two weeks. Again. *Big picture, Syd*. Louis would be with you for the long haul. And he was certainly worth the wait.

⌒

The day passed quickly, though I found myself frequently distracted by Louis' impending departure. After reading the same paragraph in a complaint letter for the fifth time, I decided I needed some serious help. I tried Kate's work line, but got her voicemail, so I tried her cell phone in desperation.

"Hey, Syd! How are you?" Thank God she picked up.

"Kate! I need a sanity check."

She laughed. "What is it this time?"

Sadly, I deserved the dig since I had required *many* sanity checks over the years. In fact, if it weren't for Kate, I wouldn't have retained any sanity at all.

"Louis has to go back to France for two weeks for work. I'm freaking out," I blurted.

"What else is new? You wouldn't be you if you didn't freak out a little. It means you care a great deal for him."

"You don't think I'm insane?" Kate's belief in my "normalcy" never ceased to amaze me.

"Syd, will you stop beating yourself up? You've always been a very emotional, very, um, *sensitive* person. It gets you hurt sometimes and causes you loads of stress, but it makes you the incredible person you are. The sooner you come to terms with this, the better."

She had a point. I guess if I started with this type of personality and then lived through a less than perfect romantic life, it would make sense that I was still a little...uncertain with Louis. After all, it had only been seven weeks, right? I wasn't a total lunatic—at least in this case.

"Thanks, Kate," I said, feeling a little better. "It helps to have you remind me of my redeeming qualities."

"Indeed, you have many redeeming qualities. *You know this*! Just do me a favor, okay?"

I hesitated. "What kind of favor?" Kate had led me through a few rather challenging favors over the years. I think the worst was when she convinced me to give a speech in front of the Bronx chapter of the Harley-Davidson Riders Club in order to conquer my fear of public speaking. I wasn't sure which scared me more—the act of public speaking or the big burly bikers. (Although pretty much everything intimidated me when I was in high school.)

"Don't get nervous," she responded. "I want you to remember that you've been through a lot over the last few years—and while your relationship with Louis has brought you great happiness, it's been a whirlwind romance to say the least. It's perfectly normal to feel unsure of things sometimes."

"You're absolutely right."

"You know I always am. When will you accept this?" she teased. "You could save yourself so much worry!" I could hear the smile in her voice. She knew I wouldn't be able to argue that point.

I laughed. "You can be *really* annoying sometimes, you know?"

"I'm your big sister. It's one of the perks of my job."

Now she really had me laughing. "I'm glad to know you

find this to be a rewarding experience."

"I do! When you were first born, I thought this whole thing was going be awful, but you've been quite entertaining over the years." A cascade of giggles confirmed her statement.

"Leave it to you to have me laughing and irritated at the same time. You have a unique array of talents, Kate."

"Don't you forget it!" she sang. "Oh! Hang on for a sec, Syd."

I heard Nick's voice in the background. I also heard...a loudspeaker? *Where were they?*

Kate came back on the line. "I'm sorry, Syd. I have to go now."

"Is everything all right? Where are you?" I felt the familiar anxiety set in.

"Everything's fine. I'll give you a call later, okay?" Her voice was calm, so I decided to believe her—for the moment.

"Okay. I love you!"

"I love you too, sweetie. 'Bye."

It was times like these that I didn't feel emotional or sensitive as Kate described, I felt like a total freak. In the span of a few minutes, I had stopped worrying about Louis' trip and started worrying about Kate. I had been so wrapped up in my own life for the past seven weeks that I hadn't paid attention to what was going on in hers. I thought about the loudspeaker I had heard in the background. It sounded like a hospital—unless there was another place that paged doctors on a regular basis. What were they doing there? I knew she told me everything was fine because she didn't want me to worry, but I didn't buy it. She was *always* protecting me. One of these days I would have to grow a pair and insist she tell me what was going on.

Was it possible to develop things like strength and confidence? Louis and Kate seemed to have both in abundance. If I was going to be a lifelong partner for Louis,

I would need to dial down the worrying and become Strong Sydney. Or perhaps Confident Sydney. I knew I had seen these attributes in myself before, even if it had been in limited supply. I would have to do my best to find them and kick them up a notch. And the first item on my list was to find out what was going on with Kate. It was time I took care of her for a change. It was time for me to be the perfect sister.

# Chapter Twenty-Three

Louis and I had a wonderful evening together before his trip, but I was still distracted by the thought of Kate being in some kind of trouble. I explained what had happened to Louis—who then shared my concern—but we were unable to get Kate on the phone. After a night of fitful sleep, I kissed Louis goodbye and made him promise to call me every day. I even had him spray his pillowcase with cologne so his scent would keep me company while he was away.

I tried reaching Kate all morning, but had no luck. I finally decided to try Nick's cell phone. I *had* to get to the bottom of this.

"Hello?" I could barely hear his voice above the static.

"Nick? It's Syd. Is everything all right?" *Rats*! I had totally overcompensated for the static by shouting.

"You don't have to yell, Syd. I haven't lost my hearing recently," he replied with a chuckle. "Everything's fine, but I can't talk now. I'm on my way to a meeting."

I made a conscious effort to lower my voice. "I'll let you go then. Just one question—do you know where Kate is? I've been calling her since last night, but she hasn't picked up."

"She's at home resting."

"Resting? Did something happen? Is she sick?" I could feel the torrent of worry threatening to unleash.

He sighed. "She's fine. Why don't you give her a call later this afternoon and she'll fill you in, okay?"

*I knew it!* Something *was* going on. "I will, but you're sure she's fine? You would tell me if she weren't, right? I can handle it."

"Yes, Syd, I would tell you. You can relax," he said, exasperation coloring his tone. That was my cue to go.

"I will. Have a good day, Nick! 'Bye!"

I hung up the phone and tried to relax. Kate was the strong one, she had never really needed much from me. I suddenly felt extremely selfish. I picked up the phone and started to dial her number when I remembered Nick asked me to call her later. I put down the phone and turned my attention back to my work. This was going to be a long few hours...

By four o'clock, I was fit to be tied. I dialed Kate's home number and waited with bated breath. Kate picked up on the fourth ring, right when I thought I was going to get the machine (and go out of my mind).

"Syd?" she murmured.

"Hi, Kate!" I cried, elated to hear her voice. *Tone it down, Sydney.* "Um, how are you?"

"Sick." She coughed. "I feel like crap."

"Have you been to the doctor?"

"No, I'm fine. I just need to rest."

I didn't buy it. "Kate..."

"Yes?"

"When I talked to you yesterday, it sounded like you were in the hospital. Are you sure you're all right?"

She was silent for a few moments. I was doing my best not to wig out, but decided if I lost the battle, so be it. Based on her hesitation, a good old-fashioned wig out might be warranted this time.

Enough with the silence. "Kate? Please say something."

"Sydney Julia Bennett, I'm *fine*! I promise. You have no reason to worry—not that this has ever stopped you before."

She picked *now* to be a smart ass? *Really*?!

I pushed my retort aside and asked, "So, you don't have cancer?"

She laughed softly. "No, I don't have cancer." She took a deep breath. "I'm pregnant."

*Pregnant?* I temporarily lost the power of speech. Clearly, Kate was enjoying my reaction since a long stream of laughter erupted from the other end of the line.

"Syd? Are you okay?" she asked in between snort laughs.

"I'm more than okay! I'm going to be an aunt!" I jumped up and did a little dance around my office.

"That's right, hon. You have some very important responsibilities coming your way. You're the only local relative which means you'll be our go-to babysitter."

"Sweet! I can't wait." Tears filled my eyes. "I'm so excited for you and Nick."

"Thanks! We're pretty excited ourselves. It's too bad I feel like crap most of the time. Morning sickness *sucks*."

Ugh. My poor sister had been suffering and I had been consumed with my relationship problems—which were mostly in my head. It all seemed so silly now.

"Why didn't you tell me sooner? You let me go on and on about my stupid stuff when you're creating a life!"

"Syd, stop it!" I could hear her rolling her eyes. "It's not like you've been dealing with minor issues. These have been major life decisions."

"Not as major as this."

"Sweetie, there is no need for comparison," she responded firmly. "And we weren't trying to keep anything from you. We're just starting to tell people about the baby. We wanted to get used to the idea first."

Now that I knew about the bundle of joy, I had a million

questions. "When is the baby due? Are you going to find out if you're having a boy or a girl? Have you chosen names yet?"

"Get a grip, Syd! The baby is due in April. We aren't going to find out what we're having because we want to be surprised. And we haven't even begun to discuss names."

I was a little disappointed. I really wanted to know if I was getting a niece or a nephew. I would definitely find out when it was my turn—but that was a *long* way off.

*Back to the present, Sydney.* "Is there anything you need, Kate? Something to help to settle your stomach?"

"Don't worry. Nick has me fully stocked. I'd love to see you though. Why don't you stop by after work?"

"Absolutely. I'll call you when I'm on my way."

"Sounds great. I'll see you soon."

"Hang on, Kate! Have you told Mom and Dad?"

She chuckled. "We told them last night. I think Dad went into shock. Mom is already planning a number of knitting projects."

"You'd better buy a *ginormous* dresser for the baby's room." Our mom loved knitting and this was her first grandchild, so the combination would yield impressive results.

"No kidding! Nick's scared. Since we're not finding out the sex of the baby, he thinks everything is going to be yellow. He's *not* a fan."

"Green and blue are fine too. Make sure to consult with mom before the knitting rampage begins. You know her creative streak runs in weird directions sometimes."

Kate snorted. "No one has forgotten the Christmas of the lavender vests." Indeed, no one had. We all got them, even the men in the family. It didn't matter how masculine you were, it was tough to carry off lavender brocade.

The blinking light on my phone signaled the end of our conversation. "I have to grab this call, Kate. I'll see you later! Congratulations again!"

"Thanks, sweetie! 'Bye!"

After I hung up from a rather extensive discussion of the possibility of pet health insurance with our newest employee, I allowed myself a moment to take in Kate's news. I couldn't believe it. I was going to be an aunt! Louis was going to be an uncle. This was insane! I couldn't wait to tell him. He promised to call before he got on the plane, but I wasn't sure how long his meetings would run.

I closed my eyes and let the news settle in. The Bennett sisters were full of life-changing news lately. I suddenly wondered how my parents were doing. They had had a lot to take in over the past two days. I decided to give them a call later to check in. I could picture my dad sitting at his desk playing solitaire while he tried to process it all. Somehow the feel of the cards in his hands helped him to make sense of everything.

The last hour of my day flew by due to spontaneous visits from a good portion of the employee population. People always had human resources issues (from the necessary to the ridiculous) and they figured while they were there, they may as well grill me a little more about my engagement. All the public details had been spilled at this point, but people hadn't tired of the story yet. It must have been a slow week for company gossip if Louis and I were still the top story.

I was about to leave for the day when the phone rang. Hoping it was Louis, I lunged for the receiver.

"Sydney Bennett, how may I help you?" I said breathlessly.

"You can tell me how much you love me, *mon coeur*."

I smiled. "I love you more than you can possibly imagine."

"I only have a quick minute, but I wanted to hear your voice before I got on the plane."

"I have some amazing news!" I squealed. "There's going to be a new addition to our family!"

Crickets. That was odd.

"Louis? Are you there?"

He cleared his throat. "I am here. A new member of the family?" he asked shakily.

Why did he sound so freaked out? *Oh.*

"I'm sorry, Bluey," I giggled. "I didn't think about how that came out. *Kate* is pregnant! You're going to be an uncle!"

He sighed with relief. "That is wonderful news! Please congratulate Kate and Nick for me."

"I will." I paused, wondering if I should ask the question. "You were pretty freaked, weren't you?"

He laughed. "Yes, I was. We have a lot on our plate right now. I was only wondering how we were going to handle a baby on top of everything else."

"Someday," I said. "Not for a few years though, right?"

"I don't know if we have that long," Louis replied. "I mean, you are kind of old..."

I choked on the water I had been sipping. "Hey! I'm not *old!*"

I had never heard Louis cackle with such gusto before. When he thought something was really funny, his voice raised a couple of octaves. This, in turn, pitched me into a fit of laugher. Anyone within a fifty foot radius of either one of us would have thought we were completely insane— which was not far off the mark.

He eventually caught his breath. "I love you so much, Syd."

I let out my last few giggles as I rolled my eyes. "I love you too. Even if you do like to mock me for sport. Nick is thrilled that he finally has a worthy ally."

"And I will do him proud." I could hear the smile in his voice. "Thank you for putting me in such a good mood before my long flight, *mon coeur.* I will call you when I get to Paris, okay?"

I sighed. I missed him already. "Okay, Bluey. Have a safe flight."

My visit with Kate after work was short-lived. Pregnancy had hit her pretty hard and the poor woman was completely exhausted. When she wasn't nauseated, she was sleeping. I delivered a bouquet of white tulips (her absolute favorite) along with Louis' congratulations and left her to rest. Nick thanked me for coming by and let me know he would have her call me tomorrow.

The next morning, I woke to find a voicemail from a worn-out Louis on my cell phone. There had been a lot of turbulence on the flight and even he—the man who claimed the army had taught him to sleep under any conditions—couldn't sleep. He said he would call me when he had gotten settled in his hotel. I listened to his message a couple more times before I got out of bed. I didn't think I would ever tire of the sound of his voice.

I finally heard from Louis in the late afternoon. I had just finished going over a very complicated claim issue with our medical insurance representative when my phone rang. The number was blocked, so I crossed my fingers and hoped it was him.

"Sydney Bennett, how may I help you?"

"*Mon coeur!* How I miss you!"

"I miss you too, Bluey," I murmured. "I'm sorry you had such a rough flight. How are you feeling?"

He yawned. "Tired, but I feel much better now that I have heard your voice."

"You have no idea how happy I am to hear *your* voice. I already want you to come home. I know it sounds awful…"

"You simply cannot help yourself, Syd. I am irresistible." His yawns kept coming.

"Have you gotten any sleep?" He had once told me that he used to go a night or two without sleep in college if his workload was high, but he was *way* out of practice.

"Just a little. I had to get up to speed on a few things before we meet with the clients tomorrow."

"You sound totally drained, Louis," I said sternly. "You'd better get some rest."

"Are you trying to get rid of me already?"

I laughed. "Not at all. I would much rather keep you on the phone, but I'm not sure you'll be able to form sentences for much longer."

"Sadly, you are right. I am not as young as I used to be."

"You're all washed up at twenty-four," I responded drily. "Maybe I should trade you in for a younger model."

"You were lucky to score me in the first place! A woman of your age?!"

"Way to be cruel," I joked. "Besides, you've made your choice. I'm afraid you're stuck with an older woman."

"And I could not feel luckier, *mon coeur*. I love you."

I smiled. "I love you too, Bluey. Now go to sleep."

"You win! I will call you tomorrow."

I hung up the phone, already wishing it was tomorrow. I wasn't looking forward to two weeks of this. I had been searching for Louis for a lifetime and now that I had found him, I didn't want to be without him for any longer than I had to be. I had plenty of things to keep me busy during his absence though—being the perfect sister for Kate and planning the perfect wedding. *Wait a minute!* Kate loved designing *anything*, so the two could overlap quite nicely...

*Chapter Twenty-Four*

Due to an unexpected visit from our largest investors, my boss and I were kept busy for the next few days planning events to impress them. From seminars by our in-house scientists on our latest technological breakthroughs to themed outings to our most popular local tourist spots, all parties involved were going to have an excellent time. The good news was I was so busy I didn't have time to miss Louis. The bad news was I didn't have much time to talk to him. My boss had two sick children at home, so I had to work through the weekend hosting all the events. Every detail had to be perfect if we had any hope of additional funding. I was ecstatic when Wednesday night arrived and the investors went home. This meant I would *finally* be able to stay in one place for an extended period of time.

My first stop was Kate and Nick's house. Nick had graciously invited me over for dinner since I hadn't been able to stop by much over the last week. The best part? He was planning to make his famous chicken cutlets. I had often tried to reproduce these cutlets, but to no avail. I didn't know exactly what his secret was because I had used the same recipe and while his results were mouthwatering, mine were mouth-spritzing at best.

I rang the doorbell and heard Nick yell, "Come in!"

I opened the door and was immediately hit with a heavenly smell. Apparently, the chocolate bar I had inhaled earlier in the afternoon hadn't done the trick because I was suddenly ravenous. I fervently hoped dinner was almost ready.

"Hi, Nick!" I grinned as I walked over to hug him.

"Hey, Syd. Dinner is almost ready." *Excellent!*

"Thanks for inviting me. I brought you some wine." I set the bottle down on the counter.

"Thanks, Syd. And what did you bring for the patient?"

Poor Kate had spent the majority of her days utterly nauseated. Most smells made her run for the bathroom (or in one case, a welcoming shrub) and very few things would stay down. I pulled a container of matzo ball soup from Max's out of the bag in my other hand.

Nick beamed. "You rock, Syd! She still loves the smell of the cutlets, but the grease is too much for her stomach to handle. This is perfect."

"Mom always made it for us when we were sick. It's the perfect thing for a delicate stomach."

Just then I heard noise from the doorway. "I thought I heard something." Kate smiled at me and extended her arms, waving me into a hug.

I embraced her gingerly. "How are you feeling?"

"The same as I look—like crap." She laughed weakly.

She wasn't kidding. She didn't look like herself at all. She was always so bright, happy and...clean. A quick once over told me she hadn't showered for a couple of days. But more than that, her eyes lacked their usual shine and her skin appeared slightly grey. *Damn.* I hoped morning sickness wasn't genetic. I wanted no part of that mess.

I carefully smoothed her hair back. "You don't look like crap. You look tired—and rightfully so. Growing a human is a lot of work!"

"You never were a very good liar, Syd. But I always loved you for it. It made it easier to torture you," she said before giving me an evil grin.

Nick came over and put his arm around Kate. "Why don't you two sit down and relax while I finish getting dinner ready?"

"Are you sure you don't need any help, Nick?" The delightful aroma was starting to take over my thoughts and I was willing to do anything to taste the cutlets as soon as possible.

"Don't worry, Syd. Nick has it covered."

I giggled. "Because Nick's your buddy."

"Nick's someone you can trust," she responded happily.

"Someone you can drink with."

Kate was barely keeping it together. "He doesn't care if you hurl in his car."

I winked at her. "Nick!"

That was it. We burst into a fit of laughter that was most unladylike. There was definitely some snorting involved. (It was well deserved though. I think we did John Cusack proud, even if we didn't get the words exactly right.)

Nick stared at us with disdain. "It never gets old, does it?"

I beamed at him, while Kate tried to recover from her fit of cackling.

"No, it doesn't!" We said in unison.

Nick pushed us out of the kitchen in disgust. While he normally took part in our movie reenactments with great pleasure, whenever we quoted this particular dialogue from *The Sure Thing,* he felt that we went a little too far. Such mockery of his name was simply not to be borne.

As we sat down on the couch, I wiped tears of laughter from my eyes and focused on my sister.

"We're so lucky to live so close to each other, Kate."

She held her arms out to me. "Come over here, Syd. I need another hug." I moved over to her end of the couch and she pulled me close. When I peeked up at her, she had real tears in her eyes.

I put my hand on the side of her face. "Kate, what's the

matter?"

"Don't mind me," she said with a roll of her eyes. "Pregnancy hormones are a bitch. I just want you to know how happy I am to have you here to share this with me."

I smiled. "I can't tell you how overjoyed *I* am to share this with you." I took her hand and held it next to my face. "I honestly don't know what I would do without you."

She sighed contentedly and put her head on my shoulder. I held her hand and we sat in silence for a few minutes. Then I heard the soft snoring. Poor Kate! This baby was sapping all of her energy.

Nick came into the room, assessed the situation and carefully scooped Kate into his arms. He motioned for me to head the kitchen before he took Kate into their bedroom. I entered the kitchen to find a platter full of delectable chicken cutlets waiting for me. I stopped for a moment and inhaled the amazing smell. *Mmm...*

Nick walked back into the kitchen and laughed. "What are you doing, Syd? I thought you were hungry? Dig in!"

He didn't have to ask me twice.

∽

The next couple of days passed in a blur and before I knew it, it was Friday. I had never been so excited by the prospect of catching up on my sleep. Of course, the bed would have been much better with Louis in it, but I would have to wait four more *long* days to see him and there certainly wouldn't be much sleeping going on...

Thankfully, Louis had been able to call me every day, which helped me miss him a little less. Each call was full of his family's latest adventures and by the end I was laughing so hard my stomach hurt. I told him he could totally turn their lives into a lucrative reality TV series, but he didn't think the American public would find the lives of French country folk very exciting. I begged to differ.

How often did your day involve chasing two dozen chickens out of your house with a broom because your dog let them out of their pen and your front door was always open?  It had taken Louis' mom a week to clean all the feathers—not to mention droppings—out of the house.  Or would you honestly expect your childhood seamstress to whip out a tape measure when she ran into you in the big city so she could measure your bust to see how much your breasts had grown in the last few years?  Louis' cousin Sophie had to brave that particular nightmare.  But my personal favorite was the day the transvestite accidentally took the bus to Louis' hometown (total population four hundred) and was told by Louis' father that the auditions for the town play had been held the week before.  They were performing *La Cage aux Folles.*  You just couldn't write this stuff!

I heard the phone ringing as I was unlocking the front door.  I ran in, threw my bags down and grabbed the receiver.  I was hoping it was Louis since I hadn't heard from him all day.

"Hello?" I said breathlessly.

"What have you been up to lately, young lady?" I could tell Louis was a little drunk and therefore, more than a little horny.

I giggled like a school girl.  "Nothing as exciting as you, my love."  I took the phone into the bedroom and collapsed onto the bed.  I needed to be in a horizontal position as soon as possible.  This week had kicked my ass.

"I am out with my cousins.  They took me to this club owned by a friend of theirs.  It is insanely crowded and there is way too much touching going on."  That explained the loud voices and the heavy drumbeat.

"Are you getting old?  I thought touching was a good thing."

"I only want to be touched by you, *mon coeur.*"

The sexy smolder in his voice sent my heart racing.  I sighed.  "I *miss* you.  I can't wait for you to come home—I mean, back to California."  I knew France would always be home for Louis.

"Wherever you are is home for me now, Syd. You are what I need."

I felt my heart swell. *We were forming our own family.* It was a thrilling, but petrifying feeling. I had always relied on my parents and my siblings as my sounding boards in decision making. Now everything would start with Louis.

"You're what I need too, Louis." My voice caught on his name.

"Are you okay, *mon coeur*?"

How embarrassing! He was out at a club having a good time and I was at home crying. *Get it together, Sydney!*

I cleared my throat. "I'm fine. It's been an exhausting week."

"At least you have time to relax now. You should take it easy this weekend. You will need a lot of energy for my return."

I laughed. Louis knew just what to say to put me in a good mood. "So, how are your parents doing?"

"My mom is in heaven," he said happily. "She has already started making plans for our wedding."

*What?!*

"Um....Louis, how could your mom start making wedding plans when we're getting married in California?" She didn't speak English! And she didn't know anyone outside his home town. And what was she doing making plans for *my* wedding without even speaking to me? My heartrate was starting to pick up for a very different reason than earlier in our conversation.

Louis was quiet for a moment. "I suppose we have not talked about specifics, have we?" I could hear the sadness in his voice.

*Oh, Sydney! You never think.*

Louis was an only child and there was no doubt his mother wanted the entire town to come to his wedding. How could I tell him that this wasn't the wedding I wanted? I mean, the man moved to a different country for me. I needed to do this for him, didn't I? I suddenly felt extremely selfish, because I really didn't want to. I had been dreaming about this day for as long as I could remember and I didn't want the wedding to take place so far away from *my* friends and family.

"No, we didn't," I replied softly. "We'll have to do that very soon."

"Indeed. Do not worry, I will talk to my mother. I am sure she will be on board with a wedding in California."

Guilt was causing a pit to form in my stomach. Louis had been so good to me, I had to do something for him. "Let's talk about it when you get back, Bluey. There has to be something we can do so everyone will be happy."

"Whatever you want, *mon coeur.*"

My mind was whirling with possibilities. "What if we have the wedding in California and then have a reception in France shortly afterward?"

"That is not a bad idea. My mom will still be able to host all the traditional events, though she may ask us to have a small reenactment ceremony." He laughed. "I am glad to say, I finally made her realize we would not be getting married in a church."

Louis had grown up in a *very* catholic household. Not only was he required to attend church every Sunday, but he also had to attend extra religion classes twice a week. Louis was well known for his use of logic and reason and was therefore disliked by the priest. He would question all tenets set forth and would not relent until he was given an answer that made sense to him. Consequently, his mother was often called in for conferences. Since Louis refused to change his behavior for the sake of his mother's reputation, he was removed from these classes after a few months. He now joked if he set foot inside a church he would burst into flames.

I snorted. "That must have been tough for her to hear."

"You got that right," he quipped. Louis had been working very hard on picking up American slang. I didn't want to tell him the expressions he used sounded totally adorable with his accent.

"You're too funny, Bluey."

"Please do not worry, *mon coeur*. We will figure this all out. I want you to enjoy your wedding day. I know how long you have been dreaming about this day in particular. I promise it will be what you want it to be."

I was marrying the most amazing man in the world. And if you stopped to think about it, I was going to end up with *two* weddings! Who wouldn't want to have a wedding in France? How beautiful and romantic! Everything would work out just fine. Besides, the main focus was that Louis and I were going to spend the rest of our lives together. I couldn't get too stuck on the details of the day that would mark the official beginning of it.

"Thank you for always taking such good care of me, my love."

"It is my job now. I take this responsibility very seriously. Your happiness is of the utmost importance to me," he responded, his voice filled with emotion.

"And your happiness is very important to me," I murmured. "If you want to be married in France, then we'll have to have two weddings. Oooh! This way, your mom can drive you nuts about one wedding and mine can drive me nuts about the other. Now that I think about it, there's no way one wedding would have been able to contain the two of them."

He laughed. "We have very luckily averted disaster."

"You got that right," I teased.

"I really miss you, Syd."

"I really miss you too, Bluey."

"You sound exhausted. Get some rest, *mon coeur*. I will call you tomorrow."

I didn't want to let him go, but he was right. I could barely keep my eyes open. "Until tomorrow then. I love you."

"I love you too. Dream of me." His voice was almost a whisper.

I sighed. "I always do. Goodnight."

After I hung up with Louis, I stayed in bed for a while, just staring at the ceiling. While I felt pretty satisfied with our plan to have two weddings, I was a little freaked out by the idea of having to consult someone in most of my decisions from this day forward. Everything would now be about compromise, which meant neither one of us would actually get what we wanted anymore. We would each have to give in to a certain extent. I had been so focused on the joys of sharing my life with someone, I hadn't thought about the drawbacks. Kate had often told me marriage was a lot of work, but I thought she told me this to make me feel better about being alone. Now I was starting to see that she was being honest with me. This relationship was certainly going to be far from perfect, but I was starting to think this was how it was supposed to be...

## Chapter Twenty-Five

The next four days dragged by at a snail's pace. I was so eager for Louis' return, I could think of nothing else. It was easy enough for me to indulge my obsession over the weekend, but once I returned to work on Monday morning, life became more complicated. I really hoped regular travel wouldn't be part of Louis' job. Otherwise, I might end up being out of one.

After what seemed like an eternity, Tuesday night arrived. I had wanted to pick Louis up from the airport, but he insisted on getting a car service. He knew traffic made me crazy and since his company paid for his travel to and from the airport, he thought it made perfect sense to keep me as happy as possible.

Little did he know that the crazy was already taking over my normally mild-mannered personality. Ever since the day he mentioned his mother initiating plans for a wedding in France, I had begun a slow descent into madness. I had heard stories about issues with mothers-in-law, but I hadn't even met her and already I felt a certain animosity toward her. I knew this was totally irrational, but I was the *bride*. Didn't she know *I* was the one to decide on all the important wedding details, like the *location*?!

Clearly, I had already been possessed by the spirit of Bridezilla. I was hoping Louis' return would help to put the pieces of my sanity back together. There was something about him that grounded me, forcing me to see the big picture instead of focusing on the minutiae. I sat on the couch waiting for him to return from the airport and tried to clear my head. I didn't want our first encounter in two weeks to be tainted by my lunatic alter ego.

I heard his key in the lock and sprinted to the door. When he finally got the door open, I nearly knocked him to the ground.

He laughed. "I am happy to see you too, *mon coeur!*"

I buried my head in his chest. "You have no idea how much I've missed you. Why didn't you call me when you landed?"

He put down his bags and held my face in his hands. "I wanted to surprise you." He grinned devilishly at me. "And I have a very good idea of how much you missed me. I have not felt whole for the last two weeks."

Louis then drew me close and kissed me hungrily. I felt like an electric current was passing through my body. I started hastily unbuttoning his shirt and steering him toward the couch.

"Wouldn't you be more comfortable on the bed?" Louis said as he kissed his way down my neck.

I unbuttoned his pants and pushed them down around his ankles. "No time. I need you now."

He grinned like a kid on Christmas, pulling me on top of him as he sat down on the couch. It was a good thing we didn't have roommates anymore, because they would have gotten quite a show over the next hour.

Louis and I lay wrapped around each other on the couch. I was so warm and happy that I never wanted to move. Then my stomach rumbled. *Hmmm. When had I eaten last?* I had been so focused on Louis' return, I had actually forgotten to eat. I had never forgotten to eat in my life. *Whoa.*

Louis raised his eyebrows. "It has been more than two hours since you last ate, has it not?"

"I had much more important things on my mind than food," I said lightly, giving him a kiss on the nose.

"Very few things are more important to you than food," he responded with a smirk. "I am humbled to make the list."

I swatted him on the back of the head. "You suck!"

He ran his hand up my thigh. "Maybe later...if you are lucky."

I swatted him again.

He raised his hands in surrender. "I am fairly hungry myself. Shall we get dressed and go get something to eat?"

"Absolutely." My stomach rumbled once more. "Do you want to go to Charlie's?"

Louis wrinkled his nose. "I am so tired of eating out. Do you mind if we go to the grocery store?" He kissed my neck slowly, focusing on my weak spot. "That way we can return to more important things much sooner."

I felt my whole body beginning to melt. "If you want to eat any time soon, you will cease and desist, *Monsieur* Durand," I murmured. "Otherwise, I cannot be held responsible for my actions."

"You win, *mon coeur*. Let us get dressed." He helped me up from the couch and we quickly put on all necessary clothing.

As we drove to the grocery store, I thought about how lucky I was. Louis had only been back in the country for a few hours and I already felt my sanity returning. I was sure we would be able to work out our wedding details (times two) without a problem. I sighed contentedly.

Louis smiled. "You seem to be in a good mood."

I put my hand on his knee. "Being around you always puts me in a good mood."

"I promise to put you in an even better mood when we get back to the apartment." He laughed darkly.

Louis parked the car and we walked into the store hand

in hand. As we walked through the aisles, I realized we needed a lot more than a few things. I had been so busy with work, I had eaten most of my meals out and hadn't stocked the house with much of anything. By the time we were done, the cart was brimming with food.

While we were unloading our booty onto the conveyor belt, Louis remembered one last item. I continued to pile our groceries on the belt as he ran to retrieve whatever item it was he couldn't live without. I was so tired, I wasn't even looking at the items as I put them down. I reached into the cart and felt something soft wrapped in plastic. It slipped out of my hands as I tried to pick it up, so I glanced over to see what it was. I carefully studied the item in question. *Wait. Were those?* I read the label. *Oh God.* I was holding a package of pig's feet. Did Louis put these in the cart? Did someone else put this in our cart as a joke? *Gross!*

I was still standing there contemplating the possibilities when Louis returned. "I see you found my pig's feet." He was fighting a serious smirk.

I regarded him suspiciously. "Were you playing a joke on me?"

"No, my grandmother used to make these for me as a child," he replied innocently, the smirk finding its way to a hearty chuckle. "I love them!"

Comprehension slowly dawned on me. "So you're enjoying the fact that I'm a closed-minded American who freaked out when she found animal hooves in her cart?"

He nodded. "Precisely."

I shook my head. "You really do suck." I paused. "And not in a good way."

That sent him into further fits of hysterical laughter. The cashier was not amused. I smiled apologetically at her and quickly paid our bill.

When we got home, Louis prepared his cherished pigs feet and made me promise to try them. I almost balked, but then I remembered I would have years of trying new and exotic foods ahead of me. I had to get used to it. I was certainly not going to be known as the ugly American who only ate hamburgers and macaroni and cheese.

The taste was...interesting. I didn't think I would voluntarily eat pig's feet again, but at least I tasted them. I was going to have to be more adventurous in all aspects of my life if I were going to be *Madame* Louis Durand. (Little did I know there would be a seemingly endless array of "delicacies" coming my way in the next year. I would be served frog's legs, snails, kangaroo, cow intestines and calf brains. I tried everything but the brains—I had to draw the line somewhere.)

When the next morning arrived, I was filled with sadness that Louis and I would be separated again so soon. But reality was reality and money had to be earned. I had just gotten out of the shower when an enormous cloud of cologne permeated the bathroom, sending me into a severe coughing fit. *What happened? Did the bottle explode in his suitcase?*

I toweled myself off as quickly as I could and opened the bathroom door. The scent was so strong, it brought tears to my eyes.

"Louis?" I couldn't stop coughing.

He raced into the bedroom with an alarmed expression on his face. "Are you all right, *mon coeur?*"

After I regained control of my breathing, I asked, "What. Is. That. Smell?"

"Smell? Oh! I put on a bit of cologne."

Normally, I found Louis' scent to be intoxicating. This was...*overbearing.*

"Did you buy a new cologne when you were in France?" And was it industrial strength?

"No. I just bought a new bottle of my cologne. I was almost out of it before I left. Good timing, no?"

I nodded weakly. "Indeed."

"Are you sure that you are okay, *mon coeur?*" he asked, his eyes filled with concern.

"I'm fine, Bluey. I was a little surprised by the, um,

*strength* of the scent."

He smiled ruefully. "I remember Jean telling me I used it a little too liberally. I was just so happy that I did not have to ration it anymore. I probably went a little overboard."

I put my hand on the side of his face, quickly realizing what a bad idea it was. I had just coated my hand in the high-octane scent.

"I love your cologne," I said softly. "I just think a little goes a long way."

He chuckled. "You will have to enforce a limit of sprays."

That was exactly what I had been thinking. "Good idea! How about a maximum of three?"

"We will give it a try tomorrow. I may need four to achieve the full power of my manly scent." He broke into a grin.

"You no longer have any need to attract anyone with your 'manly scent,'" I said sweetly.

Louis threw his head back and laughed. "I love you so much, Syd."

I carefully gave him a kiss goodbye. I didn't want to transfer any more of his cologne to my face. "I love you too."

For the next couple of days, I had to carefully monitor Louis' cologne use. He finally agreed three sprays would be sufficient, since he was now unavailable to the ladies. I knew the people in his office would thank me for making his scent less *fragrant*. As a member of a Human Resources department, I had had more than my share of discussions with employees regarding the appropriate amount of cologne/perfume to wear in an office environment. Not a fun discussion to have, but way easier than the dreaded body odor discussion.

Unfortunately for me, that evening was my turn to be the source of a scent *faux pas*. Louis and I were sitting on the couch after dinner enjoying some mind-numbing TV when I felt rumbling in my abdomen. *Uh oh.* I had been able to hide the fact that I farted from Louis thus far in our relationship, though once we started living together it had become much more complicated. I had made more than a few spontaneous trips to the balcony for "a breath of fresh air." No doubt Louis was on to me, but I wasn't ready to give up the illusion yet.

I started to extract myself from the couch for a trip to the balcony, when Louis tugged on my hand. "Where are you going, *mon coeur*? You are so snuggly. I do not want you to get up." He tried to pull me back onto the couch.

I laughed nervously. "I need a little air. I'll be right back." I tried to extract my hand from his, since my time was almost up.

He refused to release my hand while eyeing me suspiciously. "Is that truly what this is about?" he asked, a smile playing at his lips.

As I was about to answer him, a foreign sound escaped my body. *Shoot.* I had finally farted in front of Louis. I felt my face flood with heat from the humiliation. And that wasn't even the worst part. The fart was smelly, loud and— oddly enough—musical. *Oh, yes.* It came out as a high pitched note, kind of like, "Plew!"

Louis laughed so hard that he fell off the couch. He had actual tears streaming down his face from the exertion. I just stood there watching him, completely torn between laughing with him and being annoyed with him. I finally joined him on the floor and started to giggle. Every couple of minutes he would become completely still, look at me and sing, "Plew!" Then he would start laughing all over again. I decided my days of hiding farts from him were over. Although I doubted he would find it this funny every time.

The next morning, I woke up sincerely hoping Louis was not going to be on another "Plew!" kick. Last night had been more than enough for me. I groggily walked into the bathroom, stood in front of the bathroom mirror, rubbed my eyes and screamed. *Who the hell was the strange man in my bathroom?* I quickly searched the bathroom for something I could hit him with when I heard Louis' voice.

"Are you okay, Syd?" *What?!* Where did *he* come from? More importantly, what happened to the man in the bathroom?

I slowly focused on Louis' face. Something was very wrong. *No way!* He had shaved off all his facial hair! He looked like a completely different person. It was then that my sleep-addled brain comprehended, *he* was the man I had seen in the mirror.

I chuckled. "I'm sorry, Bluey. I didn't recognize you at first." I touched his face in amazement. "You look like a teenager!"

"I have such a baby face," he grumbled. "This was not intentional. The razor slipped and there was no other way to fix it."

"You're *adorable*."

He swatted me on the butt. "Not funny."

I put my arms around him. "Seriously! You're hot! Meet me at my locker after school?"

"To use your lovely expression, 'you suck,'" he retorted.

I reached up and kissed him. "I know, but you still love me."

"And you are lucky I do." He smirked. "I have to run. Have a good day, *mon coeur*."

I turned on the shower and took off my pajamas while the water was warming up. "You too, Bluey!"

Louis stopped in his tracks. "I will carry that image with me all day." He sighed and literally ran for the front door.

I threw my pajamas in the hamper and scanned the bathroom. Sharing a bathroom with Louis was a unique experience. He was neat in most other areas—his personal appearance, his car and the rest of the apartment. He always put his dishes in the dishwasher, put his clothes in the hamper and picked up all his work papers. However, he didn't feel the need to clean up a good portion of the beard hair he had trimmed, the toothpaste he had dropped or even the few stray drops of urine which fell on the floor by the toilet. (He sometimes sleepwalked into the bathroom in the middle of the night and I imagined this interfered with his ability to aim for the toilet.)

Though this kind of behavior didn't thrill me, I knew I was far from perfect. And it was certainly true that different things bothered different people. Louis and I were simply going to have to figure out what we could live with in terms of the other's behavior. In the meantime, I chose to focus on that while living with someone you believed to be your soul mate couldn't be without flaws, the love you shared was more than enough to make up for it. However, on a day-to-day basis it was a very tricky business...

# Chapter Twenty-Six

On Saturday morning, Louis called his mother to broach our American wedding/French reception idea. Thankfully, she was on board, as long as the reception wasn't long after the wedding. She was very excited at the prospect of a trip to the United States and was already telling all her friends that her son was going to have a lavish American wedding. I was thrilled she was happy with our plan and told Louis she was more than welcome to do all the planning for the French reception. Well, almost all the planning—I still wanted the responsibility of choosing my dress.

I would need a less formal wedding dress for the French countryside and after seeing many photos of Louis' mom, it was clear to me we didn't have the same style. There were going to be many photos taken that day and I had no intention of having photographic evidence of me in a dress of her choosing. Lest you think me overly judgmental, just picture Madonna circa nineteen eighty-five. Not even the hint of a joke, people.

Once this was settled, I knew I had to call my parents to break the news that our wedding would be in California. Louis and I had found a beautiful hotel on the water in Monterey and had decided on the spot that this was the perfect location for the wedding. The majority of my friends lived in the Bay Area and the rest of my friends (not to mention Louis' family) would have to travel to either New York or California for the wedding, so we thought California was the better choice.

My father wasn't going to be pleased as he was a hardcore New Yorker. He kept telling me California was going to fall into the ocean and I had better move back home before I drowned. I was also sure many of my parents' friends wouldn't travel to California, so I knew they would be disappointed. My parents had attended many of the weddings of their friends' children and they wanted their turn to show off. But ultimately, a wedding in Monterey was what Louis and I wanted, so this was what we were going to do. None of this changed the fact that I was completely petrified to make this phone call.

I decided to avoid this task by checking in with Maya— or trying to. She was becoming very difficult to pin down these days, which meant she was up to something. I was convinced her elusiveness had something to do with Jean, but she wouldn't admit a thing. And despite Louis' best efforts, he wasn't able to wheedle any information out of his former roommate. *What the hell was going on between the two of them?*

I dialed her cell phone number, fully expecting to get her voicemail instead of the rapid pick up she used to employ. To my surprise, she answered on the first ring.

"Sydney Bennett! Where have you been?"

I laughed. "I could ask you the same question, my friend. I've left you a bunch of voicemails. What have you been up to?"

She sighed. "Nothing exciting. Not all of us can live out a movie plotline."

I rolled my eyes. "Bullshit. Something's going on, Maya. You've never been shy about filling me in on all the details of your life—even the ones I didn't want to hear." Seriously, some images could never be erased.

"Come on, Syd!" she cried. "You *love* my stories. I used to provide the much-needed excitement in your life."

"I had plenty of drama of my own, thank you very much." I took a deep breath. "Just promise me that you're all right. I'm not used to being kept in the dark where you're concerned."

"I'm fine, Syd. I appreciate your concern, but there's no need to worry, okay?"

"Maya, you *know* me. I'm going to worry until you tell me what's going on."

"It's a good thing, trust me," she said with more than a hint of exasperation. "I just want to keep it to myself for a little while longer. I don't want to jinx anything."

I thought for a moment. "Fine. But tell me one thing—does it involve Jean?"

She laughed. "Bye, Syd!"

"Maya!"

She actually hung up on me! How rude! I sat and weighed my options. I knew I should respect her request and allow her some privacy, but this was such a foreign concept when it came to Maya. She had always been an open book. I felt a massive sense of frustration at not knowing what was happening and recognized I was in no state of mind to call my parents. This unpleasant task would have to be put off for a little while longer. I wondered what movies were on cable...

⌒

By late afternoon, I decided I could procrastinate no longer. I put on my big girl panties and called my mom at the store. Of course, my dad picked up right away.

"Duck, I'm so glad to know that you're still breathing." *Great.* This did not bode well for the rest of the conversation.

I silently cursed myself for not speaking with him earlier in the week when I checked in with my mom. This call would have been so much easier if I didn't already feel guilty.

I sighed. "I'm sorry, Dad. Work has been insane over the past two weeks and then I got, um, distracted by Louis' return. I've missed you though!"

"We've missed you too. How's Louis?"

*Interesting.* He didn't usually ask about Louis. Perhaps this was a good sign?

"He's doing well, Dad. He's happy to be back in California."

"More than likely, he's happy to be back with you," he observed. "Who could blame him?"

Okay, this *was* good. He sounded happy. I tested the waters further. "How are you, Dad?"

He sighed heavily. "The usual. I can't get used to these crazy teenagers who come into the store. They have these huge spikes and piercings all over their bodies. Oh! And the tattoos! This one fellow had tattoos covering his entire face!"

"Wow, Dad, that must have been bizarre for you to see," I said, mocking him just a little.

"You don't sound too surprised, Duck. Do you have piercings I don't know about?"

"Of course not!" I spluttered. "I've just seen all the things you've described pretty often."

My father gasped with gusto, pretending to be shocked. (Very little actually shocked this man.) "Where have you been spending your time lately?"

"The Bay Area is a lot more progressive than the suburb you live in, Dad. I'll take you to a few places to observe the next time you're in town."

"Sounds like a date. Now how's the wedding planning coming?"

I filled my dad in on the plan to have the wedding in the US (yes, I was a total coward) and then a reception in France. I had told my mom about our plan (again, the watered-down version) a couple of days ago, but I had been too stressed to tell my father. I knew he would have plenty to say about traveling to Europe. The idea of taking the trip didn't bother him—in fact, it seemed he was looking forward to it—but he couldn't resist pushing my buttons. It was one of his favorite things to do. And no matter how hard I tried to resist, I *always* took the bait. I really needed to find this man hobby.

"You mean I have to enter that godforsaken country?"

I sighed. He really enjoyed putting on a performance. "No, Dad, if you're that uncomfortable, I'm sure Mom would be fine going without you."

My father sighed dramatically. "No, I couldn't do that to her. She needs me. I'm her emotional rock."

I spit out the water I had been drinking and started to cough uncontrollably.

"Are you okay, Duck?" he asked in between chuckles.

It took a couple of minutes, but I was finally able to speak. "You're amazing, old man. Even after all these years, you're still able to catch me off guard."

"I'm the master, Duck," he declared. "One day you may be able to rise to my level."

I took a deep breath. "Dad? Is Mom around? I have something to discuss with both of you about the wedding." I could already feel my heartrate picking up. Why was I so freaked out about telling them the wedding would be in California? I was nearly twenty-eight years old. It was time to grow a backbone.

"Sure, Syd. She's up front cashing out the drawer. I'll give her a yell." And this was exactly what he did. Unfortunately, most of the yell ended up in my ear. (Seriously, my dad was *loud*!) I had to remember to hold the phone away from my ear when he said that. I mean, he did give me fair warning.

My mom picked up the phone. "Syd? I'm so happy to hear from you, darling. I've missed you!" I couldn't help but smile. My mom always made me feel special. It was going to make it that much harder to tell her our decision about the wedding location. *Get on with it, Sydney!*

"I've missed you too, Mom. How are you?" No, I wasn't stalling. I couldn't tell her about our wedding plans without going through some pleasantries first. The woman raised me to have manners!

"Well, business is going very well. We've booked a bunch more parties—and not just birthdays!—anniversaries, going-away parties and even one retirement party." She sounded really excited. I silently hoped I wouldn't kill her mood. Maybe I was overreacting? Maybe she would be fine with having the wedding out here. Oh, to hell with it. *Just tell them, Sydney!*

"That's great, Mom! I'm so glad to hear things are going well." I paused. "Listen, there's something I'd like to speak to you both about concerning the wedding," I said, my voice shaking ever so slightly.

"Is everything all right, Syd?" my mom asked.

I cleared my throat. "Everything's fine, Mom. Don't worry. I just wanted to let you know that Louis and I have decided to have the wedding here. In California. We found this gorgeous hotel in Monterey overlooking the water. We can have the wedding out on a big, beautiful terrace. And there's a long staircase leading down to the terrace. It's spectacular," I trailed off.

I waited with bated breath, hoping they would have something positive to say. I mean, it was my day, right? Well, technically, it was Louis' day too, but he didn't care as much about the details as I did. Besides with my family, it was *my* opinion which mattered the most. This was what I wanted and I expected them to back me. Okay, I hoped they would. I desperately wanted this.

My dad was the first to break the silence. "First you tell me I have to go to France of all places and now you tell me I have to go to California? Where I might fall into the ocean? Duck! Are you trying to kill your poor father?"

*Wait.* What just happened? Suddenly, I was cackling until I could barely breathe. My dad was a gigantic pain in the ass, but he loved me and he understood me unbelievably well. He knew exactly what to say to release my tension.

My mom giggled. "Teddy, you're *incorrigible*. Sydney, a wedding in California will be wonderful!"

I breathed a sigh of relief. I often forgot how much my mom loved California. She had lived in San Francisco for a few years in her early twenties and would have settled there if it weren't for my father—my biological father. She would have moved back to California once Kate and I moved out here, but there was no way that my father (my real father) would have moved. She told me once that she was tired of being separated from her true home by penises. No joke—she actually said, "penises."

"Which hotel did you decide on? Oh! This wedding is going to be just beautiful!" My mom was bursting with excitement.

I grinned. "The Monterey Plaza. Have you ever been there?"

"I've never stayed there, but I did have lunch with a friend there once. The view was amazing!"

I started jumping up and down. I felt like a five-year-old who had just gotten a hot fudge sundae. (But honestly, you would still get the same reaction out of me for a hot fudge sundae.)

"We have a lot of planning to do, Mom! I hope you're ready."

"Are you joking? *I can't wait!* Have you picked a date yet?" I could picture my mom dancing around her store. She always did that when she was happy about something. It used to embarrass me to no end, since she had no qualms about doing it in public.

"We're looking at next September, which gives us a full twelve months to plan."

"Oh, Syd. What a delightful wedding it will be!" She had now entered the weepy stage. That was a quick transition! Was residual menopause the culprit? *Focus, Sydney.* This was a topic for another conversation. One that did not involve my father.

My dad coughed. "Okay, Lyn, I think it's time to get you home. It's closing time and the customers don't need to see you have an emotional...thing."

My mom laughed through her tears. "You're probably right, Ted. We love you, Syd. Promise me you'll call soon so we can talk details."

"Of course, Mom. We have a lot of work to do! We'll have to bring Kate up to speed. Though I think in her current state, she'll serve us best in an advisory capacity. No strenuous work for her."

My mom sighed. "Poor Kate. I hope her morning sickness goes away soon."

"Me too," I admitted. "I love her very much, but she's one cranky pregnant woman. I want my sister back."

"Cut your sister some slack, Syd," she chided. "It takes a lot to create a life and for some women, it takes a whole lot more than we'd like. You'll find out for yourself someday."

*Gah!* I wasn't ready to think about children yet. Louis and I were already on the fast track in our relationship. Children were definitely a few years away.

"Thanks for the reminder, Mom." I chuckled. "I have *way* too many other things to think about. I think at this point in time a child would be the end of me."

"Don't even joke about that, Duck. These things have a way of happening..."

*Eww!* My dad was talking about my sex life. It was time to go.

"On that note, Dad, I must go. I love you both! I promise to call again soon."

"Say hello to Louis for us!" my mom called. "And please tell his mother how much I'm looking forward to meeting her." I could hear my dad in the background trying to get her to hang up the phone.

"Bye, Duck!" I imagined my dad trying to physically remove the phone from her hands.

"Bye, Syd!" My mom was obviously determined to get a

few last words in. "We love you!"  Click.

Clearly, my dad was trying to curtail the level of emotion that he was going to have to deal with this evening.  He found women in general to be far too irrational for his taste, but he loved my mom dearly, so he grudgingly talked through her concerns. Didn't mean he had to like it.

I laid back on the couch and closed my eyes.  I felt more relaxed than I had in a long time.  Things were starting to fall into place.  Louis and I were blissfully happy, we had a beautiful apartment and we were starting to plan a gorgeous wedding.  Life was perfect.  Now all I had to do was plan the perfect wedding.  How hard could it be?

## Chapter Twenty-Seven

The last three weeks had been a flurry of wedding research. Maya was in *heaven*. She must have purchased every bridal magazine in existence. Luckily, Kate was feeling better, so the three of us had spent many evenings buried in these magazines, discussing everything from the style of my wedding gown to the font choice for the invitations. I had never appreciated how many details there were to create the perfect wedding until I actually had to decide on them. Consequently, I was unbelievably glad I had the two of them and my mom helping me. My brand of crazy mixed with Bridezilla was a lethal combination (thank goodness they were very skilled at keeping me in check).

With all these resources, the details quickly began to fall into place. The previous week Louis and I had booked our dream hotel in Monterey for a Saturday wedding in September of next year. We were introduced to our wedding planner, Monica, and given a list of local vendors for everything from flowers to tuxedos. We set up an appointment for early next year to talk about ceremony details and to sample wedding cakes. Louis thought it was hilarious that I was most excited about the cake. But seriously, how could you *not* be excited about the opportunity to keep trying different cakes until you found the most delicious one? Fork, please!

I also had the good fortune of having my friend, Lexi, refer me to her cousin who would do our flowers for cost. I had been floored by the astronomical cost of wedding flowers, so this referral thrilled me to no end. Louis and I didn't want to spend a fortune, but I also had no intention of having carnations as my bridal bouquet. It was funny, when I was a young girl planning my wedding, it seemed like a magical experience. (Because in the fantasy, I had an endless budget.) But when I grew up, I realized that planning a wedding required *a lot* of compromise as well as economy. It was easy to see I wasn't going to have the "perfect" wedding I had dreamed of, but it would be beautiful.

I had also never imagined as a child that the true lifesaver for my wedding planning would be a website. All you had to do was enter your wedding date along with a few details and you were given a personalized calendar with task lists for each day leading all the way up to your wedding. It was pure genius! I felt a great sense of relief knowing no detail would be forgotten. In fact, I felt a closer kinship to the creator of this website than I did to some of my friends. (Who wouldn't? My interests always came first as far as the website was concerned!)

Louis was in awe of the lengthy discussions Kate, Maya and I would have on various wedding topics. He didn't understand why the process of planning a wedding had to be so complicated. I did my best to keep him in the dark, because if he actually knew the extent of our discussions, his head might explode. Men didn't understand the importance of choosing the right flowers, wedding favors, invitations, etc. They didn't appreciate how everything had to come together in just the right way in order to make us happy. And they certainly couldn't fathom that because most women hoped they would only get married once, everything *had* to be perfect. But there was no pressure or anything...

Amidst all the wedding planning, I had completely forgotten about my birthday. This spoke volumes about my level of distraction. While I was not excited about being that much closer to thirty, I *loved* celebrating my birthday. You got cake, gifts, a special birthday meal and people just fussed over you in general. (Plus, I always bought myself a gorgeous new outfit.) Celebrating my birthday lifted my spirits every year. And this year, I would have a fiancé to celebrate with! I had never had a boyfriend on the actual day, so I was looking forward to my birthday in particular this year. I was on pins and needles as I wondered what Louis had in store for me.

Finally, my birthday arrived. It was a Thursday night, so I didn't think he would plan anything crazy, but no doubt it would be romantic. I was all decked out in my birthday ensemble, anxiously waiting for him to come home. This year, I had chosen a black fitted pencil skirt, a shimmery violet blouse with a black lace camisole underneath and black high heeled boots. I decided to wear my hair down and followed Maya's detailed instructions on how to use my new sparkly makeup. I was pretty sure I did her proud this time!

When Louis walked through the door, I jumped up and ran to him. "Happy Birthday, *mon coeur*!" he sang.

I threw my arms around him and squeezed him tightly. *Hmmm.* There was a peculiar absence of flowers. I thought he might send me some at work today, but when they didn't arrive, I figured he was going to bring a bouquet home with him. Perhaps he had something special waiting for me at the restaurant he had chosen?

Louis held my face in his hands and kissed me. "How was your day?"

I grinned. "It was nice! My boss took me to lunch and then invited a bunch of people for cake in the afternoon. Oh, and Kate and Nick sent me the most beautiful flowers."

He rubbed his eyes. "Excellent. Now where would you

like to go for dinner tonight?"

Did I hear him correctly? Did he just ask me at six o'clock on the evening of my birthday where I wanted to go for dinner? Was this some kind of joke?

Okay, that might have sounded a bit harsh. It was just...Louis and I had spent a lot of time talking about our childhoods and while he had told me birthdays were never a big deal in his family, I had told him how important they were in mine. I made a huge fuss over my family and friends on their special days and I liked to have the same treatment in return.

I had shared this information with Louis in a very upfront manner. I had even told him once if he wanted to marry me, he would be expected to buy me flowers at the very least four times a year—my birthday, our anniversary, Valentine's Day and Mother's Day (when the time came). I had been *very* open and honest with him about what was important to me and did not expect him to simply know these things as many women did.

So, now my general feeling of "What the fuck?" should make a lot more sense. Please forgive my language, but profanity was absolutely necessary in this case.

I stared blankly at Louis. "You mean you haven't made reservations anywhere?"

He cocked his head to one side. "Was I supposed to?"

I was at a loss for what to say. I felt completely let down and didn't know how to handle it. My mind was suddenly filled with questions. This was the man I was going to marry? This was how I was going to be treated by my husband? Was this what I really wanted? I mean, I knew marriage involved a lot of compromise, but was it too much for him to go through a little effort for my birthday, knowing how important it was to me? How hard was it to buy some flowers and make a dinner reservation? I needed to sit down.

I walked over to the couch and eased myself into a sitting position. I felt the tears coming and didn't know what to do. Louis came over and sat next to me. He took my hand and stroked it.

"What is the matter, Syd?"

I dropped my eyes to the floor. "I'm not sure."

He grinned and took a box with a ribbon out of his pocket. "Maybe this will make you feel better?

I tried to smile. I took the box and turned it over in my hands. "Thank you, Louis."

"Go ahead! Open it."

I removed the ribbon and opened the box. Inside was a box containing a travel size bottle of Chanel No. 19. I loved this perfume, but it felt like a little bit of a letdown considering he had given me a giant bottle of Eau de Givenchy when he returned from his trip to France—just because he missed me.

I cleared my throat. "Thank you, Louis. I love this perfume."

"I am so glad you like it, *mon coeur*. Now where shall we go to dinner?"

At this point, I was barely holding it together. I glanced over at Louis and willed the tears to stay in my eyes.

"You know, Louis, I'm not feeling that well. Would you mind if we stayed here?"

He frowned. "Are you sure?"

I nodded. "I'd like to take a bath."

"Do I get to come?" he asked suggestively.

*Was he serious?* "I actually have a bit of a headache. I think I'll relax alone, if you don't mind."

"Shall I order some takeout for the birthday girl?"

I had suddenly lost my appetite. I felt completely let down and just wanted to be alone. These were the times when it was really hard to live with the person who was the source of your sadness.

"I'm not hungry," I murmured. "I guess I had too much cake today."

Louis lifted my chin with his finger and forced me to look him in the eyes. "Are you sure you are okay? You seemed fine, even happy, when I came home and then suddenly you were not."

I didn't have it in me to explain this to him. "My headache has gotten worse. I'm sure I'll be fine after resting." I wasn't sure if that was true, but I wanted to believe it.

I got up and went into the bedroom. As I started getting undressed, Louis came in, nostrils flaring. *Great.* This birthday was getting better and better.

"Sydney, if we are going to be married, you are going to have to be honest with me. What is the matter?"

*Fine.* I turned to face him. "Today is my *birthday.*"

He stared at me like I was crazy. "I know this. You love your birthday." He was clearly waiting for me to elaborate.

"I do love my birthday. And you love me, therefore, you need to love my birthday too."

He motioned for me to continue.

"Louis, I love you very, *very* much." I paused and took a deep breath. "Do you remember what I did for your birthday?"

He nodded. "You made it very special. I had never had that before. It was amazing."

"That's exactly what I wanted for you." I tried to swallow the lump in my throat. "I know how much you love me, Bluey. It just....it hurt that you didn't put more thought into my birthday."

"But I asked you where you wanted to go to dinner," he faltered. "And I gave you a gift."

I sighed. I was going to have to give it to him straight and it wasn't going to sound good.

"You asked me where I wanted to go the evening of my birthday, when it would be too hard to get into a nice restaurant without reservations. You didn't bring me any flowers and you gave me a gift that wasn't as nice as the gift you gave me when you came back from France."

"That is not good enough for you?" Louis asked angrily. "Is this what our relationship comes down to?"

I felt terrible, but if we were going to have an honest relationship, he was going to have to have a clear understanding of what was important to me.

Tears starting spilling down my cheeks. "Louis, it's not about the amount of money you spend, it's about the *effort*. Are you honestly telling me you couldn't find the time to make a dinner reservation and buy some flowers?"

I could see he was struggling with how to react, between his anger and my tears.

"What is the big deal, Syd? I will buy you flowers tomorrow. We can go to any restaurant that you choose and I will buy you another gift."

I was completely confused. What happened to my romantic Louis? Did he leave once he moved to this country? I began to freak out, wondering if I had rushed into my decision to marry him. I slowly backed away from Louis, my head spinning. The anxiety descended on me in a split second, the pressure in my chest building to the point of pain. *Crap!* Of all the times to have a panic attack!

My breathing quickened. "I....I need a minute." My knees buckled and I found myself sitting on the floor.

Louis rushed over to me. "Syd? Are you okay? What is going on? Do you need a doctor?"

I shook my head. "No need for a doctor. If you let me have some time to myself, I'll be fine."

Louis took my hand. "I don't want to leave you."

"I only need a few minutes, all right?"

Suddenly, there was a knock at the door. Louis looked at me sadly and sighed. "I will see who is there." He got up slowly and left the bedroom.

I heard Louis open the door and greet whomever was outside. They exchanged excited conversation for a few minutes and then I heard the door close. What was that about? Did he really think now was a good time for a chat? I found myself even more irritated with him than I had been a few minutes earlier.

Louis came back into the bedroom to find me sitting in

the same spot on the floor.

"Who was that?" I asked, refusing to meet his eyes.

"Sydney, please look at me."

I grudgingly peered up at his face. He had the nerve to be grinning from ear to ear. My annoyance was reaching a dangerous level. I must have had an *ugly* look on my face at that moment.

His smile did not waver. "It was a special delivery."

"Special delivery?" I asked, my curiosity piqued.

He sat down next to me on the floor and handed me a square black velvet box.

I wiped my tears with the back of my hand. "What is this?"

"Why don't you open it and find out?" he said softly.

Well, it probably wouldn't make things any worse. Opening the box took a bit of effort because my hands were shaking, but when I finally got it open, the contents took my breath away.

I stared at Louis. "When did you do this?"

"During one of your many wedding planning sessions with Kate and Maya. Do you like it?"

I was speechless. Nestled in this little black velvet box was an exact replica of the costume engagement ring I had purchased at Nordstrom. It was absolutely beautiful.

Tears filled my eyes once more, but for a very different reason. "I love it," I sobbed. "And I love you." I put my arms around his neck and started to cry.

"Why are you crying, *mon coeur*?" he asked, completely bewildered.

"*I don't know,*" I wailed.

He pulled out of the embrace and stroked my face. "Why don't you try on your ring?"

My face lit up and I held out my trembling fingers. He removed the costume ring from my finger and replaced it with the dazzling ring he had had made for me. It fit perfectly. He gazed into my eyes and smiled.

"Happy Birthday, Syd," he whispered before kissing me

tenderly on the lips.

"*Thank you*, Bluey."

He cleared his throat. "Now, I am sure you are in need of some food. Any interest in the chocolate cake that is currently in the refrigerator?"

I grinned. "Is that a trick question?"

He helped me to my feet and carried me into the kitchen. I giggled the whole way and was thankful that my birthday had vastly improved. We then sat at the dining room table and ate cake out of the box. It was the best birthday cake I had ever had.

Later in the evening, Louis explained to me that he had been so nervous I would find out about my engagement ring, he had completely forgotten to execute the birthday plans he had come up with and asked if he could have a do-over the next day. I was more than happy to take him up on his offer (And sincerely hoped Maya wouldn't kill me for canceling our plans). I managed to regain my composure and reminded myself how Louis and I were still getting to know each other; it was understandable that we would need to make some adjustments.

The next day, I came into work to find three dozen roses waiting for me. Between the flowers and my new engagement ring, the office gossip was flying once again. That night, Louis took me to Il Fornaio for dinner. After we had dessert, he took me to the garden where I had proposed to him. He told me how surprised and happy he had been that night and how no one had ever made him feel the way I did. He had tears in his eyes when he said he was the luckiest man in the world. It was an unforgettable evening. Despite the rocky start, it ended up being the perfect birthday.

*Chapter Twenty-Eight*

It was amazing how quickly time flew when you were embroiled in planning a wedding. Four weeks had passed since my birthday and we were only a few days away from flying to New York for Thanksgiving. My nerves were starting to fray. I had no idea what my dad and Charlie had in store for Louis, but I knew it wouldn't be easy. The only thing I could take comfort in was that Louis was nearly unshakable and from everything I had seen, would always come out on top. This didn't mean my dad wouldn't put in his best effort though.

Just what had I accomplished in these past four weeks? As you know, the wedding site had been booked and the florist had been secured. After a lot of hard work—and a lot of help from Kate and Maya—I had booked a photographer and a DJ, had chosen invitations and wedding favors and had even found *the* dress. *Squee*! I had found the dress I had been imagining since I was a little girl. Okay, I hadn't known exactly what it would look like, but I had a good idea. I knew it would make me feel like a princess.

The week before, Kate, Maya and I had ventured out on our first dress shopping trip. Naturally, prior to this expedition, we had spent countless hours poring over bridal magazines in order to choose the general style of the gown I wanted. After much deliberation, I decided on a pure white gown, with a full skirt and a fitted bodice. I knew I didn't want long sleeves, but wasn't sure if I wanted cap sleeves, spaghetti straps or a strapless dress. Of course, I knew this was all just theory at this point; I would have to try the dresses on to know for sure.

Maya insisted we start at the Bridal Galleria in San Francisco. She said we wouldn't find any acceptable dresses outside of the city. While I trusted her fashion expertise, I wasn't sure I could afford what this expertise would dictate I wear. Kate advised me to keep an open mind, since you never knew when someone would have some kind of crazy sample sale. She had a point, but honestly, the idea of a sample sale scared the crap out of me. I often joked about being Bridezilla, but I knew they actually existed. I also knew they could eat me for lunch. Not that Maya would let them...

We spent the first hour perusing our options. Per our pre-shopping discussion, we would each select three dresses for me to try on. (I had to impose a limit on Maya or I could easily end up with thirty or more.) Any opportunity for her to dress someone brought out her inner child—as in, time to dress my dolly! I also had to remind her that she was choosing for me, so she should select dresses *I* would like, not dresses she would like to see me wear. It was *my* wedding day, after all, *I* had to be the one to be happy with my dress choice. She could complain all she wanted!

Due to Maya's complete lack of patience, I tried on her dresses first. She had chosen an ivory satin halter with an ankle-length skirt (and a huge slit up the side), a white lace strapless dress with a calf-length skirt and a white silk short-sleeved dress with a generous scoop neck, a very fitted bodice, a full-length skirt and a crimson sash. She certainly went for variety! Unfortunately for her, I felt like a trollop in the first, a debutante in the second and a prom queen in the third. Maya could have easily pulled off any one of them, but I lacked not only her confidence but her petite frame

Kate's dresses were much more in line with my taste. She was the opposite of Maya in that she would purposely choose dresses she knew I would like, rather than trying to push me to make "daring fashion choices." Kate had chosen a white strapless chiffon gown with a full-length train and a jeweled sash, an ivory strapless organza gown with antique lace and a white satin ball gown with illusion straps and a beaded bodice. I loved them all, but if I had to choose, I would have gone with the ivory organza.

Finally, it was time to try on my gowns. I chose an ivory basket weave organza strapless gown with floral detail, a white satin off the shoulder A-line gown with a side drape bodice and a white spaghetti strap ball gown with a satin beaded bodice and a full tulle skirt. The skirt of my last gown choice was particularly beautiful as it had additional beading patterned into the tulle. The first two gowns looked lovely, but the last gown was breathtaking. It also seemed oddly familiar. Perhaps I had seen it in one of the endless parade of bridal magazines I had perused over the last couple of months?

A knock on the door to the dressing room brought me back to the present.

"Are you all right, Syd?" Kate asked. "You made a very strange noise."

I opened the door and walked out. Kate took one look at me and her mouth fell to the floor. As tears welled in her eyes, she whispered, "That's it."

I nodded. I hugged her close (carefully, of course) and felt the tears forming in my eyes as well. Something about this dress made me feel like a princess. It was just...me.

I put my nose to hers and murmured, "I'm so glad you're here with me, Kate. Everything feels more special when I'm with you."

That was when the bawling commenced. *Uh oh.* I had forgotten about the uncontrollable hormones of my pregnant sister. My heartfelt declaration had unleashed a massive amount of emotion. *Crap!* I had to find something to bring her out of it quickly. My eyes searched the room and settled on exactly what I needed. *Thank God!*

I cleared my throat. "Kate! I see a candy bowl across the room. Should we take a peek and see what we can find? I could sure use some sugar!"

She smiled and led the way to the candy bowl. I let out a sigh of relief. That was *close*. Nick would have killed me if I had brought her home in tears again. I was on serious probation after taking her to see *Pretty in Pink* last week. It was playing at the dollar theater and I thought Kate would enjoy the experience of seeing it on the big screen again. ( It was one of our favorites when we were younger. We were both in love with Andrew McCarthy, despite his heinous hair at that time.)

Unfortunately, she empathized with the characters a little too much and the resulting feelings were too overwhelming for her to contain. Apparently, it took Nick two hours to get her to stop crying. Who could possibly have predicted such a reaction? Navigating the emotions of a pregnant woman was like walking through an active mine field. You really never knew when something was going to blow up. At least I had diffused the current situation for the time being...

After we had made our selections, I realized Maya was missing Where had she gotten off to this time?

"Kate, where did Maya go?" I craned my neck, searching every part of the store within my sight, but wasn't able to locate her.

Kate shrugged. "She was *just* here. Maybe she went to the bathroom?"

"You sit tight and enjoy your snack. I'm going to see if I can find her." Granted, I had already decided I was going to buy this dress, but I still wanted her to see me in it.

I began combing the aisles for Maya. The store was relatively deserted and for some reason the silence was making me nervous. Did something happen to her? I chuckled to myself. What could possibly have happened to her in a bridal salon?

I heard a small yelp behind me. What was *that*? I quickly turned around, forgetting I was wearing a wedding dress with a huge skirt and promptly fell on my face. *Nice, Syd.* That bodes well for your wedding day. Evidently, I would have to practice walking in this dress *a lot* before the big day. I didn't need to end up on the floor in a gigantic poof ball in front of everyone I knew.

As I clumsily got to my feet, I caught a glimpse of someone in my peripheral vision. I turned around to find Maya admiring herself in a full length mirror. This in itself wasn't an unusual sight—Maya often went over her appearance with a fine-tooth comb. The odd part was that she was wearing one of the wedding gowns she had chosen for me. This was an interesting development indeed. Maya had *never* expressed any interest in getting married. I now wondered if all her bravado was simply a cover.

I stepped behind a rack of dresses and weighed my options. I was dying to know what was going on (and I was still convinced it had something to do with Jean) but I didn't want to embarrass her. I peeked around the rack and saw an expression of pure joy on her face. Maya rarely showed signs of genuine emotion. It wasn't that she didn't feel anything, she just didn't want to share her private feelings with others. I really didn't want to catch her off guard and make her feel vulnerable.

Suddenly, I heard a voice behind me. "I bet you're wondering why I'm wearing a wedding dress." It shouldn't surprise me that Maya made my decision for me.

I turned around and locked eyes with her. "I was only wondering where you went. I wanted to show you my dress."

Maya gave me a quick once over. "You're *exquisite*, Syd. This is the one?"

I nodded. "This is the one."

She smiled. "Excellent choice. By the time Kate and I are through with you, you're going to look like you just stepped off a magazine cover."

I looked...well, I tried to look at my shoes. I couldn't see them under all the poof. I had to ask Maya what was going on, but it wasn't going to be pleasant.

I raised my eyes to meet hers. "Are you going to tell me what's going on?"

She laughed. "What makes you think something is going on?"

"Uh...you're trying on wedding dresses. You have never in your life expressed *any* interest in getting married. You've always discussed marriage with a certain amount of distaste." I wrinkled my nose for emphasis.

"Syd, I only wanted to see what this dress would look like on. I mean, look at it, it's *gorgeous*." She turned back to the mirror and admired the fitted white dress with the red sash. I had to admit, she was stunning. "Besides, I did have a life before I met you. I thought about marriage then."

"Really?" I sounded more shocked than I had meant to. "I'm sorry, that didn't come out right. What changed your mind?"

She sighed. "I guess the men I met in college and the years since graduation have just turned me off to the idea. None of them were anything like the man I had imagined marrying."

I raised my eyebrows. "Does this mean you've met someone who's reminded you why you once believed in marriage?" And if so, is his name Jean?

She closed her eyes. "Maybe."

"Ah hah! I *knew* it." I giggled. "Who is he?"

She slowly opened her eyes. "Wouldn't you like to know?"

"*Are you fucking kidding me?*" I was seriously going to kill her. "You invade *every* aspect of my life, push me outside of *every* comfort zone I have, extract information I don't necessarily want to share and you won't share this with me?"

She threw her head back and laughed. "Sydney Bennett! Did you suddenly grow a backbone?"

"Are you going to tell me or not?" I grumbled.

"Calm yourself, woman. I'll tell you." She took a deep breath. "His name is Devon and he works at my company."

*Hmmm.* "You mean, it isn't Jean?"

"Get real, Syd," she retorted. "He's *so* not my type."

"Then why is it you were all over him behind a gigantic plant?" I was going to get an explanation for that night one way or the other.

"I *may* have had a little too much to drink," she admitted.

I smirked. "Oh. My. God! Are you *embarrassed?*"

She shook her head. "Of course not! I'm never embarrassed. After...*Jean*, I decided it was time to get serious about my future. So, the next day, I asked Devon out."

I was shocked. "Maya! That was weeks and weeks ago. What would possess you to keep this a secret for so long?"

"I didn't want to jinx it," she said softly. "I *really* like this guy."

Seeing Maya in such a vulnerable position was totally bizarre—but in a good way. I was relieved to know she actually wanted someone special into her life.

I hugged her close. "I'm so happy for you."

Even though I had my eyes closed and we weren't facing each other, I knew she was rolling her eyes at me. "Jesus, Syd, stop getting all mushy on me. *Eww.* You know it's not my thing." I thought it was pretty interesting that she made no attempt to pull out of the hug. Maya was such an enigma.

I suddenly remembered leaving Kate alone for at least ten minutes with a full bowl of candy. *Crap!* I was going to be in even more trouble with Nick. I quickly wrenched myself away from Maya and grabbed her hand.

"Syd!" she groaned. "Where are we going in such a hurry?"

"We have an urgent matter to attend to. Kate has had unrestricted access to a candy bowl for far too long. I'm

already on Nick's shit list, so we have to act quickly!" I raced
back to the main salon. Well, I went as fast as I could in a
gigantic, poofy wedding gown while dragging a whiny Maya
behind me. This was decidedly not a garment made to be
worn for a quick getaway.

I stopped dead in my tracks when I reached the entrance
to the salon. There on the floor of the sacred ground where
brides discover their cherished wedding gowns, was my
lovely sister, Kate, stuffing her face full of Kit Kats. As I
marveled at the sight of my perfect sister in this less than
perfect situation, I felt fear in the pit of my stomach. There
was no telling what Nick was going to do to me this time. I
shouldn't bother purchasing this gown and having it altered,
because I wasn't going to make it to my wedding day. I was
as good as dead.

## Chapter Twenty-Nine

Thankfully, I was able to return Kate to Nick in a happy state, which ensured I would actually get to fly home for Thanksgiving and introduce Louis to the rest of my family. Things were touch and go for a while, since during her candy binge, Kate had somehow managed to produce a list of no less than seventy-five items which *had* to get done before the baby was born. Apparently, she had found a stash of pink tissue paper in the bridal salon and wrote down every thought in her head. Luckily, she had crashed by the time she got home and Nick was able to dispose of the list before she remembered she had written it. I wasn't sure why she thought it was necessary to buy a cow, but Nick didn't find this amusing in the least.

With the crisis behind me, I was able to concentrate on preparing for our trip to New York. We planned to fly in on Tuesday afternoon so I would be able to spend all day Wednesday helping my mother prepare the Thanksgiving meal. Once again, she had invited too many guests and we would need extra time to prepare since Kate wouldn't be there to help. Nick had insisted they stay in California so Kate could have a restful Thanksgiving this year. She was still feeling tired and nauseated and he had no intention of exacerbating these feelings with a six hour flight and two airports full of nasty germs.

On Monday evening, I decided I had to do something to prepare Louis for meeting my family. He kept insisting he could handle anything, but he had no idea what he was in for. I was well aware he had met a wide variety of people in his lifetime and it was clear he did very well with people when he turned on his charm, but I knew he had never met anyone like my father.

"Seriously, Syd, will you relax?" Louis pleaded, his mouth twitching.

"I love you, Bluey, but you have to stop telling me to relax. You aren't taking this seriously. My father will come at you when you least expect it! You *have* to be prepared."

He put the last of his clothes in his suitcase and zipped it. "*Mon coeur*, it will all be fine. Trust me, they will ask me whatever questions they want to, I will answer them gladly and we will all have a good time."

I regarded him with pity. "Just remember, Nick won't be there to help you. And Charlie doesn't know you well enough to protect you. You'll be on your own, my friend."

Louis laughed. "You are too much, Sydney Bennett." He walked over to me and held my face in his hands. "Please stop worrying. I am very much looking forward to meeting your family."

I met his eyes and sighed. "I'll try to stop worrying. I haven't had much success with that, oh, *ever*, but I'll try."

He ran his hands down my back and whispered, "Now that we have finished packing, we can focus our attention on more pressing matters."

"You have a one-track mind, Bluey," I teased. But he had a point...

⌒

By the next morning, my nerves had multiplied. I wasn't able to deal with the idea of eating anything, so I had far too many cups of tea. No doubt, Louis was thrilled to have the winning combination of Hyper, yet Worried Sydney. Her thoughts were muddled, she spouted complete nonsense and she had to pee *constantly*. What a great choice for an air travel companion!

After we passed through airport security and arrived at the gate, I ran to the bathroom for what seemed like the millionth time. As I stood in line, I tried to pinpoint what I was actually nervous about. On a very minor scale, I was nervous about flying. I had employed my usual method of distraction and had bought the latest issues of *People* and *US Weekly*, which would get me through the first couple hours of the flight. As a result of his time in the French military, Louis could (and did) sleep anywhere, so I would be left with four remaining hours to deal with by myself. Four very dangerous hours in which I would be able to torture myself with all the possible disasters which could befall Louis' first visit with my family.

I knew in all likelihood my family would love him. Charlie would bond with him over their shared love of fixing cars, my mom would be entranced by his stories of growing up in France and Zoe would enjoy discussing the nuances of French cuisine. Everyone would have a wonderful time getting to know each other. If I were being truly honest with myself, the root of my worry was my father.

My father's main concern was that his children were happy. He had spent a great deal of time, energy and love ensuring this took place. And you had to hand it to him— he had raised six children, so he had put forth a lot of effort. Clearly, everything had happened very quickly for Louis and me and my father just wanted to confirm that I was making the right decision in marrying him. He had seen me get hurt far too many times for his taste and would do anything in his power to prevent it from happening again. What really worried me was exactly what he might do or say if he believed Louis did not genuinely care for me.

I was well aware that Crazy Sydney had now taken over

the party, but she was rather hard to get rid of. As I made my way back to the gate, I had a sinking feeling in my stomach. Louis was the first man I had ever truly loved. I knew with absolute certainty I wanted to spend the rest of my life with him. What was I going to do if my family didn't feel the same way?

I heard Louis call my name. I had gotten so lost in my thoughts, I had passed our gate. I walked back to the gate and put my arms around his neck. Nuzzling into him always made me feel better.

"What is bothering you, *mon coeur*?" he asked with concern in his eyes. "You look....sad."

I sighed. "I'm fine. I was wondering what you'll think of my family."

"I thought you were concerned about what they will think of me," he said innocently.

"I'm wondering about both of those things," I confessed.

He kissed me tenderly on the tips. "It is going to be fine. Stop worrying about your father. He is not going to scare me off."

I shook my head in amazement. "You really know me, don't you?"

"Yes, I do. And I still love you." He chuckled at his clever joke.

I swatted him on the behind. "Way to ruin the moment, Bluey."

Just then we heard the announcement for the boarding of our flight to New York. Louis looked over at me and took my hand.

"Are you ready, *mon coeur*?"

I took a deep breath. "Doubtful, but we don't have a choice. Let's do this."

Boarding the plane was a painfully slow process, which did nothing to calm my nerves. There were many screaming, overtired children accompanied by their harried parents who were given early passage to the plane to allow extra time for them to settle. When we finally got to our seats, I wondered if I would feel better if I screamed along with them. Granted, no one would allow me the courtesy of looking the other way and trying to ignore my tantrum. You lost that right when you turned seven or eight.

After an hour of trying to keep myself calm with magazines, I decided to order a glass of wine. Louis had fallen asleep promptly following takeoff (he had forced himself to stay awake until then so he could hold my hand) and was quietly snoring against the window. I was glad at least one of us was getting some rest. I hadn't slept much last night and was hoping the wine might ease me into a much-needed nap.

The wine was pretty gross, but since it provided me with a degree of calm I so desperately craved, I ordered another glass. As I sipped the wine, I idly flipped through the channels on the in-flight entertainment system, searching for something to take my mind off the worry. Unfortunately for me, Crazy Sydney was still in residence. The wine had gotten her to quiet down a little bit, but not enough to allow me a modicum of relaxation. A little more wine might help...

"Syd? Sydney, can you hear me?" Why was Louis shaking me? And more importantly, why did my head feel so heavy?

I opened my eyes to find an unnecessarily bright light flooding the room. I immediately winced and closed my eyes.

"What's going on, Louis?" The sound of my voice seemed much too loud. Something was terribly, *terribly* wrong.

Louis spoke very slowly and carefully. "I woke up right before the plane landed. You were passed out next to me."

Upon hearing this, I sat bolt upright, which was a *huge* mistake. The amount of pain that surged through my body and ended up in my head was indescribable. For a moment, I thought I was going to hurl, but thankfully I was spared that humiliation. I wasn't sure I would continue to be this lucky, so my goal immediately became changing locations.

I opened my eyes and scanned the room. It appeared to be some kind of exam room. How had we gotten off the plane? *Oh my God.* I had a *really* bad feeling about this. Slowly, some rather unsavory memories permeated my mind. *No.* I couldn't have been that stupid. *Sydney! What have you done?*

My eyes frantically searched for Louis and found him sitting in a chair next to me. "Um...Louis, how did we get here?"

He bit his lip. This was a bad sign. He only did that when he had something extremely unpleasant to tell me.

"You were put on a stretcher," he said quietly. "The EMT's couldn't wake you, so you had to be taken off the plane as quickly as possible."

I wrung my hands anxiously. I had done some pretty embarrassing things in my time, but this incident was now number one on my list. God help me if Maya ever found out. She would hold this over me for the rest of my life.

"The good news is you have been cleared to go home. We should go down to the baggage compartment now. They are holding our luggage."

I stared at Louis in horror. "How long have we been here?"

He dropped his gaze to the floor. "About two hours."

*Crap!* My parents were supposed to meet us at airport. They must have freaked out when we didn't show up! I frantically searched for my purse so I could call them and tell them not to worry. How could I have done this?

Louis took my hand. "Calm down, Syd. I have already called your parents to let them know we are fine."

I buried my face in my hands. "What did you tell them?"

"What could I tell them? I told them the truth." A small chuckle escaped him.

When I removed my hands from my eyes, Louis was desperately trying not to laugh. The amount of anger I felt at that moment was astronomical. I gradually stood up, felt completely nauseated and promptly sat back down. With no other viable options, I settled for fixing my deadliest glare on him. I was fully prepared to tear him a new one when the floodgates opened and he dissolved into hysterical laughter. I was so shocked, I didn't know how to react. I just sat there, watching him completely lose his composure and wondered what I was supposed to be feeling.

For the moment, my anger won out. "Louis! How could you tell them what really happened? You're supposed to protect me! Even when I do stupid things...*especially* when I do stupid things! You were supposed to cover for me. My parents must be so worried!"

Louis pulled himself together long enough to tell me not to worry. "Syd, your parents are not worried. Your mother wants to take you home so you can rest. And your father....your father...." The laughter was bubbling up once more. "He....what is it you always say? *He laughed his ass off.*"

And that was it. Louis laughed so hard, he fell onto the floor. That was my fiancé; the man laughing on the floor of the airport infirmary because his lovely bride-to-be couldn't hold her liquor. In all the scenarios I had imagined with regards to Louis meeting my family, this had never crossed my mind. It seemed no matter how old you got, you could still shock the hell out of yourself.

"Okay, Louis, I think it's time to get you out of here." I rose cautiously from the cot. The room swayed a little bit and I sank back down involuntarily.

"Don't worry, Syd. I got you a wheelchair." He gestured to the huge brown contraption in the corner of the room. It even had a long pole with a bright red flag shooting out of the top of one of the handles.

I closed my eyes and exhaled for a count of five. "Great."

Louis helped me into the wheelchair and handed me my

purse. "Are you ready, *mon coeur*?"

I peeked up at him. "To face the endless humiliation my father will heap on me for this? Not really, but at least it will distract him from grilling you for a little while."

It was then I realized some good would actually come from this situation. I felt like complete shit and I had embarrassed myself within an inch of my life, but if it meant that Louis' first time meeting my parents would be easier for him, then it was worth it. I had essentially sacrificed my dignity for him. Though it probably would have meant more to Louis if I had done it on purpose...

My parents were waiting in the car outside the baggage claim exit. I would later find out the airport police gave them a break since they had been waiting for nearly three hours due to my, um, medical issue. When they saw us, they both got out of the car quickly. The difference in their facial expressions was almost comical. My mother looked extremely worried and my father had an enormous grin on his face. Something about this juxtaposition struck me as horribly funny and I fell into fits of giggles. As soon as I started, my father and Louis joined in. My poor mother didn't know what to do; she probably thought that we had all lost our minds.

Once we reached the car, I slowly got up from the wheelchair. My mom came over and hugged me gingerly.

"Are you all right, honey?" The concern in her eyes made me instantly regret my burst of laughter.

I smiled. "I'm fine, Mom. I'm so sorry for worrying you."

"Duck! You always know how to make an entrance." I turned to find my dad reaching out to hug me. I threw myself into his arms. I had really missed him, even if he was about to make my life a living hell.

"Thanks, Dad. You always know just what to say." I pulled back to face him and grinned. "Now come and meet Louis."

I introduced my parents to Louis and everyone was

silent for a moment. Then my dad turned to Louis and slapped him on the back.

"Well, now that you're engaged to our daughter, it's clear you have your hands full, isn't it, Louis? Why don't we get you something to eat so you can keep your strength up?"

My mom smacked my dad on the back of the head and did her best not to smile. "Ted, that was *appalling*!"

Louis grinned at them both. "It is a task I am happy to take on. She makes it more than worth it to me."

My mom linked her arm through his. "I think I'm going to love you, Louis."

After he got my mom settled in the car, Louis helped my dad with the luggage. They were already smiling and chatting like they were old friends. As we drove away from the airport, I thought about how different this initial meeting was than I had imagined. Oddly enough, it actually turned out to be pretty positive, despite my mortifying display of drunkenness on the airplane. It reminded me very much of my relationship with Louis—completely unexpected, but perfect in its own way.

## Chapter Thirty

The next morning, I woke to find only a slight ache in my head. Thanks to my dad's hangover remedy (which smelled *and* tasted like tar), I felt almost normal. The remedy came with a price though. During each of my father's day-before-Thanksgiving phone calls to his friends, he recounted my drunken airplane adventure in painfully accurate detail. Since there was no volume control on my father, there was no location in the house to escape reliving my humiliating experience.

I was sitting in the kitchen drinking a cup of tea when my mother came in to begin her Thanksgiving dinner prep. We had a massive amount of cooking and baking ahead of us, which meant my father would have plenty of time to grill Louis. I was glad the two of them had been getting along so well, but I wasn't fooled. I knew my dad would pull out all the stops to assess Louis' true intentions toward me. Never mind the fact that we were *engaged*. There was no way my father would stop until he was satisfied. I fervently hoped Louis had the strength to withstand the barrage of questions coming his way.

"Sydney Bennett, what are you thinking about? You look so serious." She smoothed my hair away from my face.

"Oh, I was just wondering what Dad plans to put Louis through today." The possibilities were endless.

She shook her head. "Don't you worry, honey. Louis can handle anything your father has in his arsenal."

I grinned. "Do you really think so?"

"I know so!" she exclaimed. "Now let's get started on these pies."

The rest of the day passed by in a haze. There were far too many pie crusts, pans of stuffing and turkey parts. I had also prepared innumerable vegetables and appetizer trays. I was so busy, I didn't have time to think about poor Louis. I started to wonder if this was my mother's plan. She could be quite crafty when it came to her children.

After we put the last tray in the refrigerator, my father and Louis came in through the back door. I didn't even know they had left the house. I started to panic as I thought of all the horrible places my dad could have taken Louis. The crazy butcher shop with questionable items hanging from the ceiling and the faint odor of entrails, the gym where my dad likes to go to "swim" (watch the local women's' college swim team practice) or the worst possibility of all—the senior center. I shuddered in horror as I thought about my father lining up all his friends to interrogate Louis about every aspect of his background in an attempt to catch him in a lie. Nick had barely made it out alive five years ago...

I slapped a smile on my face and ran into Louis' arms.

"How was your day, *mon coeur*?" he asked, grinning from ear to ear.

I kissed him quickly on the lips. "I doubt I worked as hard as you did. Where did you two go today?"

My father cleared his throat. "Don't forget that fathers need love too, Duck." He gave me his sad eyes for good measure.

I walked over to my dad and hugged him. "I'm sorry, Dad. I only wanted to make sure you didn't put Louis through too much on his first day here."

Louis laughed. "You have no need to worry, Syd. I had a great time! Your dad is *hilarious*."

My dad patted Louis on the back fondly. "This kid has a great sense of humor. They loved him down at the center."

*Crap.* That was the worst option. I examined Louis closely. He seemed to be fine, but it was quite possible he had some horror stories to tell me later. Louis was too much of a gentleman to tell me about any misdeeds in front of my parents.

My mom came over to kiss my dad and Louis hello. "So, where did you boys have lunch?"

"I took Louis to the deli and Charlie met us there," my dad replied innocently.

*What?!* I thought Charlie was going to meet Louis *tomorrow.* They tag teamed him behind my back. Of all the devious things to do!

I narrowed my eyes at my father. "Whose idea was that, Dad?"

"Charlie and I thought it would be nice to get to know Louis in a more *intimate* setting. There will be so many people at dinner tomorrow and he deserves our undivided attention."

I frowned. "You're far too sneaky for your own good, old man."

"Do not worry, Syd," Louis soothed. "We had a great time." He came over and rubbed my back. "Charlie is great. He was telling me about this old BMW he plans to restore. It is too bad we live so far away, I would love to help him."

I searched Louis' beautiful blue eyes for any source of distress, but he seemed truly content. I smiled begrudgingly at my father.

"I took great care of him, Duck! After lunch we went to the gym and then to Vic's to pick up the meat for tomorrow's appetizers."

*Dear God.* He had hit all three appalling possibilities. Well, my dad was never one to hide anything. He made no

apologies for who he was and what he enjoyed doing.
Judging by the smile on Louis' face, he had enjoyed his day
with my dad. I decided to preserve the moment and keep
my mouth shut.

"It sounds like you boys have had quite the busy
afternoon," my mom said. "Are you ready for dinner?"

Dinner turned out to be at my mom's favorite Italian
restaurant. My dad always took her out the night before
Thanksgiving as a thank you for all the work she put in that
day—and to give his palate a taste of something different
before days and days of turkey and stuffing. The four of us
had a lovely dinner together and I slowly started to relax.
Louis and my parents were enjoying getting to know each
other and I was grateful.

On Thanksgiving morning, I woke up at five am with
my mother to help her get the turkey in the oven. I enjoyed
having this time alone with her, especially since the rest of
the day would be completely insane. As we sat on the living
room couch with our mugs of tea, my mom turned to me
with bright eyes.

"You're one lucky woman, Sydney Bennett!" The grin
on her face was obscenely large.

"Mom! You look like a crazy person." I giggled. "You
really like him, don't you?"

She nodded. "I *really* do. He's kind, intelligent, very
funny and most importantly, he loves you sincerely."

I was overjoyed that she saw him as I did and tears
quickly sprang to my eyes. I put my tea down and snuggled
up to her.

"Thanks, Mom. Your opinion means a lot to me." I
sniffled. "Has Dad shared his...*thoughts* with you?"

She laughed. "Your father won't admit it yet, but he likes
Louis as much as I do. He feels it's his responsibility to put
him through the paces, you know, test his stamina."

"Why does he feel the need to do that?" I asked.

"Because you're his little girl," she responded softly. "You kids mean the world to him. He just wants to be sure that the man you marry is worthy of you."

"I'm grateful that you married him, Mom," I murmured. "He's the most wonderful father anyone could ever have."

She hugged me tightly. "Indeed, he is. We're very lucky to have him in our lives." She sighed. "But don't tell him that. His ego barely fits in this house as it is."

As we chuckled our hearts out, I wondered what I had been so worried about. My family had more than welcomed Louis, they had found a place for him.

Seven hours later, I remembered what I had been so worried about. Appetizers were in full swing and I was trapped in the kitchen with my mother preparing the next course. Louis was in the living room with the rest of the family and I was dying to be part of the conversation. On my few trips out to distribute more *hors d'oeuvres,* I could see my aunt and cousins circling him like vultures. I wished I could be out there to protect him and hoped Charlie and Zoe would do that for me. My aunt had made a sport out of humiliating any member of my family, but I was her favorite target. She was definitely going to work the green card angle with Louis.

After another hour, I was freed from the kitchen. I practically raced over to Louis and put my arms around him. I felt an instant sense of calm when he kissed the top of my head and rubbed my shoulders.

"You must be tired, *mon coeur.* You and your mother have been quite busy for the past couple of days."

"It was all worth it," I answered, grinning at my future husband. "Um, how has it been going out here?"

He chuckled. "Charlie introduced me to everyone and then he and Zoe kept me company. He seemed particularly adamant about keeping me away from your aunt."

I searched the room for my brother and found him sitting with my father and Zoe. This would be the perfect place to sit and relax for a few minutes. We were going to need to build up our strength to get through the marathon of questions at dinner. I took Louis by the hand and led him to their safe haven.

Zoe jumped up and hugged me as soon as we were in close proximity "I love him," she whispered. "He's everything you described and *more*."

I smiled. "Thanks, Zoe. I'm thrilled to hear you approve."

"Don't forget about your big brother, Sydie." Charlie was waiting for me with open arms.

I hurried into them, just as I did when I was six years old. I loved my big brother to pieces and would always worship the ground he walked on. After I had nearly squeezed the life out of him, I pulled back and glared at him.

"You sneaky bugger! When exactly did you and Dad plot to interrogate Louis over lunch yesterday?" I surveyed him with mock horror.

Charlie laughed. "You know it was Dad's idea. My job was to protect your fiancé."

Zoe put her arms around Charlie's waist. "That's because I threatened to withhold unless he took care of your interests, Syd."

Louis and I both erupted into howls of laughter. The holidays always reminded me how much I missed Charlie and Zoe. I really hated living across the country from them—and from my parents. I had to figure out a way to get us all on the same coast. This meant I would somehow have to convince Louis, Kate and Nick to move back east because Charlie was just as bad as my father when it came to expressing the horrors of California.

Thankfully, dinner wasn't as difficult as I had imagined it would be. I had a sneaking suspicion my parents had developed a plan with Charlie and Zoe for keeping invasive questions at bay. Every time my aunt or one of my cousins tried to bring up the topic of our short courtship or the possibility of a green card marriage either my parents or Charlie changed the subject.

They had such an effective system going that my aunt eventually gave up. She definitely enjoyed the game of humiliation, but she didn't want to have to work too hard to reap results. In the end, she and her children left shortly after dessert and I found myself relaxing in the living room with my father and Charlie while Zoe and Louis helped my mother clean up the colossal mess from dinner.

As usual, my father was lying in his recliner rubbing his stomach. Charlie laughed and slapped him on the knee. "Did you eat too much again, Dad?"

My father closed his eyes and shook his head. "You know I can't resist your mother's pies. I had to sample a little of each."

I raised my eyebrows. "A little? You're the reason we had to make *two* apple pies, Dad! Otherwise no one else would get to have any."

My father feigned offense. "Once again, you exaggerate the situation. California has definitely made you more dramatic, Duck."

Charlie shook his head. "She's always been this dramatic, Dad, but don't worry, she has Louis now. He'll be able to ground her. I have faith in him."

I gawked at Charlie. "*What?*"

"Seriously, Syd, I really like him," Charlie said. "I think you made an excellent choice."

"Thank you, Charlie," I replied. "I thought you two would get along well."

My father cleared his throat. "Do any other opinions matter?"

"Yes, Dad, of course they do," I said, hiding my eye roll. "What do you think?"

He stared me straight in the eye and drawled, "I think he could do better." Then he started to laugh. My dad certainly enjoyed nothing more than being a smart-ass. He felt it was his responsibility to make our lives as difficult as we apparently made his life when we were children.

I nodded. "Thanks, Dad. I'll be sure to relay your

thoughts to Louis."

"Stop being so serious, Duck!" He threw his hands in the air in frustration. "He's a great kid and your mother and I are happy you've found each other." His smile showed me just how earnest he was.

I got up and gave him a hug. "Your opinion means even more," I whispered.

My dad held me for a long moment and when he let me go, I saw tears in his eyes. It must have been bittersweet for him to see his youngest child getting married. At least now he could rest assured that I had found a worthy man to share my life with. He was getting far too old to be able to carry out the threat of bodily harm to rogue suitors.

Following this happy thought, Louis, Zoe and my mother came into the room, laughing as though they had shared a great joke.

"How is everyone out here?" my mom asked.

After another round of applause for her incredible cooking, I said, "We're great, Mom. Dad was telling me how much he likes Louis."

Louis grinned. "The feeling is mutual, Mr. Bennett." He turned to the rest of my family. "I wanted to thank you for welcoming me into your home. I have felt so lucky since the day I met Sydney and now that I have met all of you, I feel even luckier."

My mom looked like she was going to cry. She hugged Louis quickly and went off, I suspected, to find a tissue. My dad shook Louis' hand, said something gruffly that I couldn't hear and followed her.

Charlie turned to Louis. "Nice job! You know how to clear a room."

Zoe smacked Charlie in the stomach. "Charlie! He might not know you're joking!"

"Do not worry, Zoe," Louis replied merrily. "I know Charlie pretty well already. We seem to think alike."

Zoe eyed the two of them skeptically and then turned to me. "Syd, I think we have a serious problem. These two are going to be big trouble."

"Uh, *yeah!*" I cried. I knew I would be the butt of many a joke from these two in the future, but ultimately, I was happy to see Charlie and Louis getting along so well.

"It sounds like you young people are having too much fun in here." My father came in carrying a bottle of champagne followed by my mother carrying six glasses.

Charlie whistled. "You brought out the good stuff. What are we celebrating?"

Zoe stared at him like he was crazy. "Your sister's engagement?"

He pulled Zoe into his arms. "*Oh, yeah.* I knew something important was going on here." He smiled and kissed her on the nose.

My dad smacked Charlie on the back of the head. "There will be plenty of time for that later. Now is the time to focus on your sister."

Charlie straightened his posture. "*Yes, sir.*"

I took a deep breath. My dad's toasts were legendary—mostly for embarrassing the recipients. Zoe was still recovering from the toast he gave at their engagement party nine years ago. No one had been particularly interested in hearing about my brother's escapades in college. Charlie's run in with the campus police and physical descriptions of his girlfriends before Zoe were simply not suitable for such an occasion. I knew it was my father's version of humor, but I really didn't think Zoe's grandmother appreciated the level of detail he gave. (His descriptions were surprisingly vivid.)

I closed my eyes and said a silent prayer for him to keep it clean. The myriad of inappropriate topics he could bring up flashed before my eyes. I had told Louis most of the compromising moments from my past, but I had no desire to relive them in front of my family for my father's enjoyment. The only thing I could take comfort in was that my father was unaware of the worst offenses...

The pop of the champagne cork brought me back to

reality. I locked eyes with Louis, hoping that everyone's good humor would hold through whatever revelations took place. I had a tendency to overreact (*just a little*) when I was teased sufficiently.

My mother handed me a glass of champagne. "Syd, he promised me he would keep it short and sweet."

I smiled cautiously. "Did you ask him not to embarrass me?"

"There's only so much I can do, honey."

*Lovely.* Well, at least Louis had already agreed to marry me. *And* he had already seen me behave like a nut on more than one occasion and still loved me. What could my father possibly say to change that? I was probably overreacting. Again.

My father cleared his throat and surveyed his audience while we waited patiently for him to begin. The expression on my face had to have been a mix of embarrassment, resignation and sheer terror all rolled into one. My father took one look at me and burst into laughter.

"Relax, Duck. I'll keep it brief." He grinned and turned to Louis. "Louis, we're all grateful you've come into our lives. I've never seen Sydney this happy and I'm overjoyed that the two of you have decided to spend the rest of your lives together. Welcome to the family."

My mother beamed and raised her glass. "To Sydney and Louis."

Everyone else followed her lead. I stared at my father in disbelief. He had let me off far too easily. Was he saving the truly embarrassing toast for a more public occasion, like *our wedding*?! I would have to kill him if this were the case. Having my father trot out my most questionable decisions for all our family and friends to analyze was *not* part of the plan for my perfect wedding day.

Just as we clinked our glasses, my father turned to Louis and said, "Make sure to cut off her access to liquor after the second drink. You'll save yourself a world of trouble."

And there it was. *Thanks, Dad.* He even had the nerve

to glance over and wink at me. Leave it to my father to end the evening with his perverse sense of humor.

The remainder of our visit in New York was relatively uneventful and for this, I felt quite fortunate. Zoe and Charlie had us over for dinner the night after Thanksgiving and we finally had an opportunity to relax. Zoe and I were able to catch up and Charlie and Louis talked about everything from world news to car parts. I took my mother Christmas shopping on Saturday while my father educated Louis on his knife collection. My father had over five hundred knives, so it was a very, very long—not to mention unnerving—day for Louis. He bore the entire visit surprisingly well. It seemed my fiancé could deal with just about anything.

As we rode to the airport in the backseat of my parents' car, I put my head on Louis' shoulder and sighed. He kissed the top of my head and asked, "Did you have a good time, *mon coeur?*"

I gazed up at him and smiled. "It was perfect."

He laughed and squeezed my hand. I was a little startled to discover that my definition of perfect was evolving.

# Chapter Thirty-One

The month of December went by in a blur and the new year arrived swiftly. I had used my remaining vacation time over the holidays to conduct some serious wedding planning. I reviewed the catering menus for our wedding venue and selected dishes for our tasting session, researched several options for our honeymoon, had my first dress fitting and chose a dress for my bridesmaids. I had no idea going into this experience that choosing this dress would be *much* harder than choosing my wedding dress.

Everyone had a different idea on style, color, etc. and Kate was the only one who seemed to care about my opinion. In fact, Maya was still trying to convince me that her choice of a red satin strapless mini dress was much more alluring than the plum off-the-shoulder knee-length dress I had chosen. After a lengthy argument, I pointed out that I had intended the dresses to be sophisticated—*not* alluring—and if she had any sense she would remember this was *my* wedding and she should shut her mouth. Apparently, Bridezilla Sydney had no problem coming out when pushed.

In the midst of all the wedding planning, Louis and I were able to have a nice quiet Christmas. Since it would be Kate's last chance to travel before the baby was born, she and Nick decided to head back to the east coast to visit our parents. It was a little strange not being with my parents or siblings for the holidays, but it was nice to introduce Louis to my family's favorite Christmas traditions. We trimmed our beautiful Christmas tree, baked gingerbread cookies, watched *Holiday Inn* and *The Sound of Music* and dined on roast beef and Yorkshire pudding on Christmas Day.

Going back to work was difficult after having so much time off, but I was looking forward to catching up with my boss and coworkers. I was going to have to wait until next week to do this in person though, since my boss was sending me to a five day training on our new employee database software. Before I left, I reminded Louis that I would be in downtown San Jose for the week and would only be reachable on my cell phone. He told me he had meetings all morning and would check in with me in the afternoon.

The morning passed fairly quickly as my brain attempted to absorb all the features of the new benefit tracking system. I was thankful when our morning break arrived since my eyes were burning from two hours of staring at a computer screen. I quickly ran to the bathroom and then checked my cell phone for messages. Oddly enough, there was one from Louis. Perhaps he had finished his meetings early?

From the moment I heard his voice, I knew something was wrong. While he simply asked me to call him back, his voice was...strained. It lacked his usual warmth and genial tone. I tried to remember if he had told me about any difficult projects coming up for him at work, but couldn't come up with anything. I had a sinking feeling that whatever the issue was, it was really, *really* bad.

I dialed Louis' work number and noticed my hands were shaking. He picked up on the first ring.

"*Mon coeur*, I am so glad that you called."

I cut to the chase. "Are you okay, Bluey?"

He hesitated. The anticipation was killing me. What happened? Did someone die? It was so unusual for Louis to be this concerned about anything. I couldn't wait any longer.

"Louis! What's going on? You have me really worried."
*Honestly, Syd, like that's so unusual!* I knew I shouldn't have
pressured him, but something was seriously wrong and I
needed for him to get to the point as quickly as possible.

"Syd, I got some bad news this morning."

He sounded absolutely awful. Somebody must have
died. *Oh my God!* We were going to have to go back to
France for a funeral. And I still hadn't signed up for French
lessons. I wasn't prepared to meet his family. They were
going to think I was crazy! *Okay, Sydney, this thought process is
wrong on so many levels.* Reel yourself back in. I took a deep
breath and attempted to calm my frazzled nerves.

"What happened?!" My voice was much shriller than I
had intended.

"I lost my job," he said softly. "My company had a large
scale layoff and my position was eliminated."

*What?* I wasn't expecting that. I closed my eyes and
took yet another deep breath.

"I'm so sorry, Bluey." I frowned. It seemed rather
strange for him to lose his job only a few months after he
had been transferred to the US. It was going to be hard for
him to find another job on a visa, but at least he had a little
time to figure it out.

Louis was oddly silent on the other end of the line. I
started to wonder if something else had happened. He was
never this quiet.

"Louis, is something else wrong?"

He cleared his throat. "Well, you could say that. I just
found out that my company had me on a J-1 visa, not an L-
1 visa, as I had thought. In addition, I have discovered since
we earn three year college degrees in France rather than four
year degrees, I may not qualify for an H1-B visa."

I didn't like where this was going. Immigration was one
of the functions I handled for my company, so I was
alarmingly familiar with all the options.

"I have thirty days to figure this out or I will have to

leave the country."

My head was spinning. I stared at the ceiling and willed myself not to scream. I was in a public place and felt no desire to let everyone here know how insane I was.

"Okay, there's no need to panic," I said calmly. Yes, I saw the irony in this statement coming from me. "The safest thing to do is to get married." *Did I just say that?*

"Syd, I..."

"Louis! Do you know how long I've waited for you? Seriously, you took *forever* to come into my life. I dated a parade of total losers while I was waiting for you to show up and it wasn't fun. I'll be damned if I'm going to let some stupid visa issue keep you from me for even a day." *Holy crap!* My backbone was here to stay.

He chuckled robustly. *There was my Louis!* "You are an amazing woman, Sydney Bennett."

"I know," I replied. "You tell me often enough."

"How did I get to be so lucky?"

I shook my head. The poor man still had no idea of the degree of crazy he had been saddled with. "You must have been a saint in a former life. Now, down to business. We'll go to city hall tomorrow, apply for a license and be married by the end of the week."

"But what about all the wedding plans? You have gone through a lot of effort...and it is everything you have dreamed of for so long."

"Don't be silly! We'll still have the wedding in Monterey. What does it matter if we're technically already married? It just means we won't have any jitters that day." This really wasn't such a bad plan after all.

"So instead of having two weddings, we are going to have three," Louis said matter-of-factly.

I slapped my palm to my forehead. "Yes, I suppose we will. Three weddings to the same man, Bluey! I may as well change my name to Elizabeth Taylor." Then I remembered even Elizabeth Taylor only married the same man twice.

"You realize I have no idea what you mean, right?"

I giggled. "Don't worry, Bluey, I'm just having one of my moments. It'll pass."

I noticed the trainer signaling everyone back inside. How the hell was I going to concentrate on software at a time like this?

"Louis, our training session is starting up again, so I have to go. I'll call you during our lunch break, okay?"

"Okay, *mon coeur*. I love you," he murmured. He still sounded so sad.

"I love you too. Please don't worry, Bluey. Everything is going to be fine."

After I hung up with Louis, I picked up my purse and started walking to the training room. With each step I took, the realization that I was going to have to get married in the next thirty days or send my fiancé back to France hit me right between the eyes. I had to call Kate. She would be able to talk me down from this ledge. I desperately hoped she didn't decide to pull an "I told you so" out of her arsenal. This just wasn't the moment.

I walked back to the lounge area and dialed Kate's cell phone. Thankfully, she picked up right away.

"Hey, Syd! How—"

"Kate!" I interrupted. There was no time for niceties. We had a true crisis on our hands. "I'm sorry to cut you off, but I'm really and truly freaking out here. This is *not* a drill. *I can't breathe.*"

"Sydney, you need to relax," she ordered. "I'm sure it's not as big of a deal as you think."

"Well, Kate, this is one instance in which you're *wrong*. I know this must come as a huge shock to you, because you're *never* wrong, but here we are." I exhaled very slowly. "I'm getting married."

Kate laughed. "*Duh*! What have we been planning for? Seriously, Syd. You need to take a break."

"No, you don't understand." My voice must have gone up five octaves. "I'm getting married, like, *tomorrow*." Okay, so it was a bit of an exaggeration, but I tended to do that under pressure.

The other end of the phone was silent.

"*Did you hear me, Kate?!*"

"Syd, what happened?" she asked, keeping her tone even. "You're clearly leaving out some vital information here."

"I'm sorry! I guess in my total freak-out, I forgot to make sense! Because I usually make so much sense, *right?!*" I was dangerously close to a meltdown of epic proportions. I put my head between my knees and took a few deep breaths. In the process, I dropped the phone.

"Syd? Are you all right? What's going on?" Her voice had an edge of hysteria to it that I wasn't used to hearing.

*Pull yourself together, Sydney!* You freaked out your poor pregnant sister.

I grabbed the phone and said, "I'm sorry for scaring you." I paused, doing my best to calm down. "Louis was laid off, which means he no longer has a visa, which means that either we get married immediately or he'll be deported."

Kate gasped. "Holy crap! What are you going to do? Are you sure this is your only option?"

I took a shaky breath. "From what I can tell, it *is* our only option. I thought his company had him on an L-1, but they somehow put him on a J-1, which doesn't make sense, like *at all*, and he most likely won't qualify for an H1-B due to the difference in the French education system—"

"Why are you speaking in acronyms?!" she interrupted. "Speak English, please!"

I shook my head in another vain attempt to clear it. I didn't know why I bothered. It never worked.

"Sorry! I was talking about his visa. I won't bog you down in the details, but the bottom line is due to the way his company filed his visa, there's no viable option for him to stay in the country through employer sponsorship at this point." I leaned my head against the wall. "If we don't get married soon, then he'll have to leave the country."

"Okay, Syd, this isn't what you planned, but you'll make

it work, right? You two will get married this week at city hall and you'll have the wedding you've always dreamed of in September," she declared matter-of-factly. "And then you'll get married again in October..."

"It sounds crazy, doesn't it?" I chuckled softly.

"It's, um, *unusual*, but Louis is definitely worth it."

I closed my eyes and smiled. "Yes, he is. I would do anything for him."

"As he would for you, Syd." She sniffled. *Uh oh.* The hormones had been engaged. *Think, Sydney, think!*

"Thank you for pulling me back from the edge, Kate. I know it's a lot to ask of you in your heightened emotional state." I knew I might have played right into the hormones, but it was the best I could do in my impaired state.

She laughed. *Phew.* "You're definitely worth it. I love you, Syd."

"I love you too, Kate." I paused. "I now have the unpleasant task of calling our parents and asking them to fly out here to witness my wedding in city hall."

"Oooh, I had forgotten about that. May the Force be with you, Syd."

I grimaced. "Thanks. I'll fill you in later."

I hung up with Kate and immediately dialed my mother's store before I lost my nerve. My father, of course, picked up on the second ring.

"Duck! To what do I owe the honor of your call in the middle of a work day?" He sounded very happy to hear from me. That probably wouldn't last for much longer. I was getting really tired of calling him with questionably good news.

I sighed, completely resigned to my fate. "Hi, Dad! Um, would you mind putting Mom on the phone? I'm afraid I have something to tell you both...again."

"Oy vey, Syd! Give me a second." He yelled for my mother to pick up the other phone. Thankfully, he covered the receiver this time.

"Hi, Sydney," my mom said cautiously. I didn't blame

her. I would be concerned too given my past history of phone calls.

"There's no easy way to say this, so I'm just going to tell you." I took a deep breath. "Louis was laid off from his job and if we don't get married within the next thirty days, he'll be deported."

"Shit!" my dad exclaimed. A perfect summation in my opinion.

"Oh honey, I'm so sorry," my mom murmured. "All that planning…"

"Don't worry, Mom. We're still going to have the wedding in September. I'm not giving up my dream wedding because of Louis' former company's oversight," I said firmly. "We're going down to city hall this week to get married."

"Well, at least Louis won't be deported." The disappointment in my mother's voice was overwhelming.

"Yes, and that's what's most important right now," I agreed. "But even if it isn't the real wedding, I would love it if you were both there. Is there any way you would consider flying out here? I know it's short notice, but…"

My mom didn't have to be asked twice. "You bet we'll be there! Right, Ted?"

My dad chuckled. "You sure keep things interesting, Duck. Of course we'll be there."

"You know, Sydney," my mom began, "as much fun as it would be for us to fly to California, would you consider flying here and getting married in New York?" She sounded really excited. "This way, your brother and Zoe would be there and all your friends from your childhood and, well, your father and I could have some friends come too."

*Ah*…this would allow them to have their friends attend our "wedding." I felt like I owed this to them given the fact that our second wedding (what?!) would be in California. Oh, and the third one would be in France. Was this becoming a bit ridiculous?

"Well, Mom, I would need to talk to Louis, but what

about Kate? I don't think she would ever forgive me if I got married—for the first time that is—without her. And it wouldn't feel right if she weren't there."

My mom started clicking her tongue—a sure sign she was thinking hard. "Okay, I'll check in with Kate. If her doctor won't allow her to fly, then we'll come to California. I'm sure Charlie and Zoe would love to come as well."

"It wouldn't be the same without them." I stopped to let it all sink in. "I can't believe I'm going to be '*Madame* Durand' in a week!"

"Well, I wouldn't brag about it, Duck. Are you sure you want to change your name? Bennett has such character."

I laughed. "You're too much, Dad, but I love you anyway. And I love you, Mom!" I glanced at my watch. "I have to run, but I'll call you later."

"Bye, Syd! We love you," my mom sang happily. She was a woman on a mission. If there was any way to make a wedding in New York happen, she would find it.

I hung up the phone and took a moment to catch my breath. I couldn't believe how quickly this had happened. It seemed like from the moment Louis and I met, everything had been in overdrive. And even though every step had scared the crap out of me, I felt no need to slow down. Somehow the pace was perfect.

# Chapter Thirty-Two

To my mother's great delight, not only had Louis agreed to her plan, but Kate had been cleared to fly to New York no later than the following week. Unfortunately, Louis' father had *not* been cleared to fly. He was scheduled to have liver surgery at the end of the month and his doctor didn't feel he was well enough to make the trip. Naturally, Louis' mother wanted to stay to take care of her husband, so Louis and I wouldn't be married in the presence of his parents. To make matters worse, none of Louis' extended family members would be able to come to the wedding on such short notice. My poor fiancé would be the only French person in attendance, surrounded by a sea of uncouth Americans.

Thankfully, my boss was kind enough to grant me a week off so we could carry out our last-minute plan. Louis and I planned to take the red-eye to New York the following Monday evening, apply for our marriage license on Tuesday and get married on Friday. This time frame would allow for ten days to plan a small reception. Well, it was supposed to be small, but it seemed to be growing by the minute. My parents kept adding people to the guest list who they absolutely *had* to invite for one reason or another.

Every time the phone rang with a change in the headcount, I cringed a little inside. Because of the rapid swell of the guest list, the reception went from being in my parents' home to the hotel where my high school prom was held. This bothered me on a number of levels, but that was a story for another time. And though this was going to be our *legal* wedding, it wasn't the one I wanted the majority of the world to see. But for the sake of my parents, I would simply have to grin and bear it.

As a result of our decision to get married in New York, I had the privilege of having phone calls from my mother several times a day with regards to the reception. I thought it only fair she be able to plan this one, since I was planning the reception in California and Louis' mom was planning the reception in France. It took every ounce of patience I had not to hang up on her after the fifth call of the day. The number of details my mother wanted my opinion on would have been enough to drive anyone crazy. However, for a bride who wasn't planning on getting married for another eight months, the threshold was a little...okay, *a lot*, lower. Add in the fact that I was a complete lunatic to begin with and you were just asking for trouble.

By the night before our flight to New York, I was ready to kill my mother. Each time she had called me (a whopping total of seventy-eight times in six days), I reminded her that I had given over all the decisions to her. Apparently, my father was no help to her as he would simply give her his opinion without any sort of discussion and Nick had cut off my mother's phone calls to his wife due to Kate's spiking stress levels. This meant I had to hold my mother's hand through every—and I do mean *every*—single detail of the reception.

I honestly had no interest in debating cream versus sage napkins, tulips versus lilies or chicken picatta versus beef wellington. I had to feign interest in each topic and fight every attempt to tell her I didn't consider this to be my real wedding. It wasn't that I didn't care, it was that I knew whatever she chose would be lovely. What irritated me the most was she didn't realize that I was currently experiencing a massive anxiety attack since I was getting married in a much shorter time frame than I had originally planned. (Why hadn't I been able to hold on to my idea of the perfect pace?)

In some ways, I was barely holding it together. Consequently, these lengthy discussions were becoming the bane of my existence. On the bright side, I finally understood what it must have been like for Louis during our wedding planning thus far. Although he was lucky enough to have these discussions over a four month period (with another eight to go), while I had to endure the equivalent number of conversations in the course of one week. Not to mention the fact that I had been *far* more reasonable than my mother...

Maya thought my mother's phone calls were completely hysterical and would call me every evening for a breakdown of the day. Part of me really wanted to kill her too, but I was touched that she was flying to New York to be there for our wedding *and* to help my mother with the reception. As far as I was concerned, once I arrived in New York, I would switch into full bride mode and didn't want to be bothered with problems of any kind. I figured Maya was going to be in hell for part of her visit, so I may as well indulge her curiosity now. I was well aware she wouldn't find the wedding discussions with my mother even remotely funny when she was in the middle of them. That was something *I* would find completely hysterical when the time came.

The day of our flight to New York was incredibly busy at work. I had three sexual harassment training seminars to give and these sessions always came with a myriad of questions. My brain was in overdrive by the end of the day and I was looking forward to relaxing on the plane. (No, I didn't plan on having any wine, thank you very much.) Louis had set me up with his laptop and my favorite romantic movies and I had a plethora of magazines for my amusement just in case sleep was elusive. I was going to do everything in my power to stay calm—and more importantly—to avoid an experience like the last time we flew to New York.

Before we left for the airport, I called to check in with Kate. She and Nick were flying to New York on Thursday in order to miss as much of the wedding craziness as they could without cutting things too close. As I dialed her cell phone, I thought about how Nick was doing everything in his power to be sure his wife was allowed to stay calm and well rested. The poor man looked like he needed someone to do the same for him.

"Hi, Syd!" Cheerful Kate was in residence! It seemed her hormones were off duty for the time being.

"Hi, Kate! How are you feeling?" I missed Cheerful Kate. She had been replaced lately by Tired Kate, Weepy Kate and Bitchy Kate. (You heard me.) I wasn't as fond of them as my sister, but as far as I was concerned, pregnant women got a free pass. I knew Cheerful Kate would come back to me for good someday.

"I feel great! My stomach has calmed down a lot and I've gotten some rest," she gushed. "You're so sweet to be worrying about me when you're about to get on a plane to New York and get married!"

"That's how much I love you, my dear." I took a deep breath. "I'm *nervous*."

"Of course you are! It's perfectly normal. Everything will be beautiful," she soothed.

"You're right. Mom has planned an amazing reception. There's nothing more I need to do."

She laughed. "Except buy your wedding dress! You're such a good daughter for waiting to shop with Mom."

"Well, she missed shopping for my real wedding dress, so I *had* to allow her the joy, even if it's on a smaller scale."

"It doesn't make you nervous that you're going to shop for the dress for your *first* wedding a mere three days before it takes place?"

Pregnant Kate could also be *mean*.

I bit my tongue. "It'll be fine."

She giggled. "I bet you'll find a lot of choices in the juniors department. Now's the time to shop for prom dresses!"

Uh huh. I had no response to that.

I decided to change the subject. "Louis picked up the rings today, so we're in good shape." We had selected matching plain platinum bands. I had initially thought about a band of diamonds, but given the fact that Louis didn't have employment, this wasn't the time to be extravagant.

"Will you take your band off before each future wedding?"

Nice, Kate. "I hadn't thought about it. Maybe I'll keep adding bands." Was there some kind of protocol? I honestly didn't know anyone else who had been through a similar situation. I guess I would have to figure it out as we went along. I glanced at the clock and realized I had run out of time to chat. I had a few things I wanted to do before we left for the airport and Louis would be home any minute.

"Well, Kate, it's time for me to go. The next time we see each other I'll be extremely close to becoming half French."

"You're *such* a goofball. Marrying him won't change the fact that you're a full-blooded American. And I wouldn't have it any other way. You'll make some cute half French babies though."

I winced. "Kate! It's way too soon for talk of babies. Let's get through the weddings first." There would be *three* of them, after all.

"I'm only teasing," she said, chuckling. "Have a wonderful flight! I love you, sweetie."

"I love you, too. I'll give you a call tomorrow. In the meantime, get some rest, okay? You and Nick both need some time to relax."

After I hung up with Kate, I closed my eyes and slowly breathed in and out. I kept trying to find a sense of calm, but the only thing I seemed to find was panic. One of these days I was going to have to find a way to rid myself of my neurotic tendencies once and for all. Attempting to diffuse them was absolutely exhausting.

⌒

To my great delight, the flight was completely uneventful this time. Once we landed, my parents took us to their favorite diner for breakfast and then we headed straight to the town hall to apply for our marriage license. We had already made our appointment for the ceremony on Friday, so all that was left was a trip to the mall for a very important purchase. Since Louis had already purchased his wedding suit in California, he and my father headed off to the nearest electronics store while my mom and I hit the department stores.

There was very little that interested me in Macy's or Bloomingdales, so we moved on to Nordstrom. The majority of the dresses were black and even I knew choosing one of these dresses would be extremely bad luck. I was so desperate, I even checked the juniors section, but everything was either extremely short, extremely bright or extremely bedazzled. I guess when you were a teenager even your clothes needed to be extreme.

I was beginning to lose hope entirely when I happened to notice a small boutique section in the corner near the lingerie department. The dresses were definitely more muted, but also more tasteful, so I allowed myself a modicum of excitement that I would finally find a suitable dress. I had really wanted my mother to be with me when I found the dress, but I began to think I was going to pay dearly for this desire and end up getting married in something my grandmother would have found fashionable. (There was a surprisingly large selection of sparkly pant suits.)

Nestled in the corner of the boutique was a gorgeous floor-length strapless gown. It was made of a pale gray raw silk and was both subtle and elegant—just the right degree of formal for my first wedding. Yes, it sounded crazy, but it was true. I fingered the delicate fabric with awe and tears filled my eyes knowing I would actually be a beautiful bride this time. I kept telling myself it didn't matter, that this was only for legal purposes and I had already found my true wedding dress, but I felt an instant sense of calm when I found this dress. And they had it in my size! Last minute alterations were possible given my mother's status as a master seamstress (I had rocked her dresses from elementary school through senior prom), but the added stress might be the end of her.

I called my mother over and showed her the dress. She agreed with me that it was *the* dress. After a quick confirmation in the dressing room of a perfect fit, we shopped for shoes and decided on a pair of delicate silver Mary Janes, my signature shoe, with three inch heels. This brought the hem of the dress just high enough so the skirt wouldn't brush the floor. After a celebratory tea, we met my father and Louis and headed back to my parents' house.

We only had two and a half days before the wedding and my mother still had a decent to-do list to tackle. Thankfully, Maya was taking the red-eye from California tonight. She was going to hold my mother's hand from her arrival until the wedding, thereby allowing me some time to get a grip on my sanity. I knew it was an impossible task, but I would rather spend the short time before the wedding in a spa than dealing with my mother's last minute tasks. I still had scars from the week before Kate's wedding...

Maya's arrival was exactly what my mother and I needed. She kept my mother busy and on task and she kept me on a beauty regimen which would reap amazing results—or so she promised. She had researched every salon and spa within a fifty mile radius of my parents' house and had made appointments for me with three of them for everything from full-body massages to seaweed wraps. I had been massaged, exfoliated, waxed, tweezed and scented in every possible way. Maya had somehow succeeded in pulling off the impossible. I felt totally relaxed. I hoped rather than believed I would be able to maintain this feeling through the wedding.

By the time Nick and Kate arrived, all the final details had been taken care of. The flowers had been selected, the menu had been finalized and the cake had been ordered. Maya had made appointments for herself, my mom, Kate, Zoe and me with our favorite local salon for the morning of the wedding to have our hair and nails done. Following this, Maya planned to do everyone's makeup right before the ceremony.

As we sat down for dinner that night, we breathed a collective sigh of relief. Everyone had made it to New York safe and sound, everything wedding-related had been taken care of and Louis and I would have a beautiful day to share with my family tomorrow. I felt awful knowing Louis' family wouldn't be with us, but tried to focus on the fact that Louis and Charlie were going to set up a webcam in the town hall so they could at least see the ceremony in real time. This was as close to perfect as we would be able to get for the time being.

## Chapter Thirty-Three

I woke up the next morning with a nervous stomach. Usually when this happened, I would just roll over, snuggle into Louis and instantly feel better. Unfortunately for me, my brother had kidnapped him last night. Zoe had insisted the bride and groom spend the night before the wedding apart and not see each other until the ceremony. I knew this was merely a superstition, but I felt inclined to trust a woman who had such a happy marriage. Sometimes the little things made all the difference. I also liked the heightened sense of anticipation we would experience from spending the night apart.

My mother took one look at me and made a cup of tea and a piece of toast to help settle my stomach. While I was sure this helped, she achieved better results by holding me in her arms and reminding me what an amazing man I was marrying. She stroked my hair and told me about the jitters she had felt the day she married my father. I closed my eyes and laughed as I thought about my eight-year-old self scarfing down nothing but brownies at their reception. I had only an inkling of my good fortune that day, when my father officially became my father, but became truly grateful in all the days following.

Maya arrived promptly at nine-thirty and whisked us off to the salon. She had bagels and pastries delivered so no one would have hunger pains during the long and arduous beautifying regimen. The woman was brilliant—a fact which she reminded me of often. Her gift of sustenance was exactly what everyone needed to rally together through the last few tasks before the impending wedding.

After our hair and nails had been done to perfection, we returned to my parents' house to dress and have our makeup artfully applied by a true master. Kate was kind enough to keep me company while Maya did Zoe's and my mother's makeup. My childhood bedroom had been set up as a waiting room since all the work took place in my mother's bedroom—the largest in the house. Maya insisted on space to allow her "creative genius" to be at its best.

Kate walked over, plopped herself down next to me on the bed and tapped me on the nose.

"How are you feeling, Syd?"

I smiled nervously. "Fabulous!"

She put her hand on mine and sighed. "You don't have to pretend for me. I'd be surprised if you *weren't* nervous. This is a big day, sweetie."

I took a shaky breath. "I know. And I *am* nervous. But I'm also really happy." I closed my eyes. "I just need to focus on that instead."

"Your hair looks amazing, Syd," she murmured. "Your dress is absolutely gorgeous. You'll look *perfect*."

I got up and walked over to the mirror. I had decided to wear my hair down this time, since I would wear my hair up for the next wedding. Big poofy white dresses with veils were definitely complimented by fancy updos, while my pale gray dress looked lovely with my hair in loose waves down my back.

Maya came up behind me and put her hands on my shoulders. "It's your turn, Syd. Are you ready?"

I turned to her, doing my best to seem confident. "Let's do this!"

"You're going to be a beautiful bride," she said, her eyes twinkling.

Maya was true to her word. She used a light foundation with a hint of shimmer, faint rose-colored blush, sparkly silver eye shadow, charcoal eyeliner, volumizing mascara and luscious red lipstick. The end result was breathtaking.

I gasped when I saw my reflection in the mirror. "Maya, I…" I couldn't find the words to express how I felt at that moment. I hugged her gently and whispered, "Thank you."

"Well, I did promise Louis a smokin' bride." She winked suggestively at me.

I burst into a fit of giggles. Maya often had just the right expression in her arsenal. "You're too much. And I love you for it."

My mother came bustling in with my garment bag and stopped dead in her tracks when she saw me. She beamed at me while tears glistened in her eyes.

"You look *gorgeous*, Sydney."

I felt myself starting to well up. "Thanks, Mom."

Maya cleared her throat. "May I please have everyone's attention?" Zoe came running in and the four of us focused on her with rapt attention.

"The ceremony is in less than an hour," she said with authority. "All we need to do is get Sydney dressed and accessorized. The main thing we need to do now is make sure she *does not cry*. Her makeup has been applied to perfection and it must stay that way at least until she walks down the aisle. Are we all clear?"

Everyone nodded. She stared at me pointedly. "Sydney?"

I nodded more vigorously. She held up her right index finger and pointed at me. "Absolutely *no* crying."

My mom laughed and took out my wedding dress. As I slipped it on over my numerous lacy undergarments (This was my first wedding night, after all.), I was happy to see it looked even more beautiful on me today than it had when I tried it on at the store. I was sure most of that was due to hair and makeup, but I could have sworn it was also a sort of glow. (Yes, I said it. I thought I had a bridal glow.)

After twirling with gusto, I surveyed the room for opinions. Every single one of them was welling up. It was unbelievably sweet, but it made it that much harder for me not to cry

My mother wiped the tears from her eyes (totally smearing her makeup) and walked over to me with a small jewelry pouch in her hands. She took out her diamond solitaire necklace and matching earrings. These pieces were only worn on *very* special occasions and I had looked forward to wearing them on my wedding day for a long time. I couldn't believe the day was finally here! *Hold it together, Sydney!* It was becoming progressively more difficult not to cry.

After my mom helped me put on the necklace and I managed to fasten the earrings with shaking hands, she considered my appearance.

"Something is missing, Syd." She frowned. "Your dress is your something new. The diamonds are your something old. The garter Maya gave you is your something blue, but what about your something borrowed?"

My eyes must have bugged out of my head. *How did I miss this? Was this bad luck?* Everything had happened so quickly and I was juggling so many things that I completely forgot! I could feel the sweat forming on the back of my neck and started to wrack my brain for something borrowed. Technically my mother's diamonds were old *and* borrowed But...could you do that? Was it okay to double dip on your "somethings" on your wedding day? I shook my head and decided it wouldn't be a good idea. I had to think of something else.

In a panic, I scanned the room for possibilities. I could borrow my mother's scarf! No, it would look ridiculous with my dress. Maybe I could stuff it in my bra? There was no rule which says anyone has to *see* it; simply having it on me was enough, right? No, the dress was tight enough as it was, I wouldn't be able to breathe. Or I could borrow Maya's shoes! She and I wore the same size! It didn't matter that she was wearing big black boots! My dress was really long, so people wouldn't be able to see much of my feet...

Kate giggled. "Stop panicking, Syd. I have it covered." She shook her head at my mother and walked toward me, holding up the white gold and diamond bracelet I had borrowed from her the night I had proposed to Louis. It was *perfect*.

I couldn't find my voice. I gazed up at her and smiled. She hugged me tenderly. "You make an absolutely beautiful bride."

I felt the tears coming and willed myself not to cry. It was close, but I was able to stem the tide. I reminded myself firmly that I couldn't cry until the ceremony—then all bets were off.

Kate placed the bracelet on my wrist just as my father came into the room. For a few seconds he was uncharacteristically speechless.

"Look at my little Duck! You're magnificent!"

I tried to clear the lump from my throat. "Thanks, Dad." I put my arms around him and whispered, "I'm so glad you're here."

He pulled out of the hug and gently took my face in his hands. "Never has a father been so lucky, Duck. You three were a gift."

Maya sighed. The level of emotion in the room was becoming far too high for her comfort level, not to mention that it was in danger of damaging all her hard work as the wedding's makeup artist. "Okay! Time to load up the cars, everyone!"

My mother helped me into my coat and handed me my bouquet. We had selected red roses with a generous dose of baby's breath. My mother had found gorgeous gray and crimson ribbons which she had fashioned around the stems. I smiled and wondered if there were anything my mom couldn't create beauty with. I took one last look in the mirror before we left. It was true that I looked pretty, but did I look like a bride? I shook my head in my usual clearing attempt. *Did it really matter?*

Ten minutes later, we were walking up the steps of the town hall. We gave our coats to my father and went to check out the main gallery, where the ceremony would be held. Kate and I walked in and my jaw dropped. I didn't expect the Ritz Carlton, but *this*? Clearly, the decor hadn't been updated since the seventies. The carpet was a sickly gold (replete with stains), the walls were covered in dark wood paneling and hung on top of the scary paneling were numerous wood carvings of pilgrims.

I didn't have the best feeling about getting married in this room. Maybe this was a sign? I couldn't possibly be meant to marry the love of my life here, could I? *Just breathe, Sydney.* Remember the mantra. I closed my eyes and tried to slow my heartrate. The outrageous error in judgment made in selecting the design concept for this room wasn't important. What *was* important was that Louis and I were getting married today. I slowly opened my eyes and then snapped them back shut. My little speech didn't do a damn thing. I was still getting married in the Brady Bunch's long lost basement.

Kate grabbed my hand. "Sydney, come with me." She swiftly pulled me out of the offensive room and steered me to the ladies' room. She was surprisingly speedy for a pregnant woman.

Once inside the restroom, she planted me in front of the mirror. "Look at her, Syd."

"Look at who?" I cried. "*We're the only people in here.*"

She rolled her eyes. "Look at *yourself* in the mirror."

I followed her command. "Okay, what am I supposed to see?"

She came up behind me and put her arms around my waist. "You look breathtakingly beautiful."

I suddenly had a goofy smile on my face along with the usual blushing.

She turned me to face her and held my hands. "No one in there is going to be focusing on anything other than you. You are the single best distraction from that *appalling* room."

I giggled. "It *is* truly appalling." I leaned my forehead carefully against hers. "Thanks, Kate."

She grinned. "Relax and focus on Louis. Are you ready?"

I nodded and took her hand. "Ready."

As Kate and I came out of the bathroom, we saw two of my father's friends standing outside the entrance to the main gallery. Mike and Bob were speaking in low voices, but due to our supersonic hearing, both of us caught the content of their discussion. They believed since my father told them I wasn't pregnant, Louis must be marrying me for a green card. I didn't know them very well, but if they were invited to the ceremony, they qualified as his close friends. (The "general public" was only invited to the reception.) I made a mental note to have a serious discussion with my father about the quality of his close friends.

Though I knew their words weren't true, hearing them spoken right before the ceremony had caused a great deal of damage to my fragile mind. I suddenly felt ill at the thought of the widespread speculation taking place as a result of our expeditious marriage.

"None of them think this is real," I babbled. "They all think I'm marrying him to get him a green card. Like in that movie!"

Kate held my face in her hands. "Syd, who gives a crap what they think? *You* know why you're marrying Louis. All the people who matter know it too." She lowered her voice. "Don't let their small-minded opinions ruin your day. We're all *thrilled* for you! We can't wait for Louis to be a part of our family. You've made a wonderful choice...and I think you know that."

I focused on Kate's face and felt my sanity gradually return. I started to laugh and immediately wondered if Kate thought I had finally gone crazy. (Seriously, it was only a matter of time.)

"Syd, are you all right?" she asked, concern showing in her eyes.

I sighed. "How many times are you going to have to save my ass?" It was becoming *really* embarrassing.

She breathed a sigh of relief. "As many times as it takes. It's my job and I take it very seriously."

My mother came charging up to us. "Where have you two been? It's time to start!" She made some kind of bizarre gesture I had never seen before and ran back down the hallway toward the offensive room.

Kate and I scrambled after her. When we reached the door, she squeezed my hand and kissed me on the cheek. Then she turned to my father and said, "Don't give her any shit right now. She's in a delicate state."

She quickly adjusted her calla lily bouquet and started walking down the aisle behind Zoe. Maya was already seated in the front row.

My father peeked at me with innocent eyes and whispered, "What else is new?"

"Teddy!" my bother snapped. Then she turned to me, smiled warmly, adjusted a few locks of my hair and took my right arm.

I elbowed my father in the ribs with my other arm and winked at him. He laughed and offered me his right arm. I carefully wrapped my arm around his, centered my bouquet and then closed my eyes and tried to center myself. When that didn't work, I opened my eyes, looked from my mom to my dad and whispered, "I love you both so much."

My father kissed me on the forehead. "We love you too, Duck."

As the three of us walked down the aisle, I realized Kate was right about the focus not being on the hideous decor of the room. From the moment we entered it, all I see was Louis. He was wearing a dark-blue suit, a French blue shirt, a white tie and the biggest smile I had ever seen on his face. Quite simply, he took my breath away. I grinned back at him happily.

When my father gave my hand to Louis, a collective gasp followed by a round of applause was heard from the laptop on the table next to the judge. That must have been where Charlie and Louis had set up the webcam for Louis' family. At least I hoped this was the case—otherwise I had some serious questions for the judge about the town's privacy policy. For the time being, I decided to believe it was indeed Louis' family and found their warm reaction allowed me my second genuine smile of the day.

The ceremony was short and sweet, much like our courtship. I missed a decent portion of what the judge said because I got lost in Louis' beautiful blue eyes. It was one of my favorite places to be and I planned to return there often over the course of my lifetime. When the judge starting talking about rings, I pulled myself back to the present since I would actually have to do something other than gaze at Louis...

The judge instructed Louis to repeat after her as he put the ring on my finger. He smiled mischievously at me as Charlie handed him a thin band of diamonds. (Did I forget to mention that Louis asked Charlie to be his best man?) I stared at Louis in shock. This was not the band I had chosen at the jewelry store and I had never mentioned to him how badly I wanted a diamond wedding band. Somehow he always knew what I wanted. I felt tears spill down my face as he put the ring on my finger, promising his love and fidelity for as long as we both lived.

Of course, when my turn came, both my hands and my voice were shaking. But for once in my life, I didn't care about what anyone else thought. Louis and I were meant for each other and that was all that mattered. As the judge pronounced us man and wife, I kissed my husband knowing every moment we had together would be our version of perfect. And that was more than good enough for me.

## *Epilogue*

Though the town hall was not my first choice for a wedding site (or even my thousandth choice), the image would remain distinctly in my memory as the place where I became Louis' wife. The photos would have quite the heinous background, but as far as I was concerned, the joy on everyone's faces would overshadow this in spades. Due to my father's forthright thinking in bringing a bottle of champagne to the town hall, we were able to have a brief toast immediately following the ceremony and added a few stains to the scary gold carpet. My mother was horrified, but I found it to be a fitting turn of events. The Bennett family left its mark wherever they went.

The Bennett family also didn't disappoint when it came to a party. My mom ran a little, shall we say, *high* on emotion during the planning process, but once the event arrived, my dad supplied her with enough alcohol to keep her in a happy state. In fact, the entire Bennett family tended to imbibe rather generously leading to various degrees of hijinks. Our wedding, it would seem, would be no different. I could only hope *I* wouldn't be an active participant in any of said hijinks this time.

The antics began once we arrived at the hotel for our

wedding reception. It just so happened the *one* girl in Kate's high school class who didn't like her (you heard me—there was only one) worked at the front desk of the hotel. Melissa had been hopelessly in love with Kate's high school boyfriend, Derek, and had done everything in her power to drive the two of them apart. Her efforts were never successful and Melissa's resentment of Kate became astronomical by the time they graduated. To Nick's horror, Melissa flirted shamelessly with him throughout the check-in process.

When Melissa handed Nick their room key, Kate finally snapped. She slammed her hand down on the counter and proclaimed that if Melissa so much as *looked* at her husband for the duration of our stay in the hotel she would make her wish she had never been born. It was the most unKatelike statement I had ever heard her make and it was *awesome*. It turned out pregnancy hormones could be fun! I laughed for a good five minutes straight. It was an excellent way to begin the wedding reception.

Then about halfway through dinner, I received an unexpected gift from my father. My aunt had been making her usual string of veiled insults regarding all the hard work my mom had put in for our wedding reception. Once she had beaten that to death, she moved on to insinuations about both my being pregnant and Louis needing a green card. (Clearly, she shouldn't have been invited to *any* family events, but the guilt always got to my mother.) Just as my father was about to begin a champagne toast, he accidentally tripped and sent my aunt flying into a serving bowl full of salad. It was going to take a *long* time for her to get the Caesar dressing out of her hair. And even longer to rid herself of the scent of garlic!

After we had all partaken in the amazing three tiered chocolate wedding cake that Zoe and Charlie had given us, a very tipsy Zoe and even more tipsy Maya joined the band on stage for a rendition of "Love Shack." While that in itself was pretty damn funny, the dancing which accompanied the singing was over-the-top hilarious. Zoe had somehow found a top hat and was shaking it around while doing some kind cf tap dance, while Maya had gotten hold of a feather boa ard was doing something that looked a lot like it could turn into an impromptu strip tease. While Louis made sure to remove Maya from the stage before she actually removed any clothing, he managed to take a video of her performance and planned to use it to embarrass her at a later date. Payback was a real bitch, my friend.

The most bizarre turn of the evening came when our party was crashed by an out-of-town fishing club. My father originally approached the six well-dressed gentlemen to ask them to leave, but as he was a fisherman himself, he was easily drawn into a conversation regarding current New York State fishing laws. After a few rounds of drinks, the fishing club moved on and my father began singing his favorite marching songs from the army. This was a sight I hadn't seen before. I was going to peg it as the funniest moment of the night, until my father suspenders somehow malfunctioned and his pants ended up around his ankles. Luckily for him, Louis and I were the only ones who witnessed this. I laughed so hard Louis had to catch me before I fell over.

Sadly, I wasn't immune to tales of hilarity. I was filled with so much joy in my new role as Louis' wife that I had too much to drink. I thought a glass of wine or two would be fine, but the more wine I had, the happier I got, which meant I drank even more. This process coupled with the glass or two of champagne I had consumed during the wedding toast made me fairly drunk. I, of course, had a great time. Louis had a great time the next morning telling me that not only did I ask him to brush my teeth (because it was too difficult a task for me to manage myself), but I had fallen out of bed in the middle of the night and he had a hell of a time picking my sorry ass up and getting it back into bed. What a hot wedding night it was!

But the best story of all came from my lovely cousin,

Cynthia. It seemed she *too* had become fairly inebriated and ended up hurling in the flower beds in front of the hotel. What made this even more priceless was that my father's buddies from the fishing club were driving by in their rented limo and decided to stop to take photos—which they emailed to my father. (I had the stroke of genius to have them blown up for my aunt's surprise birthday party the following month. Cynthia managed to dispose of the full-sized posters, but we retained the digital images. Imagine our surprise when they somehow found their way into the slideshow of family photos shown during the cocktail hour. It was my aunt's best party yet!)

In the end, our first wedding was far from perfect, but I had the perfect groom, and that was more than I could ever ask for. As I danced with Louis to our wedding song, "At Last" by Etta James, I thought about how different my life had become since I had met him. In the last six months, I had experienced many things I had never experienced before. I had been pushed further than ever before. And I had become someone who I never imagined I would be: a remarkably sane and courageous woman (with just a hint of lunatic). Even though our romance felt like a crazy roller coaster ride—and there were several times when I was scared shitless—I wouldn't have changed any part of our story. My adventure with Louis had brought out newfound confidence and I knew in my heart we were going to have a wonderful, if slightly imperfect, life together.

I took a deep breath and closed my eyes as I rested my head on Louis' shoulder. After such a flurry of activity, I was looking forward to living life in the slow lane for a while. Then it dawned on me that I still had to finish planning my perfect wedding. I sighed. One wedding down, two more to go. What could possibly go wrong?

# Author's Note

Thank you so much for reading *French Twist*! If Sydney wormed her way into your heart, or perhaps tickled your funny bone just a little, I would be grateful if you took a few moments to write a review of your reading experience. Amazon or Goodreads; take your pick! Your time, effort and thoughtful words are greatly appreciated! Who knows? You may even wrangle a few unsuspecting folks into giving Sydney's brand of humor a try!

# Acknowledgments

I owe a debt of gratitude to my wonderful family for their generous love and support throughout this eye opening journey.

To my amazing husband, Sebastien, for sharing his life with me, for loving me unconditionally and for reminding me (often) that I could do justice to our story.

To my beautiful boys, Ryan and Xander, for filling my heart with so much joy.

To my sister, Megan, for championing my effort from the very beginning. Thank you for being my sounding board, my cheerleader, my story editor and my cover designer all rolled into one. You are the best sister a girl could ever ask for.

To my sister-in-law Jen, for sharing my excitement and delving into editing with gusto! Thank you for your inspiring ideas and for being a willing participant in our crazy family.

To my brother Colin, for having such a huge heart and for always making me laugh.

To my brother-in-law, Josh, for cheerfully reading this book despite its lack of zombies and aliens. Your kind words and keen insights into the realm of romantic comedy are greatly appreciated!

To my nieces, Sabrina and Skyler, for their unbridled enthusiasm, their creative input and their firm belief that a movie studio would purchase the film rights.

To my nephews, Jackson and Evan, for making me feel like a rock star for writing this book.

Thank you all for believing in me.

# About the Author

After thirteen years in the human resources industry, Glynis was inspired to create a work of fiction rather than continue to listen to employees' fabricated complaints each day. In her debut novel, *French Twist*, she chronicles the accelerated courtship and marriage to her husband, Sebastien - with a little judicious editing. When she's not writing, she's usually rushing to the gym, wracking her brain to remember 3rd grade math to help her son with his homework, rescuing toys from certain destruction down the toilet or trying not to burn dinner. She currently lives in Westchester, New York with her incredibly romantic French husband and two angelic sons.

# Connect with Glynis Astie

Blog: www.glynisastie.com

Twitter: https://twitter.com/GlynisAstie

Pinterest: http://www.pinterest.com/glynisastie/

Facebook:

https://www.facebook.com/glynisastieauthor

# Also by Glynis Astie

*French Toast*

## *French Toast*

Sydney Bennett is back! And her pursuit of perfection is alive and well. Naïve to the core, Sydney believed that when she finally married the man of her dreams, the hard part was over. Following a civil ceremony as a means to keep Louis from being deported, Sydney continues to plan the fairytale wedding that she had dreamed of since the age of five. Much to her chagrin, she discovers that her mother-in-law is planning what seems to be a rival wedding in France that SHE has been dreaming about for her only child since before he was born. How will poor Sydney be able to ensure two perfect weddings in the midst of Louis' fruitless job search? Especially when her mother-in-law's idea of perfection appears to be having Sydney embarrass herself in front of hundreds of French people that she has never met?

As if she didn't have enough on her mind already, Sydney finds herself faced with the trials and tribulations of being a wife. Sydney had always heard that marriage was hard, but she thought that this was just a ruse that married couples portrayed in a bid to make single girls feel less desperate. But as the bills pile up and emotions run high, she realizes that there may just be some truth to this statement. And as she watches Louis' perfection fade away before her very eyes, she begins to wonder if she made a rash decision in marrying a man that she had known for a mere six months.

With all of the obstacles that Sydney and Louis will encounter, will they be raising their glasses in celebration or watching their impulsive marriage crash and burn? One thing is for certain, Sydney and Louis Durand are headed for one hell of a toast...

"Both *French Twist* and *French Toast* are lighthearted fun reads that will keep you in stitches and make you a believer that fairytale romances really do exist ... even when real life puts obstacles in the way!"

-Kathleen Anderson, Jersey Girl Book Reviews

"This novel has a refreshing story line and is a fun, enjoyable read that will make you laugh, and leave you with a feeling of a little exhaustion as Sydney shares the preparations taking place for multiple wedding ceremonies."

-Edythe Hamilton, Ski-Wee's Book Corner

"French Toast, the second book of the French Twist series by Glynis Astie, was a delightful book...The mishaps and issues that crop up for this poor couple made me laugh out loud many times...I look forward to reading book three!"

-Heather McCoubrey, author of *To Love Twice* and *Back to December*

"This was a terrific sequel to *French Twist* and I enjoyed it a great deal. Much of it was laugh-out-loud funny, and her characters were appealing and convincing as were her situations.

-Reader